THE LAST
WORTHLESS EVENING

four novellas and two stories by

ANDRE DUBUS

D0168397

Crown Publishers, Inc.

New York

Deaths at Sea first appeared in *Quarterly West*; "After the Game" in *Fiction Network*; "Dressed Like Summer Leaves" in *The Sewanee Review*; *Land Where My Fathers Died* in *Antaeus* and as a limited edition published by Palaemon Press; *Molly* in *Crazyhorse*; and *Rose* in *Ploughshares*.

I am grateful to the National Endowment for the Arts, and the Creative Writing Program and the Department of English at the University of Alabama.

Grateful acknowledgment is made for permission to reprint excerpts from the following songs:
"I Should Care," by Sammy Cahn, Paul Weston, and Axel Stordahl, © 1944 (renewed) by Dorsey Bros. Music. Used by permission of Warner Bros. Music. All rights reserved. "Lush Life," Billy Strayhorn, composer, Tempo Music, Inc., publisher. All rights reserved. Used by permission. "I Get a Kick out of You," by Cole Porter © 1934 (renewed) Warner Bros. Inc. All rights reserved. Used by permission. "Just One of Those Things," by Cole Porter © 1935 (renewed) Warner Bros. Inc. All rights reserved. Used by permission.

Published in 1987 by Crown Publishers, Inc., 225 Park Avenue South, New York, New York 10003 by arrangement with David R. Godine Publishers, Inc.

CROWN is a trademark of Crown Publishers, Inc.

Manufactured in the United States of America

Library of Congress Cataloging-in-Publication Data

Dubus, Andre, 1936–
The last worthless evening.

I. Title.
[PS3554.U265L3 1987]   813'.54   87-9026
ISBN 0-517-56625-7

10 9 8 7 6 5 4 3 2 1

First Paperback Edition

The Last Worthless Evening, four novellas and two stories, establishes Andre Dubus as one of America's finest writers.

Dubus's growing legion of admirers will relish his newest work; it breaks new ground in feeling, style, and range. The novellas begin in the Navy, where two young officers, one black, one white, discover each other as friends amid the residual racism of the 1960s. Another novella offers shrewd homage to the detective story in Dubus's patented territory northwest of Boston. Yet another evokes the life of a suburban girl coming beautifully of age as her mother declines; and the last novella, "Rose," is an eloquent defense of her life and children by a woman who refuses defeat at the hands of a brutal husband. The stories tell about a Hispanic shortstop lost among the gringos on a major-league team and what happens to an eleven-year-old kid when he meets up with a broken, angry, and decidedly dangerous Vietnam vet who takes him into a local bar for a treat.

Andre Dubus has forged an enduring, even heroic place for himself in American literature as a writer of eloquence, passion, and strength.

ANDRE DUBUS is the author of *The Times Are Never So Bad, Finding a Girl in America, Adultery & Other Choices, Separate Flights, We Don't Live Here Anymore: The Novellas of Andre Dubus,* and *Voices from the Moon.* He has served in the Marine Corps, was a Guggenheim Fellow, a member of the Writer's Workshop at the University of Iowa, and has won an NEA Fellowship. He lives with his family in Haverhill, Massachusetts.

to Cadence

CONTENTS

. . . that whole hopeful continent dedicated as a refuge and sanctuary of liberty and freedom from what you called the old world's worthless evening . . . and He could have repudiated them since they were his creation now and forever throughout all their generations until not only that old world from which He had rescued them but this new one too which He had revealed and led them to as a sanctuary and refuge were become the same worthless tideless rock cooling in the last crimson evening . . .

—William Faulkner, *The Bear*

Deaths at Sea

for William B. Goodman

2 July 1961
At sea

Hello Camille:

I suppose we fled the South. I still don't know. Maybe it was just time for us to leave, and be together away from Lafayette, where so many people have known us since we were babies. We've talked about this for four years, so why do I mention it again? Because of Willie Brooks.

And I think of you, alone in a quonset hut in Alameda, California, with officers' wives and not a Negro among them. And I'm on an aircraft carrier in the Western Pacific, and Filipino stewards are the Navy's Negroes. They do the cooking and serving in the officers' wardroom, and they clean the officers' staterooms. It's like the life you and I, thank God, never had at home: those affluent people who had Negroes doing everything for them. Now, after my first months aboard the *Ranger*, I believe my count is accurate: there are three Negro officers. Out of a ship's crew of thirty-five hundred men, and I don't know how many people in the Air Group we have aboard. Ah: I see you reading this, saying Wait a minute. And you're right. I did tell you there were only two, and both were with the squadrons, and were not part of the ship's company; and one is a flight surgeon, the other a personnel officer. No Negro pilot. But now we have a lieutenant junior grade of our own. He is in public relations. (He wants to work in radio or television when he gets out.) He is from Philadelphia. His name is Wilson Jason Brooks. And, Camille, he is my roommate.

Fate? God? Bill was transferred to a destroyer. That left a bunk in my room. Then Willie came aboard. So my flight from the South, if that's what it was, has indeed brought me further away. At first, when he knocked on the door and I opened it and saw his black face, hesitant but smiling, I believed I had come back full circle. But very soon, by the time I had shown him his desk next to mine, pointed out that we had our own lavatory and shaving mirror— which of course he could see, but I was talking talking *talk*ing, in my shyness, my excitement, and yes: my fear—and by the time I had told him I slept in the upper bunk, but it didn't matter to me and he could sleep in whichever was more comfortable for him, I knew I had not come full circle. Because I was as far now from the South as I could imagine: I had a Negro roommate. Then I knew he would also be my friend, when he said: "I'll take the lower. You may have problems enough, without giving up your bed."

"Problems?"

"You didn't get that accent in New Jersey."

"I'm Catholic," I said.

He looked at me as if I had said I'm married, or I'm five-eleven, or I'm twenty-six years old. Then he laughed, a short one, but not forced: it came up from his chest, and he was smiling.

"Is that why you offered me your bed? Pope told you to?"

"I meant I was from south Louisiana. Cajuns and Creoles. French Catholics. I thought I talked like one."

"Well, you don't sound like a cracker. But there *is* a trace, Gerry. Must've been some mean *Bap*tists hanging out in your neighborhood."

"Are we going to shake hands?" I said. "Or stand here trying to guess how bad it could be?"

He extended his hand, a large one, and we squeezed each other, the way men do. *Never shake hands like a dead fish*, Mother told me. Why her, and not Daddy?

"Did I just get a cherry?" he said.

"Nope. Integrated college for my last three years. And in summer I worked construction with Negroes. And there was a man when I was a boy. Leonard. He mowed the lawn once a week. I liked him. And there *were* some mean Southern Baptists around. Mean Catholics too."

"Calm down, man. It'll be all right. I'm scared shitless too."

"Have you had trouble?"

"Who, me?"

Probably this sounds to you, reading a letter, more like a confrontation than a meeting. But it wasn't. You see—and you've told me that my face always shows what I'm feeling—he *knew* how I felt. He could see it; almost smell it, he told me later. He said there was guilt in the very air of the room, and he knew from my eyes that I had not earned it but had simply grown up with it. Or, as he said later, in a bar in Yokosuka, I was like a man who had seen a lynching once and tried to stop it and got beat up and didn't get killed only because he was white and they already had a Negro to hang; and I blamed myself still, and could not stop blaming myself for throwing rocks at a wheatfield and not breaking one stalk.

We were at sea when Willie arrived. They flew him to the ship, and we stayed out for another week before going to Yokosuka. During the day, except Saturday afternoons and Sundays, we rarely saw each other. We woke together. We wake to his alarm now, because its ringing is softer than mine. That's almost a metaphor, isn't it? For—Oh, God, Camille; damn this distance and these letters. I want to hold you, let you hear me and feel me while I tell you this: I've told him all of it: about you, and me, and the two of us and Emmett Till and the night in the bar when I held my knife against that ignorant bastard's throat. Willie liked that. I mean, he was moved. But he covered it up quickly by saying: "And with a knife. I thought only my people carried blades."

And I was relieved. For there was too much emotion between us that night, his fourth or fifth in our stateroom. Or too much of mine, as I told him of our sorrow and anger as witnesses, told this to a victim, but without guilt, as though we were talking about a disease he had survived, and I was telling of others suffering with it and dying, and I could do nothing for them but watch. That's it: we could have been talking of the flu epidemic in 1918. We were sitting in our desk chairs, the chairs turned so we faced each other. Then he said: "I'm glad you didn't kill him."

He laid his hand on mine, resting on my desk. Then he lifted my hand and turned it, my palm to his, and squeezed.

"The old ten percent," he said.

"What?"

"People like you. When will it be ninety? And ninety of me, for that matter. We had no money, but my parents got us through college. I'm a Naval officer. You can't know what that means to them. They'll never have to put up new wallpaper. Not in my old bedroom, anyway. Unless they take down all those pictures of their boy Willie. In khakis. Blues. Whites. That's the funny one."

"I understand."

"I know you do."

"But not about the ten percent like you."

"That was bitterness. Sometimes you get so angry at the ones keeping you down, you get angry at your people who stay down. No. It's not ten percent. We're not Indians yet. They kept us alive."

We wake together, and take turns shaving. He's a tall, broad man and, no, I haven't seen him naked yet, so forget that myth for a while. My devout Catholic and concupiscent Cajun wife. We have breakfast in the wardroom. Then I go to the Gunnery Department and he goes to the Public Relations Office and we meet again for lunch. I proposed this for the first few days, as I would to any new roommate, and at noon we wait for each other in the passageway outside the wardroom.

On the second or third day, as I waited for him, I realized that my excitement did not come only from finally having a chance to do more for Negroes than pray; I felt that redemption was at hand, for I could finally show my feelings, and the history of my feelings, to a Negro at close quarters. As close as his body is to mine. With only a smile, a greeting, a shared lunch. After work we get to the stateroom at four-thirty or so, and talk or read, then go to dinner at six. Since Bill left, I'm the senior lieutenant junior grade in the junior officers' wardroom; so, after the ringing of four bells, I must start the meal with the blessing. I say the only one I know, the Catholic one, and Willie enjoys this, sitting to my left or right—I sit at the head of the center table—and says he likes the prayer's brevity. And that I look like an aging altar boy when I say it.

26 July 1961
At sea

. . . and after eight days of it, two of those spent dry aboard ship because I was on duty, I do believe I'm still hung over. It's strange what being at sea does to you. Sometimes at sea, for even two weeks, I *think* of a beer once in a while. But I don't need one. Then we hit port and I go mad, drink as though I'm preparing for hibernation. Wonderful Japanese beer: Asahi, Kirin. Saki. Or Willie and I bring a fifth of Gordon's gin—for a dollar and a quarter—from the base to a bar where they sell us set-ups. Every time I go to sea I write you this, but I can't stop: like the need for booze, my loneliness is worse when I'm in port. Of course, because in every bar there are Japanese bar girls, and it is not their faces and bodies and their kimonos and obis, lovely as all of those are, that make my loneliness so deep that it approaches grief. It's their voices, whether in faltering and comic English, or chattering (or so it seems) in that rapid falling and rising like surf—if surf sang like a bird. I can read French and Spanish and Latin and can even converse, slowly, in all three, but even now, on my fourth Pacific tour, I cannot distinguish Japanese syllables, detect the end of a sentence or the start of one. Still, it is their voices. And, as I told you on my very first deployment out here, I do not feel lust. Lust would be easier to deal with. My hand. And I no longer confess it; I do not believe God concerns Himself with the built-up semen of sailors. I did *not* mean that as a pun. No, not lust: loneliness. And no hand can assuage it; nor could the body of another woman. I want to be home, and I wonder whether I can actually stay for twenty or twenty-five years in the Navy. But how else can I work on the sea? There must be a way. If there isn't, I'm afraid I'll become landlocked; or maybe I can teach history near at least a coast. Soon now I'll be a full lieutenant.

I think booze and loneliness are paradoxically much less of a problem at sea than in port because I change when I board the ship, knowing we'll be out for a week, ten days, two weeks. It's like taking a minor vow, like the senior retreat in high school, when for three days we could not speak, except to pray and to confess. Then we return to port and most of us drink too much and many husbands are unfaithful, and perhaps their wives or other wives are too in Alameda, and I cannot find blame in any of them. Willie is married, and they have a year-old son, and he and I do what my (faithful) married friends and I have always done: we don't drink with the women. Willie's wife is Louisa, and she's still in San Diego, his last port before coming to the *Ranger*, and she won't move up to Alameda till we return from sea in January. I wish she would move there now. So you could meet her. Their son is Jimmy.

In Yokosuka Willie eased my loneliness. Not as my other friends do, by sharing it, by talking of their wives and children. (When will we have a child? We're the only practicing Catholics we know who don't even use rhythm and are still childless, while the others have babies year after year and are in despair and moving closer to a time when they will leave the Church. Everything is mysterious. Perhaps that is why I love the sea.) No, Willie eased my loneliness by being a Negro, giving me the blessing of drinking and talking with him, giving me a reprieve from my childhood when I could only watch them and listen. A reprieve too from our last three years in college when, finally integrated, there was too much history for us and the Negro students to overcome; we were overwhelmed by it, and we softly crept over its surface, by speaking politely to each other, by nodding and smiling in the halls and on the campus grounds. The Japanese girls want Willie: they are childlike, gleeful, and shy with him; and some want to press their small palms against his. He allows this, and courteously tells them he is married and a *papa-san* and no butterfly boy. Too bad, they say, and tell him their names. Maybe next time *Lanegah* come Yokosuka you change mind. Then Willie and I drink.

All his life he has had white friends, so I think it is only my discomfort that makes his eyes shift from mine; a difficult evasion, for him, since mine are shifting too. But discomfort is of course not the right word for what I bring to our booths, our chairs at the bars, our room aboard ship. And he knows it, and understands my need to tell him all I can remember—with you, and before you: those horrors I saw and heard as a child, an adolescent, and whatever I was in college. I told him of imagining Christ in the electric chair, as I said the rosary on the night they electrocuted Sonny Broussard; then, with the terror and grief of the boy I was, seeing myself, through Christ and so through Sonny, strapped into the chair. Willie is not religious. Or, more precisely, he does not belong to a religion. But I am able to talk with him about saying a rosary for Sonny, trying to meditate on the Agony in the Garden, the Scourging at the Pillar, the Crowning with Thorns, the Carrying of the Cross, and the Crucifixion and Death. As I am able to tell him that I grew up with hardly any bigotry at all, because of the Christian Brothers' school and my parents—I think especially Daddy, with his contained and quiet sorrow about Negroes, while as a Southern man (Daddy would even say gentleman, since in the South money isn't a prerequisite for that) he followed the old ways, the traditions, the rules, but with an uneasiness I could sense even as a boy.

Almost no bigotry at all, save what I acquired simply by being there, by listening to—and telling—the jokes; by watching and hearing Negroes from that great distance between us, whether at their rear section of the bus or standing before me: Leonard taking the plate of food I gave him at the back door so he could eat under the sycamore's shade in the noon sun, while I watched (sometimes) from our dining-room window, and the oscillating floor fan blew on me and my family. Willie listens to all of this: from Christ, to Sonny Broussard's terror and final pain for raping a white girl, to Emmett Till, to Leonard, and the Negro section of town whose smells I rode through on my bicycle, going that hot summer afternoon with my friend on his paper route. And the Negro boys and girls going up to the balcony to watch from above us, as my friends and I sat downstairs for the Saturday serial and western movie. So

he understands my need to—I was going to write "unburden myself." But I shall use the real word: Willie understands my need to
confess.

And like Christ, Willie's yoke is easy, his burden is light, and
he gives me rest. On the second or third or whatever night in a
booth in a bar in Yokosuka, I nearly cried when I told him about
Daddy going outside, alone with his bourbon and water, when
news came that Emmett Till was dead. So I muttered the male
exorcism of tears.

"Fuck it," I said, and completed the ritual: I swallowed some
beer, and lit a cigarette. Then I looked at Willie, and he smiled.

"Did you tell your Daddy you almost stuck a knife in that guy?"

"No."

"Pretty decent family, for crackers."

"I'm not a cracker. I'm a Cajun. We're known to be tolerant,
cheerful—let the *bon temps roulé*—and hot-tempered."

"Carry blades too, I hear. You talk French to the slaves down
there?"

"Always. Called them *bête noires*."

"I hear we have a distinct smell. Maybe just to the cracker nose."

"They did."

"Did it smell a little bit like poverty?"

"Their part of town did. And neglect."

"They do seem to go hand in hand. Smell like fear maybe too?
Like a dog at the vet's?"

"I don't know. Sweat, maybe."

"Ah: a little of both, then. Because they was workin' theah black
asses off fo' the *cub*nel, choppin' his cotton and wet-nuhsin' his
chillun an' fetchin' him mint *joo*leps own the ve*ran*dah. White people
smell like milk. We get nauseated in a theater full of white people."

"They didn't have that problem at home."

"Oh I *reck*on not. Smell *gun* powdah if dey go to a movie wif de
white folks."

"Do I smell like milk?"

"Right now you smell like Asahi. At sea you smell like wet
dreams."

"You too."

"But dreams that stimulate a huge cock." He held his hands apart, as though showing the length of a fish that fought him for thirty minutes and then threw the hook. "Actually I'm an insult to my people. Louisa thinks I've got a cracker in my woodpile."

"You can dance, though."

"Sing too. Want to hear something from *Porgy and Bess*? Or *Showboat*?"

"Want to hear a Southern joke?"

"They have those?"

"It's sociological."

"It ought to be."

"Maybe it's even philosophical. Maybe Eleanor Roosevelt started it. Sent a chain letter to Negroes."

"I didn't know they could get mail down there. Can't read enough to vote, how can they get mail?"

"It's very complex. There are heroic deliveries."

"Night riders?"

"Of the New Frontier."

So I told him those two jokes. There in the booth, which was small like everything, it seems, in Japan; our feet and legs bumped and drew back and shifted beneath the low table. In that bar lit by softened red lights, much like the passageways aboard ship, to protect the pilots' night vision. But the lights were softer, and came from behind the bar and perhaps a couple of dim ceiling lights. Faces at nearby tables were shapes with vague features. Cigarettes rose to them, glowed, descended. My eyes burned. At the tables and in booths and sitting at the bar were officers in civilian suits and ties (Willie and I had taken off our coats, unbuttoned our collars, loosened our ties), and sailors and Marines in uniform, some with women, some waiting their chance, a few oblivious. The waitresses carried trays among the tables as if they did not need to see. They were slender shapes in kimonos, wide sleeves moving like shadows with substance, their hair darker than the darkness of the room, their faces in the light a pale glow, with brightly darkened lips and eyes. While men stumbled and bumped their way to the toilet, these women glided, like the figures a child is afraid he will wake to see entering his bedroom and, without a sound of breath or feet, crossing its floor.

"There's this boy living on a cotton plantation, and he goes off to college, and after a while he writes to his daddy and says everybody in the fraternity has a monkey and will his daddy buy him one too. So the man buys his son a monkey, and the boy brings him home on vacations, and when he's finished college he asks his daddy if he can leave the monkey at home, because he's going out into the world. So his daddy says sure, son, that'll be fine. So the boy leaves and the monkey stays, and one day the man goes outside and sees the monkey out in the cotton field. He's carrying a gunny sack and going down the rows, picking cotton and putting it in the sack, and the man watches him for a while, going down the rows and filling sacks, and then he says to himself, Now if I had me a hunnerd monkies like that, I wouldn't have to pay nobody to pick my cotton. So he goes to the pet store and orders a hundred monkies, and the owner of the pet store wants to know what he's going to do with one hundred monkies. So the man tells him, and the owner says: Nossir, I ain't goin' to order you them monkies, and I'll tell you why. The next fellow down the road'll see them monkies in your field, and he'll get to thinking, and he's goin' to order him two hunnerd. Then some old boy with a bigger plantation he's goin' to order three hunnerd, and pretty soon the South'll be overrun with monkies, and some damn Yankee lawyer's goin' to come down here and turn 'em loose and they'll go to school with my chilren."

Willie laughed. He laughed till his eyes watered, while so many of my white friends, from the Northeast and West and Midwest, had never given it more than a courteous sound resembling laughter, and some had frowned and said: Bad, Gerry, bad. But Willie understood the true butt of the joke.

"It's economic," he said. "So I guess that makes it sociological. Even philosophical. Course it generally is economic."

"Sure. It was an agrarian society. An aristocracy even, with—"

"Not just Negroes and whites. It's generally economic when somebody's shitting on somebody else."

"I suppose it is."

"Northern mills went South after the Civil War. You think it was for the climate?"

"Cheap labor."

"Cheap white labor. That's how Shoeless Joe Jackson got started playing ball. Played for a mill. Baseball was good for the mo*rale*. Fat cats always have ideas about how to keep poor folks happy without signing a check. You think those mills have unions yet?"

"Nope. But I have another joke."

"From down home?"

"Again."

"Sounds to me like you hung out with some liberals. I thought the good old boys kicked their asses on Saturday nights, till they all went North."

"I seem to be in Yokosuka myself."

"Indeed you do, my friend, indeed you do. You going to retire down there? If you can stand this Navy bullshit for twenty years?"

"Never," I said. Then: "I don't think so, anyway."

Because we haven't even talked about it, you and I, and until Willie asked me I had not known I had thought about it at all. But something in me had. Or had at least made a decision without telling the rest of me about it, through the process we call thinking. (Maybe all murders are premeditated but the killer never knows it.) Because I said *never* at once, with firmness and certainty and, in my heart, the awakening of an old dread that had slept, but lightly, on the edge of insomnia. As though Willie had asked me whether I would sleep with a coral snake.

"Some of my people miss it," he said. "They go down at Christmas. My grandparents went back to Alabama last year, to stay."

"I didn't know you were from Alabama."

"I'm not. My parents were born in Philadelphia."

"Why did they go back?"

His shoulders tightened, and just as quickly his eyes were angry. He said: "Social Security buys more down there." Then his eyes softened, and his shoulders relaxed—no: slumped toward the table that was so low I could see his belt—and he said: "To see their people. To die at home. They left it to have my father and aunts and uncles in the North. But Alabama was always home. Isn't it strange? Home? How it can shield you from all the shit out there? The evening meal of the poor—beans and greens and cornbread and rice—and the old bed and the tarpaper roof."

"You've been down there?"

"No. I wouldn't be able to stand it. I couldn't get leave anyway. My father wrote to me, after they went down last Christmas."

"Did he say it was bad?"

"Hell, no. It was a happy letter. He said compared to the sixth floor of a tenement, it was a Goddamn resort. A little house with a little yard with flowers, and they have a vegetable garden, and two oak trees, and a dirt road, and a front porch with a swing where they can sit. And friends. Old people. They gather on the porch at night and drink coffee and talk. No gangs of punks. No junkies. No dealers. Sometimes there's a fight at the bar."

"That's the best kind."

"Of fight?"

"Of bar."

"I forgot. You don't like the officers' club. Mean-ass Cajun carries a knife. Holds it at a redneck. Poor guy's celebrating. Just being happy because they found what the fish and the river left of Emmett Till."

"A pocket knife. For fishing and hunting. And in general."

"In general."

"I've always had one. Since Daddy gave me my first one—"

"When you were two."

"Eight. To go with my first long pants."

"No button on it? Makes the blade come out smelling blood?"

"Here."

I twisted in the seat and tried to put my hand in my pocket, but he said: "Shit no, man. Don't pull that thing in here. This is your kind of place, not mine. I like quiet plastic bars. I don't need some drunk Marine charging over with a bayonet. Just happens to be taped to his leg. Tell your joke."

"You're not kidding, are you?"

"About what?"

"Violence."

"Not at all, friend. If it weren't for the draft, I wouldn't even be a public relations man in a fucking uniform."

"I think—"

Then I stopped, and looked away, at the reddened darkness and the moving shapes of people.

"You think what?"

I looked at him.

"That if I were a Negro I'd be dead now."

"Or you would have learned how to stay alive. The joke, Mr. Fontenot. And I hope it's not as complex as you are."

"I'm not complex."

"No," he said. "You're not." He finished his beer, looked at my near-empty glass, and raised his hand without looking at the bar, or at the waitress when she somehow and at once noticed him and came and he ordered Asahis. He was looking at me, at my eyes. "My Cajun shipmate," he said.

"There's a monkey walking down the road. In the South, a gravel road, a country road, and he's walking on the side of it. He hears a pickup coming behind him, and he looks around, and there's a white man at the wheel, speeding up and aiming at the monkey, and the monkey jumps off the road just in time and lands in a deep ditch. Truck goes on and the monkey climbs out and brushes himself off and shakes his head. Then he starts walking down the road again. After about a mile he sees a car coming toward him, on the other side of the road. There's a Negro driving, and when he sees the monkey he comes across the road at him, and the monkey jumps in the ditch and the car misses him and goes on by. Monkey climbs out of the ditch again. He brushes off the dust and watches the car driving away, and shakes his head and says: My people, my people . . ."

Again Willie laughed, even as the waitress appeared suddenly out of the dark and noise, and he reached back for his wallet, doubling forward with that motion and his laughter too, and gave her some yen and shook his head and held his hand up to refuse the change and she thanked him in Japanese—I can't spell the word; its sound is *arrigato*—then he stopped laughing and drew on his cigarette but he laughed again as he inhaled, then he coughed. I was laughing and he waved a hand at me to stop so he could clear his throat and breathe, but I couldn't stop, for still I was seeing that Darwinian monkey on the dusty gravel road, in the hot afternoon of summer, shaking his head, bewildered and sad. Willie coughed again, breathed clearly a couple of times, swallowed some beer; and then, as though he saw too what I did—that puzzled and doleful monkey—he was laughing.

There is something about true laughter. Or at least about laughter whose source is not really comic. Like yesterday at sea—I was going to get to this but I can't stop writing about being ashore with Willie—when we were firing live rounds with VT fuses from the five-inch fifty-four gun mount, and during the firing exercise the magazine jammed and the sailors in my gun crew had to unload it by hand, carrying one shell at a time, cradled in their arms and held against their chests, having to carry the round to the turret's hatch and hand it to a sailor waiting at the top of the gun mount's ladder, then that sailor had to back down the short but vertical ladder and carry the round across the small deck, then down and down the series of angled ladders going below decks, where he could at last hand it to someone else to store. The danger of this is dropping it. The VT fuse at the head of the round is a variable time fuse, meaning once the round is fired from the gun the fuse is activated and will explode not on contact but when it approaches something—fifty feet away, thirty feet, whatever, depending on the fuse's setting. I was of course frightened, as the sailors were, and I stayed with them, so if a sailor dropped a round and set the fuse into action and it exploded he'd at least know his officer's meat and bones would join his on the bulkheads of the turret, which had always seemed comfortably large, with enough space for men to move about in, but as each sailor removed a round and carried it to the man on the ladder, our place seemed smaller and smaller, just enough to contain all the force of an explosion and what was left of the two men who before the sound and flash had been standing, breathing, speaking.

Do not think of me as brave. It was simply required. Besides, there was a detachment about my fear. I was watching myself doing my work as it ought to be done, and I concentrated more on that than on images of my body in flung pieces, and never seeing you again, or the sea and the sun, and all else that I love. Then a sailor, a seaman by rank, a lanky and gentle man from Idaho named Mattingly, dropped a round. He had just removed it from the gun's magazine, had turned toward me to pass me and hand it to the sailor on the ladder. It simply fell, as though his arms decided to uncurl from its weight. It struck the steel deck and slid perhaps a foot between us, then stopped. Its fuse was bent at nearly a forty-five-degree angle. It had hit the deck loudly, and there was the sound of its slide, then Mattingly and I looked at each other in a moment of new and absolute silence, though outside the turret, now that the firing exercise was over, planes were catapulting from the flight deck. Mattingly's face was pale, like that of a man who without warning is about to vomit. Probably mine was too. I know my mouth had opened, as Mattingly's had. Then he bent for the round, and I spoke before I knew that I could.

"Don't touch it," I said.

We watched it. Then I turned to the sailor on the ladder, only his head and shoulders appearing above the hatch. The sun was on his face, but his flesh was pale too, as though he had been in the engine room for months.

"Get off the ladder," I said. "Take the other men off the deck. Then lock the hatch behind you. Don't let anyone out here. Wait. Except Ensign Stark. You know him? The EOD officer?" The sailor nodded. "And his chief. He'll probably bring his chief. But nobody else. Do you understand? Mattingly's going with you too."

"Mr. Fontenot," Mattingly said.

"Go on."

"I'm the one dropped it."

"Go on, Mattingly."

"Yes sir."

There was not relief in his voice; or fear either; or any tone that implied hurry. He spoke like a man obeying someone at a funeral. Then he was gone, and on the phone at the bulkhead I dialed Stark's number and told him.

"You said VT?"

"Yes."

"And it's bent? The fuse? Where are you?"

"Standing here looking at it."

"We're on the way. And you get out of there."

"I want to make sure it doesn't move."

"On this big fucking ship? A grocery cart wouldn't move. I'm there," and he hung up.

He and his chief came with a manual. Stark was first up the

ladder, the color still in his face (and I hoped mine was restored, if in fact it had left), and in one hand he was holding the book. His starched khakis were crumpled. He stood looking at our companion on the deck, at its bent fuse. He pushed up the visor of his cap, and blond curls showed at his forehead. Everett Stark is twenty-two years old, married just before we sailed, and he is my drinking friend. He is a cheerful drinker and is the ship's explosive ordinance disposal officer and also our diver, scuba and deep-sea. His chief stood beside him, a dark wiry man nearing forty. He had a tool kit with him; he nodded at me once, and looked at the round. We could have been standing over a corpse, not of a friend, but of a man we had all known. Stark said: "Did you call the OOD?"

"Yes."

"What did he say?"

"To keep him informed."

"Should have told him just to keep his ears open. He'd be the first to know."

The chief took off his khaki cap, tossed it to the deck, and said: "The fourth." Then he kneeled beside the round and, with one finger, touched it. "At least it ain't a fucking misfire," he said. "Fucker's cold as my old lady."

Stark grinned and kneeled beside him.

"Good thing it's not as hot as mine."

"Mr. Stark's a bridegroom," the chief said, looking at the fuse while Stark read the table of contents of his manual.

"I know," I said.

"You can go," Stark said. "In case you need to call the OOD."

"In case he can't hear a big bang," the chief said.

"So you can write the report."

"In triplicate," the chief said.

"I'll stay."

Stark shrugged. "What the fuck. It won't be the first last call we've had."

"Mr. Stark," the chief said. "Is that book talking to you yet?"

"Not yet."

I did move toward the hatch, close enough to be blown up, far enough to feel that at least I wasn't as close as they were, at least I wasn't touching it.

"Here it is," Stark said. "Want to hear it?"

"I can't understand that shit. Just read it to yourself and tell me what it says. If you don't mind."

Stark read, then talked to the chief, his voice low until he finished; then he laughed and slapped the chief on the shoulder.

"I think it says be careful," he said.

"Seems to be the message. Maybe Mr. Fontenot could call the OOD, inform him we're being careful. In accordance with the manual."

I wanted to. Because it had become bizarre. Only a few feet outside the hatch was the sea, and I wanted to pick up the round and go down the ladder and to the rail and drop it into the Pacific. But Stark and the chief had to know whether the fuse had been activated and was ready to explode as soon as it looked at something, and for some reason had simply chosen not to yet, but might at any time: as it was carried past a bulkhead, or through a hatch. They worked quietly. They murmured to each other, passed and received screwdrivers and pliers, finally spoke hardly at all: *Okay*, they said, or *That's that*, and once Stark picked up the open manual and looked at a diagram and showed it to the chief who nodded and leaned over again with his screwdriver. There was such concentration in their faces that it seemed their bodies existed only to keep their faces alive. And their hands, their fingers. Then the fuse was off, resting bent in the chief's hand, looking as lethal still as it had on the round. Then at once Stark and the chief started laughing. I watched them. Then I smiled.

"Gerry," Stark said, between his laughter. "Call the OOD."

"Tell him," the chief said, one hand on Stark's shoulder, the other rubbing the fuse, as a gold prospector might hold and fondle a nugget, "tell him we got him a paperweight."

"To put under his cap," Stark said.

"Inside his skull," the chief said. "Give him something to roll around in there."

Together they stood, arms about each other's shoulders, laughing as though indeed they had drunk that lethal and lovely last call that would send them singing into the streets, howling at the moon, ready for fighting, lovemaking, or a bottle to share sitting on a curb. They even moved drunkenly to the hatch, and the chief leaned out of it and, sidearm, threw the fuse over the rail, into the sea. Then he released Stark and went backward down the ladder, smiling, shaking his head, then laughing again as he stopped midway and reached his hands through the hatch.

"Here you go, Mr. Stark."

Stark brought the round to the hatch and lowered it into the chief's hands. He backed down the ladder, went to the rail, looked at the water, then up at us standing at the hatch.

"You gentlemen want a forward pass or a drop kick?"

"Sissy stuff," Stark said. "See if you can throw it off the starboard side."

The chief looked up at the edge of the flight deck above the gun mount.

"I don't know. I'd have to clear the flight deck. And miss the bridge or go over it. Fuck it."

His back was to the sea. He bent his knees, then straightened them, and with both arms threw the round over his head, his straining face, and spun to watch it splash and sink.

"Beautiful," Stark said.

"Mr. Stark? Would you bring my cap down with you?" He put a cigarette between his lips, patted the pockets of his khaki shirt. "And your lighter. And that funny little manual. What's this gun? Mount eight?"

I nodded.

"Mr. Stark, don't accept no more calls from this mount."

"Hazardous duty pay, Chief."

"They never said you had to *be* hazardous. And read a fucking manual that *tells* you you're hazardous."

Stark turned from the hatch and picked up the chief's cap and the manual. He was grinning again, and he called out to the chief: "Don't you want the tools?"

"Shit," the chief said. "Might's well leave them. We'll probably be back."

Stark took the tool kit and at the hatch he patted my shoulder with the cap and manual.

"Great guy," he said, "the chief. You can inform the OOD that the motherfucker is defused and at the bottom. See you at chow."

He stepped onto the ladder, and the chief came and took the kit and cap and manual from him so Stark could use both hands going down. I phoned the OOD, watching Stark and the chief smoking at the rail, the chief holding the manual before them, and they were looking at it and smiling, talking, sometimes laughing again, like two men looking at a photograph someone had taken of them in an instant of drunken foolishness.

That was going to be a separate letter, but Willie and I laughing so long at the joke, the monkey on the road, reminded me of it. For our laughter did not spring from the recognition of anything funny. No more than Stark's and his chief's did, as they laughed at the manual and their having to use it not only to do their jobs, but to save their lives. And mine too, but I was excluded from their mirth because I had merely chosen to watch, while they had done the work they had learned to do but probably had forgotten, because neither of them expected ever to handle a VT fuse that might be activated, because an activated VT fuse was supposed to be the nose of a round already propelled high into the air, well beyond their responsibilities, their lives.

Willie and I laughed at another death: not one that comes in an explosion's instant, but a minute-by-minute, day-by-day-for-centuries death of health, justice, and hope for an entire race of Americans, and the lesser—because the suffering is less, even imperceptible—death of the white race as well. If one believes, as you and I do and as Willie does, that you cannot perpetrate or even tolerate or even close your eyes to evil without paying a price.

Later, as we drank what we called our last beer, he said: "When I get out of the Navy, I'm going to be Jason."

"Won't it feel strange? After—what, twenty-five years?"

"It's my middle name."

"I know. But most of the time I don't even remember I have one."

"What is it?"

"Francis. For Francis of Assisi. My mother's favorite saint."

"Was he the rich guy who gave it all up?"

"That's him."

"Want to give up some yen for a beer? I've run out."

"Might as well. We'll be fucked up tomorrow anyway."

I raised my hand into the noises of louder, drunker voices, and the dark and smoke that seemed to hover over our booth like something my fingers could touch and penetrate.

"I'm tired of being Willie," he said.

I waited for words. Then she was there, so small that her throat and chin were level with my vision. I ordered the Asahis; and in that pause, that turning away from Willie, I was relieved, grateful, for suddenly I knew the words that I had nearly spoken, and would have spoken had I drunk gin instead of beer, or perhaps even three more beers. I had nearly said to him: There's always Willie Mays. I had beer left in my glass, and I drank it before looking at him. Then I said: "I like it. Jason Brooks. Has style. Goes better with your boy's name too, Jimmy. Jason and James and Louisa."

"You really like it?"

"It's a strong name."

"That's what I've been thinking."

"Jason, Louisa, and Jimmy Brooks. Shit. I got to have a kid."

"A boy?"

The waitress came and I gave her all my yen but the taxi fare, a *beau geste* of a tip. I didn't count it; her eyes and smile and repeated *arrigato*s told me.

"Boy, girl," I said. "Doesn't matter. Hell, two or three of each."

In the taxi, one of those blurred rides when you're drunk and know the motion of the car will get you there, but that's all you know, sitting in that speeding and slowing forward movement over streets and past lighted bars you don't see and would not recognize anyway, Willie said: "Okay, let me see it."

"See what?"

"That knife."

"Oh." I lifted and turned my hips and pulled the knife from my pocket. "Here."

He held it in front of his face, in the light from cars and the street, and looked at its brown wooden handle and dark gray folded blade.

"It's not even long."

"Legal size. I told you it's—"

"Yes, I know. How did it feel?"

He was still looking at the knife, holding it in two hands now, a thumb and forefinger at either end.

"I had the point at his artery. I pressed it a little, not enough to even draw blood."

"Was he bigger than you?"

"I don't know. All I saw was his eyes. And how still he was. He wasn't looking at me. His eyes went down and to his left. Toward the knife. Course he couldn't see it."

"I guess that's where a man would look."

"It was pure. My feelings. Like everything was in harmony, for the first time in my life. Everything I'd ever seen or heard of done to Negroes. Right there in that fucker's face. In his throat."

He lowered the knife to his lap, and held it in one open hand in the dark beneath the car window.

"And it was like it was just him and me. Finally it was all concrete, all defined in one man. And I had him. For an end to all of it. It was a fucking catharsis, is what it was."

He looked down at the knife, and unfolded the blade.

"It's just a plain old knife," he said. "Carbon steel." He moved his thumb across the edge of the blade. "Sharp, too."

"It needs some work. But I haven't been fishing in—Goddammit, how can you live on a ship and never get a chance to fish?"

We had to hold the rails of the brow as we climbed it to the waiting sober Officer of the Deck, and next morning was . . .

16 August 1961
Iwakuni, at anchor

Hello Camille:

Last night was the ship's officers' party for the Air Group. I'm alone now in our stateroom, waiting for dinner. I don't know where Willie is. This morning when the alarm rang he turned it off and went back to sleep, and I shaved and dressed and went to work. He either skipped lunch or was on liberty today and went ashore to walk around Iwakuni.

It was a formal party. No civilian jackets and ties like they make us wear off the base so communists won't know we're officers and kidnap us and torture all manner of information from us. I have no information, except that we're not supposed to bring nuclear weapons into a Japanese port, but that's what our planes carry and I assume when officers of the Japanese National Defense Force come aboard as guests they know our planes carry nuclear bombs, and I further assume that only the Japanese people don't know this, and if there are any communists waiting in alleys they're not going to grab one Cajun lieutenant (j.g.) and interrogate his young ass about what they already know. Only a few senior officers are supposed to know what our next Japanese port will be, but the bar girls do: the ones in Yokosuka will say, "You go Sasebo now," and in Sasebo they say, "*Lanegah* go Kobe," and so on. No: the Navy doesn't allow us to wear uniforms in town because what they're really afraid of is an identifiable Naval officer becoming disgracefully drunk in public. Last night's party was confined to the base: at the Officers' Club, and we wore our whites.

Willie and I dressed together, fastened each other's high stiff collars, then with his cap under his arm Willie stood before the mirror above the lavatory. In the glass were his face, the collar that stiffened his neck, his broad shoulders in white and the navy-blue shoulder boards with the gold stripe and a half, and his deep white chest with the brass buttons going down it to his narrow waist and hips, which did not show in the mirror. I stood to his side, looking from him to his reflection, back to him. An expression was forming on his face, and I waited. Then he grinned.

"I look like a chocolate sundae," he said, and laughed, shortly, and in his throat.

"May as well put on the cap and gloves," I said. "Go all the way."

"Gloves?"

"I think we have to carry the fuckers."

"Shit. I forgot to wash them."

I was about to say it, but he looked away from the mirror, at me, as though he could read the words across my brow.

"I know," he said. "No one will notice."

"They won't be *on* your hands. Just *in* one of them."

"Maybe I should have joined the Air Force."

"Maybe they have whites too."

"We still talking uniforms?"

"I think we're talking gin. Let's do it to it."

He put on his cap, adjusting it in the mirror, and took a nearly immaculate pair of white gloves from the shelf of his wall locker, and we left the room and climbed ladders and walked passageways and climbed ladders to the quarterdeck, where a lucky ensign was the OOD, though he probably thought he was missing festivities rather than being spared them, and we smartly saluted and as smartly requested permission to leave the ship, then faced the stern and saluted the flag, and went down the accommodation ladder and joined the others sitting in the officers' launch, gently rolling in the *Ranger*'s shadow. When the coxswain got underway we all took off our caps and held them, and Willie and I turned our faces to the sunlit breeze. Japanese taxis waited at the pier and took us to the club. Willie and I stayed outside for a cigarette in the setting sun. Then we went in, to the long wide room reserved for the party. So already you can see it: hundreds of white uniforms and Caucasian faces, though few truly white but pink, florid, olive, tan, all colored by duty at sea or in the air or booze or ancestral blood, and the three black faces: the flight surgeon and the personnel officer from the Air Group, and Willie: faces which in truth looked better than all of ours, the black skin richer, somehow stronger, juxtaposed with the length and breadth and depth of the uniforms as white as altar cloths.

Late in the party Willie talked to the wrong man; or the lieutenant-commander, a pilot, saw him, stalked him, cornered him. By the time I joined them, and stayed for the rest of it, then went outside with Willie, then sat beside him in the taxi and then on the launch going out to the lights and silhouette of the ship, there was no longer reason to ask who had, as the saying goes, struck up the conversation. *Struck* is the right word, and I suspect it was the lieutenant-commander who, compelled by booze and the undeniable voices in his blood, saw Willie for the twelfth or twentieth time of the evening, and went to him. During the entire party, pilots talked to each other in groups, and often a hand was in the air, moving like a jet turning, diving, climbing. We of the ship's company stayed with each other too, except the Captain and Executive Officer, who talked with the Air Group Commander and his squadron commanders; and the Admiral, who moved about, patting people's backs, always with that smile of authority, confident of welcome, confident that no one will say or do anything to alter the spreading lips, the mellow voice. I imagine the lieutenant-commander standing at the bar, talking with pilots, glancing to his side and seeing Willie again, and this time he had to make his congee from the gold-winged brethren and follow or be drawn by his history. I see his walk across the room as a series of geometric angles and half-circles around men standing unnaturally erect while talking shop. Yet his true azimuth, that of his heart, was as straight as a carpenter's chalk line.

Willie and I had started drinking together, but the hors d'oeuvres table, the bar, and other friends separated us for a drink, for two, until gradually we were together only for a few minutes at a time, and I had forgotten him for perhaps a half-hour when I saw them. They were some seventy feet away, a young forest of white uniforms between us. They were of equal height, Willie standing straight, the lieutenant-commander leaning toward him, his sunburned face close to Willie's, his hands moving: the one with the drink swinging back and forth as he spoke, or his free hand rising and falling. Willie's left arm was at his side; he held a drink in his right hand, his arm at a forty-five-degree angle, near-motionless, as though he were assuming some military stance. Twice, as I watched, he raised the glass and sipped; then he lowered the drink and his elbow stopped his forearm and held it level, stationary. I left the people I was with and went to him, my route as angled and skirting as I have imagined the lieutenant-commander's was, and my true course as straight as I have imagined his, and also following or being drawn by history.

Beneath the lieutenant-commander's gold pilot's wings were ribbons from Korea; he stopped talking to turn, hear my name from Willie, shake my hand as Willie said: "And this is Lieutenant-Commander Percy." His eyes were brown and had that wet brightness, that intensity, of alcohol and vocal excitement. He said: "Pleased to meet you, Gerry." My concern for Willie dissolved in adrenaline. Percy was from the South. Then I knew I had already known it, from his lips: they were thin and shaped by his pronunciation into a near-pout, as if they slouched toward his chin, and their corners drooped. They would have been sensual, were it not for a lethargic certainty about them, making him look pampered. They also grinned widely. And when he was intent, as he listened to my name and looked me up and down without appearing to, weighing my character, my worth as an officer, and later as he listened to me, or to Willie the one time he spoke, his lips were straight and grim, a mouth you would expect beneath eyes looking at you over a pistol barrel. I was trying to place his drawl when Willie said: "The Lieutenant-Commander is from Georgia."

"Atlanta?" I said.

"Oh hell no. Place called Rome. Little place. You're a Southern boy yourself."

"Yes sir. Louisiana. Sorry I said Atlanta. I'm from Lafayette— a little place—but people always think I'm from New Orleans. I mean even after I've told them."

"That's because they don't know us. Atlanta. New Orleans. Memphis. Words to them. Cities. They don't know our culture."

"Little Rock," I said.

He missed the expression on my face (or the one I felt there) and the tone of my voice (or the one I heard there); I believed I was cold and challenging.

"Right," Percy said. "Little Rock. They saw it on *T-V*. Saw the 82nd Airborne following the orders of their Commander-in-Chief." He looked at Willie. "Which I would have done too. Like that." He snapped his thumb and a finger damp from stirring his bourbon and ice, then with his cocktail napkin wiped the drops from his palm. (Yes: I am not adding that as a prop; I could smell his drink, probably sour mash.) He wore a gold wedding ring. "Same as if Kennedy sends me to Russia. People up North didn't see Little Rock. They saw a dumb governor and some dumb high-school kids and God knows what all, come to look at the soldiers. But they didn't see our culture, that's what they don't know anything about. Little places like Rome and Lafayette. In the bayou country, weren't you?"

"Yes sir."

"How long you been in now?"

"Four years and a couple of months."

His eyebrows raised and he cocked his head, looking at me with something like warmth. Hair in his eyebrows was bleached by the sun, but they were mostly brown, like his short hair.

"Almost a lieutenant. You staying in, then?"

"Yes sir."

"You two are roommates."

"Willie puts up with me."

"See?" He looked at Willie, then back to me. "You two boys're shipmates. Liberty buddies. Go ashore and get drunk together. Right?"

I told him yes, sir, we did some of that.

"That's what I been telling Willie here." He looked at Willie; then he shifted his feet to face him, leaving me as a point in the triangle, watching them. "The real Southerner is like Gerry. Not some poor ignorant son of a bitch that can't get along with Jesus Christ Himself, and's never learned you judge a man by what he is. Not by what he looks like. Or what he's called. Course I worked with more colored people growing up back home than I have in the Navy. But that'll change. Among the officers, I mean. We got plenty enlisted colored people."

"Negroes," I said.

He looked at me, with those shining eyes. Then his lips changed. They were open, perhaps on the last syllable of *people*. But they closed, straightened, and for a moment I could sense his absolute command over the demons in his soul. Then he grinned and with a turn of the head brought the grin to Willie. I watched Willie.

"Fine with me," Percy said. "I don't care what a man wants to be called. Long as he does his work, and does it the best he can. 'Sailor' is what I call them, whether they're black or purple or green. Or a pale scrawny white boy grew up in New York City. *But—*" he raised his glass so it was level with Willie's face, his nose and eyes, and pointed the forefinger. Willie looked at it. "*But*. If they fuck up, I come down. And I mean I come down hard. We got planes to fly, Willie. Them's not laying hens on that flight deck. And there's pilots in them. And two other men aboard the big ones. And we know what all those planes are for: one purpose, and one purpose alone. Get the fuck on that catapult and up in the air and drop the loads. There won't be a ship left to come home to. You know that. Gerry knows that. You boys'll get nuked up the ass by the big fish. About thirty minutes after the whistle blows. At *most*. And we'll run out of fuel. But *af*ter Moscow. We all know that.

So when a sailor fucks up I call him a bunch of things. But I'll tell you this: if that man is a Negrah, Walt Percy don't call him a nigger. I might call him a worthless dumb son of a bitch. But not nigger. If you'll pardon the word. Because I'm trying to make a point."

Willie wanted to hit him. Or his body did; but he does not believe in it, so what Willie wanted to do, wanted to be allowed to do, was tell Percy, loudly and articulately and for a long time, that he was full of shit. Willie wanted to be a civilian, wanted Percy to be one too. Even if, as civilians, Percy were Willie's boss. Willie could tell him what he had to say, and quit his job. Yet there in the club, and aboard ship, or *any*where, in or out of uniform, Percy was not Willie's boss, only a senior officer, and still he constricted Willie as surely as a straitjacket; and Willie had to yield to the constriction, even help it with his own will. He was breathing deeply and his tight blouse showed each breath; the skin of his face was taut over his cheekbones and jaw, and his nostrils widened with his breathing. For his mouth was closed and I knew from his jaw and the muscle in front of his ear that his teeth were tightly pressed together, his tongue heavy and strong behind them, a wild animal he wanted to set free.

"Willie, we weren't allowed to say that word in our home. My big brother did. Just once. Name's Boyd. He was maybe fifteen, sixteen. Big old country boy. My daddy didn't scold him. No sir. And Boyd was a bit too big, too old, for a spanking. My daddy didn't slap him either. Or shake him till his head wanted to come loose, like he did to me once when he thought I lied to him. I did lie, but not as much as he thought. Had to do with some car trouble and getting home late from being out with a girl. No sir, Willie. My daddy didn't say a word to Boyd. We were at supper. He put down his fork and got up from where he was sitting, at the head of the table, there in the kitchen. He went to Boyd's chair. Boyd was sitting at one side of the table, next to me. We had a big family, three boys on one side of the table, I was the youngest, and three girls on the other side. I saw it coming. Boyd didn't. He was working on his supper and maybe thought Daddy was going to piss or something. Daddy took hold of Boyd's chair and pulled it straight back—with one hand—and turned it, so he was looking down at Boyd. All I could see was Boyd's back and Daddy's face and shoulders, but I could feel it in Boyd's spine, coming at me like a radio signal: let me tell you, he knew now. Daddy pulled him up from the chair with his left hand and turned him so his back was to the wall. I guess so Boyd wouldn't fall on me and my plate, waste all that food. Maybe break my nose. Then he hit him. With his fist, Willie. Coming up from way down. Sounded like a bat hitting a softball. Not quite a baseball, but a new hard softball. Old Boyd hit the wall and went down on the floor. He could still see and hear, but not much, and he sure as hell wasn't about to move. 'Boyd,' Daddy said, 'we don't say that word in this house. You want to talk like poor white trash, you know where you can find them. Maybe they'll even take you in.' Then he went back to his chair and finished his supper. Old Boyd got up and went on to bed. And that man—my daddy—went to school for seven years. That's it. Seventh-grade education. After that he stayed home and worked with his daddy on the farm."

Then Percy smiled and, oblivious of Willie's glare, his taut face, held Willie's bicep.

"Willie, I bet anytime old Boyd starts to say that word his jaw shuts him up, it starts hurting so bad." Maybe then he noticed Willie's face. He withdrew his hand, and looked at me, a friendly look, and at Willie again. "Hell, you know what I'm trying to say. A Southerner—a *real* one, mind you, not one of them no-counts doesn't have a pot to piss in or a window to throw it out of, and doesn't respect anybody or anything because he doesn't even respect himself, but a *real* Southerner—respects the South. Loves the South. And that means"—he looked at me—"Atlanta, New Orleans, Memphis, *Mo*bile—" Then he winked at me, smiled, lightly punched my rigid arm, and said: "We don't count Mi*am*i."

His right hand with the drink swept away from me, past Willie's chest, as though turning Percy's head to face Willie. Willie gazed into his eyes. Gazed, not glared, and I believed (and still do) that Willie was seeing sharply every detail of Percy's face, hearing every inflection of his voice, and was also seeing and feeling too the years he had been carried and shoulder-pushed, then crawled and then walked as a Negro in America, and seeing as well the years beyond these minutes with Percy, the long years ahead of him and Louisa and Jimmy and his children still to come.

"And Rome and Lafayette," Percy said. "All the little towns Yankees like to poke fun at, little towns with decent people making do. And the farms and hills and swamps and, by God, mountains. But Willie—" Again he raised his glass, pointed the forefinger at Willie's nose or mouth or between his eyes. "What the Southerner respects most, and that's why we took on the Yankees in a war, is the individual. The individual as part of a whole way of life. We respect a man's right to work for his family, put a roof over their heads, whether it's a Goddamn mansion or a little old shotgun house on a patch of ground wouldn't make a decent-size parking lot. And to raise his kids as he sees fit. Believe it or not, and by God I hope I'm helping you believe it, the Southerner most of all wants to leave people alone. And be left alone. Hell, that's why my family and everybody I know down there's always voted Republican. Tell you something else too, since we've gone this far. Slavery was a bad thing. Everybody knows that. But there's something not many Yankees know. Your slave was not mistreated. Why in hell would a man whip or starve the people that kept him rich? Hell, those old boys sent their sons to the War Between the States, but not their slaves. No sir. The slave was a valuable piece of *prop*erty. You see what I mean?"

"Yes sir," Willie said. He had not spoken in so long that I was surprised, and expectant, and I watched his mouth and waited. His voice was soft and respectful, and still was when he said: "We Americans have always placed a high value on property."

Percy was confused. The words themselves were sarcastic, and Percy's lips straightened and were tight and thin. But Willie's voice must have changed the meaning of the words in Percy's sour-mashed brain. His lips eased into their drooping pucker, then spread to a smile.

"There you go," he said. "Then they were free and that was an awful mess. *A*wful. Lynchings, *bull*ying. I'll tolerate the opinion of nearly any man, and even the action he takes to back it up. Depending on the action. But I can't stand a man who has to join with others, get help with his dirty work. I would personally shoot any KKK son of a bitch showed up with his gang of walking bedsheets. Shoot him dead center in his Goddamn hood and not even read the newspaper next day to see who the son of a bitch was. But we got past Black Reconstruction. And into a new century. Now we're over halfway through it. And it'll be good in the South. For your people. I can promise you that. Make bet on it. Because people like me and Gerry here *know* the Negrahs. You can't send them up North—I know, I know, they had damn good reason to leave home. But it doesn't work. Negrahs in a Northern urban environment. It hasn't worked, and it won't. What did they get? No money, and raising their children in Goddamn ghettos. Bad as it still is down home, a Negrah man can work for a little house to live in, have him a little yard for his children. And how many times, Gerry"—he only glanced at me—"you seen a Negrah daddy taking his boy down a country road, going fishing? Bamboo poles. Or going hunting? I don't think a Negrah man can walk down a city street up North, him and his boy carrying shotguns. It's going to work, Goddammit. Gradual integration. Starting with the little kids, the first-graders. Because those little white kids' daddies, like me and Gerry, and *our* daddies, we *know* the Negrahs. We've worked with them, we've *played* with them—"

He paused. He had not finished the sentence. It hung there in the middle of our triangle, its pitch still raised for more words, but they did not come; we stood suspended in silence, in a sense of incompletion, as though none of us could speak or even move until Percy finished the sentence, lowered his pitch to lead to the period that would allow us to do more than simply breathe. I did not know where to look. My eyes settled on Percy's ribbons: he had a Distinguished Flying Cross. I looked at the two and a half gold bars on his shoulder boards. We all lit cigarettes, Percy holding his Zippo for us, an old one with raised flier's wings on its worn surface, the color of a dime from the first march of them.

"Well," he said. His smile to Willie was tentative. He held the smile, looking at Willie's face; but his eyes now were like those of a man studying a statue, trying to know from the bronze eyes and mouth and nose and jaw what sort of man the artist had sculpted: to know if he was wise, courageous in battle, a lover of women; to know whether or not he would be a good man to drink with; to know what voices were most constant in his mind.

"Well, gentlemen. Willie—" He nodded to Willie. "Gerry—" He turned his face and nodded to me. "I'm confronted with a glass has more ice than Jack Daniel's in it. I've enjoyed our talk. Now I'll go see the real highest-ranking man at the party. That portly bartender."

He put his glass in his left hand and extended the right to Willie. Who took it. I watched Willie's knuckles and fingers. He firmly shook Percy's hand. Then the hand came to me and I did too.

"I hope we'll chat again," Percy said. "All it takes. More talks like this one."

Then he was gone. And you know what? Not only had he drunk enough to be forgiven his babble, but it didn't matter anyway. Not to Percy. For he would have no remorse next morning. *This* morning, ten hours ago. I know he did not wake, as I have so many times, as you have a few times, and lie in his bunk while the party's sounds and images were first blurred, then distinct, chronological even, until he remembered Willie and thought: *Oh my God I can't believe I—* No. He woke and remembered Willie and he was glad, even grateful to himself or God, that finally he had talked to Willie. He had been an officer and a (Southern) gentleman. He had given much of his evening to a young Negro officer from the ship's company. (Had the flight surgeon and the personnel officer in the Air Group had their share of him too, on other, earlier evenings?) He was a Navy pilot. He had distinguished himself in the air over Korea. He was proudly ready at any moment to climb into his cockpit and be catapulted into his final flight to Moscow. Last night he had left his jet-pilot friends, their unity so true and deep that, to an observer, it resembles love. He had left them to talk to the colored officer, the Negro, the Negrah, and to say that Willie was not as singular as he appeared, among the Caucasian faces and white uniforms. To say that he, Percy, with his Georgian speech, was not an enemy. That no Southerner, simply because he was a Southerner, was convicted. That all the evidence was not in; that the color of a man's flesh did not touch Percy's heart; and the place of a man's birth and childhood should not touch Willie's. He had done his best. Perhaps he woke this morning with a headache, and phlegm from too many Camels.

Willie woke to his alarm and turned it off. I imagine its ringing shot through his brain and blood and heart, and returned him to the last hours of the night. So he shut his eyes and, only because he was blessed with a hangover, he was able within minutes to return to the unconscious state those last hours earned for him; to retreat into the morning of sleep he deserved.

When Percy left us, I said to Willie: "Let's get a fucking drink."

He did not look at me. I stood at the point of the triangle Percy's leaving had abolished, and Willie stared at the space where, seconds ago, Percy's flesh and voice had been.

"I'm going outside," he said. Still he looked at that air in front of him, as though it held Percy's shape. Then he walked through it.

"I'll bring them out," I said to his back.

I could not see his face. His back was erect, his shoulders squared, his strides long, purposeful, like a man on his way to settle a score, to confront someone who may badly hurt him, or take away his livelihood, even kill him, but the risk was nothing to him now, for he could no longer tolerate or even bear himself until he faced with the purity and freedom of just anger that man whose presence on the earth fouled his every breath. I hurried around people toward the bar, but watching Willie, so I grazed some men and bumped others and begged their pardons and continued on, guided by peripheral vision and a strange instinct that warned me of men in my path, and saw Willie taking his cap and gloves from the hat-check girl and, without looking back at the party, or to his left or right, walking to the door, pushing the crash bar, and going out. The door was slowly closing behind him when I reached the bar and waved to the bartender (probably a chief, a man in his late thirties; he was large but I would not have called him portly), and I nodded and even answered when friends spoke to me. I ordered two double gin-and-tonics. Watching the door, watching the bartender pouring gin on ice in the large glasses, I replied to people and saw Percy at the right end of the bar, standing with other pilots, grinning at a laughing lieutenant whose hand climbed at a low angle, as though from a flight deck, and sharply rose into the air. Then the bartender was in front of me, sweating, working fast, and I told him to keep the change from my five, not generosity but hurry (the bill was two dollars), and, sweating, he smiled and thumped the bar with his knuckles.

At the coat-check booth I overtipped for the same reason, gave to the young kimonoed Japanese girl two dollars that came out of my pocket in my plunging and grabbing hand, broke the club rules by putting on my cap indoors, then held my gloves between my left arm and ribs and, with a glass in each hand, pushed the crash bar and door with my side, turned through the opening, and was out before the door could close on my right hand holding Willie's drink that seemed so precious. Willie had not gone far. He was to my left, walking parallel to the long room whose walls and windows gave a muted immediacy to the loud and unharnessed voices of men drinking together. He walked slowly now, his steps short, his posture settling toward the pull of the earth, his white-capped head lowered. I could see the gloves in his left hand. I called his name. He nearly stopped: he was about thirty yards away, and I could see his back hesitate, an instant's motion as though not his ears but his back heard me, and it almost straightened, almost halted his legs. But he did not stop, and he did not turn to look over his shoulder, and he did not lift his face from its gaze at the ground, or whatever he saw there.

So I went to him, as quickly as I could, holding level the cold glasses, while gin and tonic dripped down their sides onto my hands, and I kept my gloves pressed between my bicep and ribs. I could not hear my feet on the grass and earth. I heard beyond the wall laughter and voices without words, sounds that had been merry until Percy, but were mocking now. *So*, I said to myself. *This is what it is. To be outside.* I could hear our drinks too: their soft fizz and the dull clicking of ice in liquid. Willie knew I was coming. I don't believe he could hear me, but he knew. When I drew within five or six paces of him, walking on his right so I could step beside him and put a drink into his hand free of gloves, I saw that, while his bent neck and head were nearly still, his shoulders and his arms at his sides were moving up and down, not jerking, but with the involuntary and rhythmless motion of resisted weeping. Then I was beside him. I did not want to violate him by looking at his face, but my eyes moved to it and quickly away from the tears on his cheeks, and I looked down at his hand. I lowered the drink in my right hand, touched the knuckles and back of his hand with it. We were still walking. He took the drink and brought it to his lips, sniffing deeply and spitting before his first swallow. I took my gloves from under my arm, then could drink. He stopped and said: "I'm out of cigarettes."

Still he looked ahead. I shifted my drink to the hand with the gloves and pulled a flattened pack from my trouser pocket and shook it till a cigarette pointed at Willie. He turned to me and took it. But as with my lips I pulled another from the pack, he faced again the direction he had walked. I held my lighter to his cigarette, then to mine, and drank with my gloves wrapped around my glass, as Willie did. I faced his side, watching now his wet eyes and cheeks, his open mouth breathing against the tears he still held back.

"I *hate* white people," he said, and they came then, loudly, his waist bending, straightening, bending, his upper arms pressed tightly against his sides, while his hands with drink and cigarette trembled beneath his face. Now I could not look away from that face. Nor could I touch him. All my life I have seen girls and boys and women cry, but until last night the only man I had seen cry—really cry, not damp eyes at a movie's end or when a man is talking with love about one of his children—was Daddy the night his brother died. I was fourteen then, and all I could do was sit across the room and watch him convulse in his chair, trying to keep his palms over his face, but his neck writhed away from them, his arms fell to his heart, his belly, and pressed them. Yet I have seen my mother and aunts and sisters and you crying at some pain of the heart, even keening, and still able to walk, to move from one room to another, even to the kitchen to boil water and make coffee or tea, even to speak with coherence—broken by sobs, yes, but still coherence. Yet I've never seen a man do that. Willie's face was both younger and older than he was. His control of it while listening to Percy was gone, and with that control something else was gone too, as if the flow of tears and the wet moaning—*oh oh aah*—as he both fought and surrendered to crying, were taking from him all the strength he had developed in his twenty-five years on earth: not only the strength to be resilient, but to be humorous too, and gentle. He had the face of a brokenhearted child. Yet at the same time he looked old: old as the infirm look, finished, done in by something as inexorable as nature.

Then I was touching him, and it was my flesh that closed the short space between us while my mind held back, bound by its inertia, by its wish that none of this from the seventeenth century until 1961 had ever happened in America, by its sad desire to be no part of it, to have seen and heard none of it since my birth in 1936, and by its conviction that the pigmentation I was born with was, against my strongest will, responsible for every tear falling from his face, every moan he could not contain, every quick and terrible motion of his arms and head and stomach and chest, so that he looked like a man fighting for his life against an enemy neither visible nor large: some preternatural opponent clawing and biting the skin and bone that covered Willie's heart. But my flesh ignored my mind. It dropped my cigarette, and my left hand and arm slid across Willie's back, drawing my body to his, my hand pushing itself between his left arm and side, and though I did not weep but only watched his face, my body moved as though it wept with him, for I held him so tightly, and my torso rocked back and forth, and my waist bent and straightened, and pulled my face down and up.

"All of you," he said. His eyes were closed. I watched their lids, and his open mouth that still held tears, but his voice was more dry now. Then abruptly he looked at me. I was startled out of the silence our bodies had given my mind, and I could feel it gathering itself again to pull me away from Willie, to make again that space between our shoulders and sides and arms so I would stand alone and become under the night sky of Japan the apotheosis of slave traders and owners and the Klan and murderers and Negro-beaters and those who inflict their torment economically, or with the tongue, or with silence, and eyes that look at a Negro as if he were not even a tree or rain but only air. So I held him more tightly. My squeeze made him gasp, and with his sound my brain emptied, was pure, clean, primordial, and Willie's eyes changed: their bright anguish softened, and they focused on my face, and I felt, I *knew*, Camille, that suddenly he saw not a white man but me.

"I have to tell Jimmy," he said. He stopped to breathe: a deep breath, then another. If all his tears had not been spent, he would have cried again. But only his voice did: soft, nearly a whisper. "Someday I have to tell my son he's a nigger." Again he breathed. Then his right arm pushed backward between us, and I lightened my grip on him so it could move around my waist, and then I tightly held him as his hand holding his drink pressed into my right side, and his arm pulled me to him. "One year old. I have to tell him, Gerry. Soon. Too soon. But before he finds out."

Our free arms rose together as we turned to face each other and embraced with both arms and I could not hear the party inside, only our breathing and the faint scraping of our whiskered cheeks. We stood for a minute, perhaps less. Then we stepped back and drank, our glasses lacking at least a swallow spilled, and I drew out my cigarettes, more flattened now, and we shaped them round, and smoked and drank in silence as we walked toward the entrance of the club. Walked slowly, I looking at my watch—the taxis for those who were leaving the party early would arrive at ten-thirty, only eight minutes away—and Willie wiping his face with his gloves.

We got the first taxi that came and quietly finished our drinks in the back seat, tossed ice and limes out the windows, and left the glasses to roll on the floor. At the pier we waited for the others, the small taxis of officers who wanted the eleven-o'clock launch. We heard it coming, its engine low out on the water. We stood at the edge of the pier, on the opposite side from where the launch would tie up, and looked down at the dark water that always seems fathoms deep at night, and we looked out to sea at the lights of the *Ranger*. I had one cigarette left, a Pall Mall, and I broke it in half and handed Willie his. Taxis came in a fast column, their headlights shining for an instant on our faces. Willie's face now was the one I had known until tonight: an expression of repose, though now I saw clearly what I must have seen on the night he first entered our room, though I had not remarked it then, for my life, my past, had taught me to expect it. Now his face reminded me of a painting I saw long ago of an American Indian, a Cheyenne or Sioux, an old chief: he wore his war bonnet, and in the set of his jaw and lips, the years in his eyes, even in the wrinkles on his face, was the dignity of a man, sorrowful yet without self-pity, who has endured a defeat that will be part of him, in his heart, until he dies.

Officers climbed loudly out of taxis, slammed doors, called to friends standing on the pier or sliding and twisting out of other cabs. The launch's engine had grown louder, and now it slowed as the coxswain approached the pier. Behind Willie and me the officers clustered. The launch drew alongside, and Willie and I turned together and followed the others into the boat, and took off our caps. Men talked above the wind. For a while I looked at the *Ranger;* then I looked away from it, high above the faces across from me, at the stars and the silent sky, and the wind blew on my face and dried the sweat in my hair. Willie and I were last to leave the launch. I walked behind him up the accommodation ladder. On the quarterdeck he saluted aft, then the OOD, and spoke for the first time since we stood outside the club. He requested permission to come aboard.

We went quietly to our room, abreast in the passageways, Willie going first down the ladders, and the ship itself quiet, its steel having absorbed and separated the others returning from the party. He entered the room first too, and we quietly undressed, as we had on other nights when we came back to the ship so drunk and tired that merely undressing was a bother, and hanging the clothes in our lockers a task. He got into his bunk and I turned off the light and walked from the door in the dark toward the bunks, then saw them, and climbed the ladder near Willie's feet and crawled onto the mattress and pushed my legs under the blanket and between the crisp sheets a Filipino had tucked with a hospital fold during the day. I shut my eyes and saw and heard Percy, saw Willie's face as Percy talked, and his face later, outside the club, and I opened my eyes to the gray overhead in the dark.

"Gerry." It was his voice again, the one I had known. "I'm sorry I said that."

"Fuck sorry."

"The man got to me."

"You don't need to tell me that."

"Yes I do."

"Okay. But just once, Jason."

I closed my eyes and remembered the wind on my face in the launch coming back, tried to feel it moving over my skin in the closed and air-conditioned room, and I saw the stars again, in the sky larger than the sea. They began to disappear, as though rising from the sea and the earth and my vision, and I saw the black of sleep coming, when below me Willie made a sound like laughter, a humorous grunt, and said: "My people, my people . . ."

He shifted, rolled to his side, and I lay on my back and for moments with closed eyes saw the stars again and focused on them until I knew from his breathing that Willie was asleep, then I let go of their tiny silver lights and received the dark.

11 September 1961
Okinawa, at anchor

Hello Camille:

There is not only a mystery in night itself, but it is intensified at sea. I am standing the eight-to-midnight watch, not the OOD on the quarterdeck, but the Duty Officer at the accommodation ladder for enlisted men. I drink coffee and smoke (not allowed on the quarterdeck, or here either, but not seen on this deck, at least not by officers). My assistant is a seaman second class, and he is also quiet. Our duties are simple enough. Every hour the enlisted men's liberty boat comes alongside from Okinawa, and we stand at the top of the ladder and as each sailor steps aboard he salutes aft, then salutes me and requests permission etc., and I grant it and he goes below. Our only important duty is to make sure a friend or, lacking that, one of the Masters-at-Arms takes below and puts to bed a sailor who is dangerously drunk: helps him down the steep ladders, and lies him in his bunk, on his side, so he won't drown if he vomits while asleep. Some of them have been drinking ashore since liberty call at noon.

And there is an interesting instruction left with the log for the oncoming Duty Officer: we are told to watch for sea snakes, which have been seen near the ladder. So Gantner (the seaman second class) and I peer down at the water as the liberty boat approaches. We are unarmed. Instructions like these make me wonder why they are not accompanied by a shotgun. The Navy seems to trust only the ship's Marines to handle any firearm smaller than a five-inch fifty-four. Ha: they don't know that tonight's Duty Officer, shepherd of the young and drunk and recently laid, is a slayer of many cottonmouths and copperheads with his cheap but accurate Hi-Standard .22 revolver. I'm not only at sea and can't fish, I can't even shoot a sea-going cottonmouth. A very lethal one at that. So Gantner and I watch the water beneath the ladder that angles out from the ship, so we can yell to some poor bastard stepping from the boat to the ladder that he is about to be struck by a terrible snake, and before he even hears us he will have in his blood a poison that, as far as I know, does not have an antidote. But it adds excitement, or at least alertness, to our hourly stand at the head of the ladder. And at times makes me nostalgic for my snake-infested boyhood: a sure sign that the night and sea are at work on me, for in truth I have little nostalgia for that boyhood, and none at all for the sudden appearance of a poisonous snake in my path or, worse, beside or behind the spot where I have just stepped. What quick— no: startled—draws from the holster, what terrified fusillades with the .22. Remember? How many times did we picnic on a bluff over a bayou, or row a skiff on one, without coming as close to a cottonmouth as city people do to pigeons?

At night I feel more deeply. And my loneliness now is also like the feeling I sometimes have at Mass, at the Consecration or while singing or receiving the Host; and sometimes watching the sun set; or sometimes taking the hook from a fish's mouth; and always picking up a dove I have shot and holding its warm body and stroking its soft gray feathers; or listening to jazz, a female vocalist, in a dark club with people at every table but quiet and listening too. So it is not true loneliness, like Ernie's when I was on the *St. Paul* and for the seven months of our deployment his wife did not write to him and when we got home to the band playing on the pier and you waiting in your red dress and all the wives and children and lovers waiting she was not there, and he stayed on the pier till he was alone on it, then took a taxi to the apartment he knew had not been his home for months; he only did not know precisely why; and the key was under the mat and the apartment was empty save for his things in cartons on the bare living-room floor, and taped to one of the boxes a letter saying she had left him for a doctor she met and fell in love with at the hospital where she was a pretty twenty-two-year-old nurse coming home alone at night for seven months out of every twelve, to letters from the Western Pacific, silk from Hong Kong, pearls from Kobe, colored photographs of ports as the ship approached them, a kimono and happy shirts from Japanese markets, and the stereo he had brought home the year before. I remember the day he rode the train from Yokosuka to Tokyo and back and carried the stereo aboard.

So mine is not true loneliness, but closer to the love that saints feel for God: a sad and joyful longing. Like St. Teresa of Avila, whose heart held so much love of God that, in harmony with the earth, she transcended it too, was beyond it, reaching for union with Him. If Teresa imagined ascending through the sky I stand under tonight, then wife-lover that I am, abiding companion of Camille, my strong and wise and gentle woman, I traverse the sky to sit with you at breakfast. For about now you are in that cramped kitchen, and I can see you, smell your morning flesh and hair, and your first coffee and cigarette, and the bacon slowly frying and the biscuits in the oven as you read the *Chronicle* and enter your day.

I believe at night the world leaves us. We do not see it. It is gone. We are left with what little of it we can see, and without those distractions lit by day, our focus does more than simply narrow: it sharpens on what for most of us is the world—our selves. So the malaise that is held at bay by the visible motion and stillness under sunlight—people and cars and buildings and highways and woods and fields and water—can in the enclosing dark of night become despair. What does Ernie do now, at watch on the bridge at night, or in Japanese cities? Could bars stay in business if we all worked from midnight till eight, going to whatever home in the morning sun rising with promise, instead of the setting sun, harbinger of twilight and dusk, then night?

So now, seeing little more than the small deck I stand on, and its rail, and hearing only the water gently washing at the ship's hull, I receive the world less through my senses than through my spirit. But with the lovely smell of the sea. And I look at it too, unable to see anything that is not a prominent silhouette on its surface: another ship, a small boat; I cannot see the myriad waves, only a softly swelling darkness and a swath of moon-shimmer. Far beyond my vision of it, the Pacific ends at the sky, a horizon I see only because of the stars. They are low in the sky at the dark line of the ocean. I am writing on the podium that holds the log, and I stop for minutes between sentences, even words, to look up at the sky covering you like a soft sheet, though it is mid-morning in Alameda, and you are awake, you are in motion. I am on the starboard side, facing east, but I may be looking toward Oregon or Mazatlan. But these stars in their sheet cover you. As I cover you: in the ocean that touches the earth where you sit in the kitchen, and under the sky that is above you and east of you too, I am with you. My spirit, my love, move in the water, and through the air beneath the stars. Perhaps St. Teresa felt this about God during the day, praying, eating, talking to a nun about whether it would rain before noon or the clouds would blow.

I wrote all that, or got to the last sentence of it, at about ten-fifteen. Now it's eleven-forty-five. Romantic, spiritual, whatever the mood was, it's gone now, as distant as last month. I stopped writing because the OOD phoned and told me to watch for a sailor on the liberty boat that left the pier at ten o'clock. A Negro sailor, in a wet uniform. The Shore Patrol had radioed the OOD, told him there had been a fight on the pier, between a white sailor and a Negro sailor, and they had fallen into the water. The Negro had come out and climbed onto the pier and then into the liberty boat. The white sailor was still underwater, and divers were looking for him. The OOD told me to arrest the Negro, get his statement, and have the original delivered to him. He said there was no need to send the Negro to the brig.

The phone is on the podium with the log. I went to the hatch of the compartment where Gantner sat in one of two chairs: a small place with a gray wall locker, a coffee percolator, white mugs from the mess hall, a desk with strewn memorandums, ashtrays made from coffee cans, a typewriter. Gantner looked up at me standing at the hatch. He is a tall, lean man, probably my age. For moments we looked at each other. Then he stood and swallowed coffee without lowering his eyes from mine. Then I told him and he drained the cup and wiped his lips with the back of his hand and said: "Shit."

He put on his cap and followed me to the top of the ladder and we stood at the rail, looking east at the sea, listening for the liberty boat. Soon we heard its engine, distant, to our left, beyond the bow. We lit cigarettes.

"You know those Goddamn piers," he said. He was not nervous, or expectant, or, as many men would be, excited. His voice was bitter, and I looked at his face and then back at the sea, wondering where he had been, what he had seen in his life. "A lot of drunk guys. A lot of guys just worked up about being ashore, just a little drunk. Everybody crowded together. Just guys. You ever notice that, how it's different when it's just guys?" I looked at him but he was listening to the engine, steady and louder, and staring over the water, perhaps at the horizon. I looked at the sky above it. "Somebody bumps somebody. That's all. And it flares up like a gasoline fire. Shit." He drew on his cigarette, then threw it down at the water, threw it with enough force to break something, if it had not been a cigarette, and if the sea could break. "Some poor fucking drunk kid."

I leaned over the rail and dropped my cigarette and watched its glow falling, watched it instantly darken, and twice the cigarette washed against the hull, then disintegrated, and I could not see the last inch of paper. I knew from the engine that the boat was making its turn, and there it was, a long boat coming widely around our bow, and I felt Gantner watching it with me as it came out of its port turn and was broadside to us, then turned starboard and came with slowing engine toward us from the stern, and I watched its red and green running lights and listened to the engine slowing, then it was idling with its port side at our ladder, and I stepped away from Gantner and stood at my post. I heard him step behind me, felt his weary sadness, like that of a young man who has been to war, or who as a child lived too much for too long with cruelty or poverty or death, and I felt that he was not in his twenties, but older than the Ship's Captain, older than the Admiral, half at least as old as the sky and sea.

They walked up one at a time, performed their protocol, men ranging in age from eighteen to forty, and all of them to some degree drunk. But tonight they did not even have to try to disguise it. They were men whose bodies were still drunk, yet their faces were sober, some marked with that exaggerated and suddenly aging solemnity of a drunken man who has just heard bad news. Not one, even the youngest, spoke to me with the alcoholic warmth that, like an old friendship, is heedless of rank. Not one smiled. They saluted aft where in daylight the flag would fly, they turned and saluted me and said, "Request permission to come aboard, sir," and I said "Permission granted," and they walked quickly off the deck, through the hatch, and down into the huge ship that sat as still as a building on land. The Negro was one of the last to come aboard. His white uniform clung to his skin, and he was shivering with cold, and I could feel him forcing his arms to his sides, away from his chest that wanted their hug and its semblance of warmth. His cap, tilted cockily forward over his right brow, was dry, except for its sides that had soaked water from his hair. It must have fallen off on the pier, before he went into the water. He turned his back to me and saluted the darkness, then faced me and saluted and before he spoke I said: "Just step behind me, sailor. Until the others have come aboard."

Two more sailors stepped on deck before I realized I could do something for the man whose shivering behind me I either heard or believed I did. I looked over my shoulder at Gantner, standing beside the Negro, watching me, looking as if he did not know whether he was a policeman or bystander or even a paraclete.

"Take him inside," I said. "Give him some coffee. And see if there's a foul-weather jacket in that locker."

He did not answer. I heard their steps on the steel deck, both of them slow, but I could detect the firmness of Gantner's, his feet coming down hard like those of an angry man, but one resigned to destiny; and the other's, soft, wet, and cold, wanting not motion but to be dry and prone between sheets and under blankets, his knees for a while drawn toward his belly, then, as he warmed, straightening until he lay at full length, even the memory of cold gone from his flesh. Soon the last sailor, a seaman first class who gave me the only sign I received from any of them—an abrupt and frowning shake of his head as his arm rose from his side to salute— disappeared through the hatch and left me alone on the deck. I stood at the railing and watched the liberty boat pull away from the ship.

Then I went through the other hatch, into the compartment: the Negro sat huddled in a chair, wearing a foul-weather jacket that was too large but not by much, its front closed above his wet trousers. His cap was on the desk beside his mug of coffee, and he was smoking one of Gantner's cigarettes and his other hand was wrapped around the mug. For warmth, I suppose. Gantner sat beside him, almost in the same pose, dry and warm but looking cold, looking near-huddled, and I thought of a blanket for him and fleetingly of the sky I saw as a starlit sheet covering you, then the Negro looked up and started to rise but with my hand I motioned him to sit, my palm pushing in his direction as though it touched his chest, not air. Then as Gantner's feet shifted to stand I pushed again at him, and he settled back. I asked him if he could type and he nodded and said yes sir and I told him to get carbon paper for an original and two.

Then the Negro moved. He was quick—motions of efficiency, not fear: he stood and carried his chair away from the desk, and Gantner, still sitting, pulled his chair to the typewriter and got paper and carbons from the desk drawer; I watched him roll them onto the carriage. The Negro stood behind Gantner and to his right, stood behind the chair, holding its back. He was directly in front of me, looking at me, his face more quizzical than afraid; but he was frightened too, and I knew then that Gantner had not spoken to him; then I knew, though I treated it as a guess, that he did not know the other sailor was dead. I told him to sit down, to have coffee, to smoke, and he pushed the chair closer to the desk and reached for his mug, but Gantner picked it up first and, twisting to his left, filled it at the percolator and placed it back on the desk, in the circle it had made before. The Negro took it. Gantner raised my mug toward me. I shook my head. He put his cigarettes and lighter and an ashtray on the edge of the desk near the Negro, then filled his coffee mug and lit a cigarette, and the Negro did too, then Gantner rested his on the ashtray, and his hands settled on the typewriter keys, so softly that not one key moved. Then I looked at the Negro, at his waiting eyes.

"I'm placing you under arrest," I said. "That does not mean the brig. You will simply go to your bunk. Tomorrow an investigating officer will talk to you." He was no longer quizzical, and he wasn't more frightened yet either: he was alert and he was thinking, with the look of a man trying to remember something crucial, and I imagined the pictures in his mind and then the last one, the one that changed his face: a sudden slackening, and now he was afraid, and more: in his eyes was a new knowledge, a recognition that his entire life, in this very moment, was finished; that is, his life as it had been, as he had known it. "You're free to make a statement," I said. "Gantner will type it and you can sign it. And you must understand this perfectly: anything you say can be used against you in a court-martial." Gantner began to type; I paused, then understood he was typing the beginning of such statements: *Having been informed of my rights* and so forth *I do hereby make the following voluntary statement . . .* "You can also remain silent. You can say nothing at all. Just get up and go below and get out of that wet uniform and take a hot shower. And go to bed. That won't be held against you either."

"Mister—"

"Fontenot."

"Mister Fontenot? What am I charged with?"

He was from the North.

"The other sailor. The one you fought with. He didn't come up."

"He didn't come up?" Now the knowledge, the recognition, was deeper, it was all of him, and I felt he was sitting in an electric chair watching me at the switch. "How come? How come he didn't just swim on up?"

"They don't know. They're looking for him."

"Wasn't *sharks* in the water. They sure he never swam to the pier? I mean, I never looked for him. I just made it to the liberty boat. I didn't even know the man. Just a white boy on the pier. I looked around the boat, once we was underway, but I didn't look real good. I was cold. I just tried to stay warm."

"Nobody said anything to you? On the boat?"

"No, Mister—"

"Fontenot."

"Mister Fontenot. No, sir."

"I think they knew."

"I don't know." He shook his head once, looked again as though he were trying to remember. "I just wanted to get to the ship, and do like you said."

"Like I said?"

"Yes sir. A hot shower and—"

"Oh."

He started to rise, but not to stand: his arms straightened and pressed down on the sides of the chair, so his weight shifted up and toward me.

"They *sure* that white boy didn't come up?"

"Nobody saw him. The Shore Patrol was there. They didn't see him. What's your name?"

He eased down on the chair.

"Seaman apprentice Ellis. Kenneth Ellis."

"Middle initial?"

"D. It's for Dalton."

"Where are you from, Ellis?"

"Detroit. Mr. Fontenot."

"Do you want to make a statement?"

"Yes sir. Yessir, I'll make a statement." He reached for his mug and cigarette, almost burned down now, and his fingers trembled. He looked at Gantner. "Want me to go slow?"

Gantner did not look up from the page in the typewriter.

"I'm fast," he said. "Don't worry about me. Take a cigarette when you want one. I got a carton in my locker and there's enough here to get me through this fucking watch."

He quickly looked up at me, apologetic, then defiant as his face lowered to the page.

"We was on the pier," Ellis said, and Gantner was typing. "I was by myself. I mean I left my buddies in the bar. I was tired. I was going broke too. I mean, they'd pay for me, but you know how it is. So I was standing on the pier, watching the boat coming. It was crowded, you know." He had been looking directly at me, and he still did but now his eyes were not really seeing mine, and his voice softened, as memory drew him back to the pier, and the man he was there, with the life he had there. "People close up against one another." I saw a motion to my right and looked at it: Gantner's face rising from the words under the keys, his eyes looking at mine. "There was some loud ones behind me. Southern boys.

But they wasn't saying nothing. To me, I mean. Or doing nothing. After a while I forgot they was even there. They was loud, but I didn't hear hear it no more. I was just watching them running lights and thinking about sleeping and tomorrow." Gantner was very fast; it seemed that Ellis's words themselves struck the keys. "I got liberty tomorrow too. I had liberty tomorrow. I was thinking about where to go, and how much money I ought to bring. When was the next payday, and would it be before the next port. I must have stepped back. I guess I did. No reason. I was just thinking and I stepped back. I bumped one of the white boys. One of the Southern boys. He said— He called me nigger. Something about 'Watch what you doing, nigger.' Something like that. So I turned on him. Mister —" His eyes came back from memory, focused on mine. "Fontenot. Nobody's called me that since I was too little to do nothing. When I got my size maybe two, maybe three guys, they called me that. But they didn't come out so good." His size was not height, or in his shoulders and chest; he was a normal young man, five-nine or so, a hundred and sixty, but I knew he was telling the truth about the two or maybe three. It was in his eyes. He'd hang on like they say a snapping turtle does, and even if you finally beat him on strength alone, you'd end up wishing you had never seen him, and you'd make certain you didn't see him again. He lowered his head, looked at the space of deck between his thighs. Then slowly he shook his head. Twice, three times, more. He did not raise it when he spoke again. "But that white boy. On the pier. I wish— We didn't even hit one another. I grabbed him and got him in a head-lock. He was a heavy boy. We was kind of turning. Like spinning round, and I was holding onto his head. Then we went off the side. The water's deep there. We went down a ways before he let go my body. He had me around here." Still looking between his thighs, he pointed at his waist. Then he said it: "Around my waist." Under Gantner's quick fingers the keys clicked to a ring, and he slid the carriage back and the keys clicked again, dulled by the three pages and two sheets of carbon paper. "Soon as he let go I did. I swam right up. I was scared too. I mean, I didn't take a big breath to go underwater. I didn't know I was going under no water. I didn't have any air left. I started getting scared I was swimming to the bottom 'stead of the top. Then I was at the top and breathing.

I mean that's all I could do, was breathe. And swim to the pier and grab the ladder. I wasn't even thinking about that white boy. I climbed up and—" Still he looked at the deck, but his head twitched upward, his neck tightened; then he let them ease down again. "Mister Fontenot's right. They must have known, on the boat. There was people on the pier. Sailors looking down at the water. When I come up the ladder. I just didn't think nothing then. I just wanted to keep sucking air, and get out of the water. Get on the liberty boat. And then the Shore Patrol come behind everybody and was yelling everybody get on the boat. So that's what we did. When I got on I checked for my wallet and I still had it. My watch was still ticking too. Then I just sat low as I could, keep out of the wind. I guess that's it."

Still he looked down. Gantner typed three more lines, and there was no ringing when he finished the last one. Then he spaced twice and typed faster than I could count but I knew the letters before they came, so I heard with each click the spelling of Kenneth D. Ellis. Then the room was silent. Gantner lit a cigarette, and Ellis looked up at me.

"Do you want to sign this?" I said.

"Sure, I'll sign it. Mister Fontenot, sir."

"Ellis."

"Sir?"

"Nothing will happen."

"Looks like a lot is happening. And a lot going to happen."

"Listen to me, Ellis. If they thought you were a man who goes around killing people, they'd have told me to put you in the brig. They didn't, did they?"

"No sir."

"So being under arrest is just a formality. I'm charging you with disorderly conduct. They'll appoint an investigating officer. To-morrow, to get it done with. When he's talked to you, you'll be free. To go on liberty. You can do whatever you want till he sees you. You just have to stay aboard."

"What about that boy?"

"You didn't drown him."

"We went into the—"

"Ellis. Somebody provoked you. You wrestled with him. You

both fell in the water. You swam out. He didn't. It's not like you held him under till he was dead."

"But—" Then all fear and confusion and his resignation to whatever fate he had imagined left his eyes, and they showed sadness, not of grief but remorse.

"You didn't kill him, Ellis. They won't even charge you with assault and battery. I'm sure of it."

"That's not it."

"I know it's not."

We looked at each other, his eyes imploring mine for forgiveness I could not grant, because I was not his friend; and imploring me too for some cleansing, some blessing short of removing him from the pier and restoring him with both energy and money to the bar with his friends, where he would drink with them and catch a later boat, long after the white boy who called him nigger was asleep in his bunk.

"Why don't you read that and sign it," I said. "Then get that shower. And some warm sleep."

As though rising after a long illness, he slowly pushed himself up from the chair, straightened his back, and was standing. Gantner pulled the sheets of paper from the typewriter and handed them to Ellis; then he stood and put on his cap and stepped toward the hatch, and I moved aside for him. He crossed the deck and stood at the rail. I looked at Ellis reading. Then I went out too and stood beside Gantner; we did not speak. After a while, and at the same time, we bent our waists and leaned on the rail, looking down at the sea, and I remembered as a boy loving to stand on those old wooden bridges over bayous, standing for an hour or more, watching the current.

Stark and his chief were on the eleven-o'clock liberty boat. I looked down into it and saw Stark, in his sport jacket and loosened tie. They came up last, Stark first up the ladder, then the chief, who was in uniform but did not salute either aft or me; and Stark, in civilian clothes and bareheaded that forbade saluting, did not go through the performance of standing at attention to face aft, then me, either. Nor did they request permission to board the ship.

"We got him," Stark said. "Where's your coffee?"

We followed Gantner into the compartment and he got two clean mugs and filled them. The chief took off his cap and tossed it on the desk.

"They put us to work," the chief said. "We were shitfaced."

"We started at noon. Lunch. Saki, and then everything."

"It was vodka. Nothing but vodka after the saki. We're sitting on the pier. Waiting for the first boat going to the ship. We'll stow away on the Captain's gig, if that's first. We don't give a shit: we're going home, set the eyelid integrity watch before we drop dead. Here comes the Shore Patrol. And Mr. Stark, he's eager, he volunteers."

"Bullshit, volunteered."

"Mr. Stark, when you say, 'Over here,' that's volunteering."

"He's right. I volunteered."

"I was about to myself," the chief said. "See, at first we thought the kid was alive. Shore Patrol guys running around, armbands, duty belts, nightsticks. Hollering. 'Is there a qualified diver on the pier?' Mr. Fontenot, try sometime hollering, 'Is there a qualified diver on the pier.' That is very official cop-like hollering. So Mr. Stark says, 'Over here.' He raises his hand too. So do I. Trouble was standing up."

"That's when I told them maybe we were not in the proper condition for underwater work."

"His exact words. Swear to God. Then they tell us the poor son of a bitch's been under there fifteen or twenty minutes. So Mr. Stark says our gear's aboard our ship. This don't work with the fucking Shore Patrol. Guy says, 'We have gear in the shed.' Leads us off to his little shack, opens some lockers, out comes all this fucking scuba gear. Even knives. So we drop our clothes and put on the suits and the guy hands me a knife. I say what am I going to do with it? He says he don't know, it's part of the gear. So I say, 'Think of some place to stick it.' He just looks at me. Mr. Stark puts his on the desk in here. I say, 'Think hard.' He don't get it. He's looking at a drunk old chief dressed up like a reptile. I think they're soft, those Shore Patrol guys."

I looked at Gantner sitting on the desk; he had pushed the typewriter against the bulkhead, and his buttocks touched it. He looked at the chief and said: "So who was he?"

"The poor son of a bitch at the bottom? Kid named Andrew

Taylor. Eighteen fucking years old. Mr. Stark found him. Mr. Stark has all the luck: he is a happy man with his wife, and thank the good Lord he is also the one to find the guy. Holy shit, Mr. Stark."

"What."

"Every time we fall into shit, your friend Mr. Fontenot, he's right there with us."

I said: "Where was he from?"

"Mississippi," Stark said.

"It was a Negro," I said. "The white kid—"

"I know," Stark said. "They told us. They got witnesses up the ass. Guys from some other ship, waiting for their boat. Let me tell you, man. I'm still fucked up. I've never seen a dead man outside of a coffin. And at the bottom of the water, and at night. There was a barge tied up at the pier. So apparently—apparently, shit: it's the only way—Taylor came up under the Goddamn barge. Probably he panicked then."

"They didn't go in holding their breath," I said.

"There you go," he said, and looked at the chief, who nodded and drank some coffee, then looked at his cap on the desk.

"We went under the barge first," Stark said to me. "Chief went one way, I went the other. I've got fucking vodka and rice wine in my blood and I'm scared I'll find him. I went down, it's muddy around the pier, and all I can see is what the light hits. And I can see the chief's light down at the other end. I keep moving and shining the light on the bottom. Then, Jesus, I see his hands. They're at the end of my light. That's all I can see. These white hands. Reaching up, and moving back and forth with the tide. Like this." He put his coffee on the desk and extended both arms straight at me, his hands vertical, the upturned palms toward my face; when he slowly moved them from side to side, his body swayed. Then he dropped his arms and expelled breath, and picked up his mug and drank. "I turned my light to the chief and waved it up and down till I saw his light coming. Then we brought him up."

The chief was looking out the hatch, his eyes focused above the deck and past the bulkhead, on the night above the sea.

It's past midnight now, and I'm sitting at my desk. Willie left its fluorescent light on so I could find my way. I crept into the stateroom and took off my uniform and I'm sitting here wearing that silk kimono and trying not to hate Andrew Taylor's father, or his mother, or whoever first said in front of him or allowed him to use out of habit the word that killed him. I can even say out of habit, though its source is greed for money or hatred or arrogance or some need to have inferiors, but all of these sound too simple, so perhaps I shall remain with the awful complexity of habit. And with fate too, though maybe after all fate is the conclusion of the patterns of history, and not a toss of cubes by the dark dicemen. But whatever it is, comprehensible or without meaning, it not only placed Kenneth Ellis and Andrew Taylor on the same pier at the same time and gave them long enough together on that pier for Ellis to step backward and bump or only touch Taylor, and for Taylor to say something, one hardly provocative sentence that ended with the word *nigger;* but it also put them both on an aircraft carrier that, simply because of its size, can only moor at the pier at Yokosuka, and must anchor off the other ports, and so forced Ellis and Taylor to return to it in a boat. Had they been stationed on the same destroyer they would have gone to it tonight, walked separately on the pier where their ship was tied, and separately boarded it, for the deep long sleep of boys.

In the darkness of our bunks Willie sleeps, and I cannot. I write, and listen to his soft breathing. He is on his left side now, facing the bulkhead, his back to me and my shaded light. It is his final position when he sleeps, though later I shall hear him shift a leg or move an arm, or turn his body once or twice, while I lie above him. I had hoped he would be awake when I came to our room. But I was relieved when I saw his shape under the blanket and sheet, and the back of his neck and head on the pillow. Yet I also wanted to tell him, and before writing to you I sat here watching him, and wondering whether he would want me to wake him and tell him now, or wait till morning. And having written this I wish he had been writing to Louisa, or reading in his bunk when I opened our door. But he sleeps. So I will turn off this light and quietly climb to my bunk above him, and quietly get under the covers, and take care to move lightly on the mattress while I lie awake and smoke and see Ellis in the chair looking at me but seeing himself standing on the pier, thinking of sleep and tomorrow's liberty and money, and while I see Taylor's hands, their palms turned upward to the surface of the sea, to air, to the dark bottom of the barge, and moving in Stark's light as gently as petals of a gardenia, floating with the ebb and flow of the tide. I shall let Willie sleep until the alarm wakes him.

After the Game

I WASN'T IN the clubhouse when Joaquin Quintana went crazy. At least I wasn't there for the start of it, because I pitched that night and went nine innings and won, and the color man interviewed me after the game. He is Duke Simpson, and last year he was our first baseman. He came down from the broadcasting booth, and while the guys were going into the clubhouse, and cops and ushers were standing like soldiers in a V from first to third, facing the crowd leaving the park, I stood in front of the dugout with my jacket on, and Duke and I looked at the camera, and he said: "I'm here with Billy Wells."

This was August and we were still in it, four games back, one and a half out of second. It was the time of year when everybody is tired and a lot are hurt and playing anyway. I wanted a shower and a beer, and to go to my apartment for one more beer and then sleep. I sleep very well after I've pitched a good game, not so well after a bad one, and I sleep very badly the night before I pitch, and the day of the game I force myself to eat. It's one of the things that makes the game exciting, but a lot of times, especially in late season, I long for the time when I'll have a job I can predict, can wake up on the ranch knowing what I'm going to do and that I'm not going to fail. I know most jobs are like that, and the people who have them don't look like they've had a rush of adrenaline since the time somebody ran a stop sign and just missed colliding broadside with them, but there's always a trade-off and, on some days in late season, their lives seem worth it. Duke and I talked about pitching, and our catcher Jesse Wade and what a good game he called behind the plate, so later that night I thought it was strange, that Joaquin was going crazy while Duke and I were talking about Jesse, because during the winter the club had traded Manuel Fernandez, a good relief pitcher, to the Yankees for Jesse. Manuel had been Joaquin's roommate, and they always sat together on the plane and the bus, and ate together. Neither one could speak much English. From shortstop, Joaquin used to call to Manuel out on the mound: *Baja y rapido.*

We ended the interview shaking hands and patting each other on the back, then I went between the cops and ushers but there were some fans waiting for autographs at one end of the dugout, so I went over there and signed three baseballs and a dozen score-cards and said thank you twenty or thirty times, and shook it seemed more hands than there were people, then went into the dugout and down the tunnel to the clubhouse. I knew something was wrong, but I wasn't alert to it, wanting a beer, and I was thinking maybe I'd put my arm in ice for a while, so I saw as if out of the corner of my eye, though I was looking right at it, that nobody was at the food table. There was pizza. Then I heard them and looked that way, down between two rows of lockers. They were bunched down there, the ones on the outside standing on benches or on tiptoes on the floor, stretching and looking, and the ones on the inside talking, not to each other but to whoever was in the middle, and I could hear the manager Bobby Drew, and Terry Morgan the trainer. The guys' voices were low, so I couldn't make out the words, and urgent, so I wondered who had been fighting and why now, with things going well for us, and we hadn't had trouble on the club since Duke retired; he was a good ballplayer, but often a pain in the ass. I went to the back of the crowd but couldn't see, so took off my spikes and stepped behind Bruce Green on a bench. Bruce is the only black on the club, and plays right field. I held his waist for balance as I brought my other foot from the floor. I stay in good running shape all year round, and I am overly careful about accidents, like falling off a bench onto my pitching elbow.

I kept my hands on Bruce's waist and looked over his shoulder and there was Joaquin Quintana, our shortstop, standing in front of his locker, naked except for his sweat socks and jockstrap and his gold Catholic medal, breathing through his mouth like he was in the middle of a sentence he didn't finish. He was as black as Bruce, so people who didn't know him took him for a black man, but Manuel told us he was from the Dominican Republic and did not think of himself as a black, and was pissed off when people did; though it seemed to me he was a black from down there, as Bruce was a black from Newark. His left arm was at his side, and his right forearm was out in front of him like he was reaching for something, or to shake hands, and in that hand he held his spikes. It was the right shoe.

Bruce looked at me over his shoulder.

"They can't move him," he said. Bruce was wearing his uniform pants and no shirt. I came to Boston in 1955, as a minor-league player to be named later in a trade with Detroit, when I was in that organization, and I have played all my seven years of major-league ball with the Red Sox; I grew up in San Antonio, so Bruce is the only black I've ever really known. People were talking to Joaquin. Or the people in front were trying to, and others farther back called to him to have some pizza, a beer, a shower, telling him it was all right, everything was all right, telling him settle down, be cool, take it easy, the girls are waiting at the parking lot. Nobody was wet or wrapped in a towel. Some still wore the uniform and some, like Bruce, wore parts of it, and a few had taken off as much as Joaquin. Most of the lockers were open. So was Joaquin's, and he stood staring at Bobby Drew and Terry Morgan, both of them talking, and Bobby doing most of it, being the manager. He was talking softly and telling Joaquin to give him the shoe and come in his office and lie down on the couch in there. He kept talking about the shoe, as if it was a weapon, though Joaquin held it with his hand under it, and not gripped for swinging, but like he was holding it out to give to someone. But I knew why Bobby wanted him to put it down. I felt the same: if he would just drop that shoe, things would get better. Looking at the scuffed toe and the soft dusty leather and the laces untied and pulled wider across the tongue folded up and over, and the spikes, silver down at their edges, resting on his palm, I wanted to talk that shoe out of his hand too, and I started talking with the others below me, and on the bench across the aisle from me and Bruce, and the benches on the other side of the group around Joaquin.

That is when I saw what he was staring at, when I told him to come on and put down that shoe and let's go get some dinner, it was on me, and all the drinks too, for turning that double-play in the seventh; and Bruce said And the bunt, and Jesse said Perfect fucking bunt, and I saw that Joaquin was not staring at Bobby or Terry, but at nothing at all, as if he saw something we couldn't, but it was as clear to him as a picture hanging in the air right in front of his face.

I lowered myself off the bench and worked my way through the guys, most of them growing quiet while some still tried to break Joaquin out of it. A few were saying their favorite curse, to themselves, shaking their heads or looking at the floor. Everyone I touched was standing tense and solid, but they were easy to part from each other, like pushing aside branches that smelled of sweat. I stepped between Bobby and Terry. They were still dressed, Bobby in his uniform and cap, Terry in his red slacks and white tee shirt.

"Quintana," I said. "Joaquin: it's me, old buddy. It's Billy."

I stared into his eyes but they were not looking back at me; they were looking at something, and they chilled the backs of my knees. I had to stop my hands from going up and feeling the air between us, grabbing for it, pushing it away.

There is something about being naked. Duke Simpson and Tommy Lutring got in a fight last year, in front of Duke's locker, when they had just got out of the shower, and it was not like seeing a fight on the field when the guys are dressed and rolling in the dirt. It seemed worse. Once in a hotel in Chicago a girl and I started fighting in bed and quick enough we were out of bed and putting on our underpants; the madder we got the more clothes we put on, and when she ended the fight by walking out, I was wearing everything but my socks and shoes. I wished Joaquin was dressed.

"Joaquin," I said. "Joaquin, I'm going to take the shoe."

Some of the guys told him to give Billy the shoe. I put my hand on it and he didn't move; then I tried to lift it, and his arm swung a few degrees, but that was all. His bicep was swollen and showing veins.

"Come on, Joaquin. Let it go now. That's a boy."

I put my other hand on it and jerked, and his arm swung and his body swayed and my hands slipped off the shoe. He was staring. I looked at Bobby and Terry, then at the guys on both sides; my eyes met Bruce's, so I said to him: "He doesn't even know I'm here."

"Poor bastard," Bobby said.

Somebody said we ought to carry him to Bobby's couch, and Terry said we couldn't because he was stiff as iron, and lightly, with his fingertips, he jabbed Joaquin's thighs and belly and arms and shoulders, and put his palms on Joaquin's cheeks. Terry said we had to wait for Doc Segura, and Bobby told old Will Hammersley, the clubhouse man, to go tell the press he was sorry but they couldn't come in tonight.

Then we stood waiting. I smelled Joaquin's sweat and listened to his breathing, and looked up and down his good body, and at the medal hanging from his neck, and past his eyes, into his locker: the shaving kit and underwear and socks on the top shelf, with his wallet and gold-banded wristwatch and box of cigars. A couple of his silk shirts hung in the locker, one aqua and one maroon, and a sport coat that was pale yellow, near the color of cream; under it some black pants were folded over the hanger. I wondered what it was like being him all the time. I don't know where the Dominican Republic is. I know it's in the Caribbean, but not where. Over the voices around me, Tommy Lutring said: "Why the *fuck* did we trade Ma*nuel*?" Then he said: "Sorry, Jesse."

"I wish he was here," Jesse said.

The guys near Jesse patted him on the shoulders and back. Lutring is the second baseman and he loves working with Joaquin. They are something to see, and I like watching them take infield practice. In a game it happens very fast, and you feel the excitement in the moments it takes Joaquin and Tommy to turn a double-play, and before you can absorb it, the pitcher's ready to throw again. In practice you get to anticipate, and watch them poised for the groundball, then they're moving, one to the bag, one to the ball, and they always know where the other guy is and where his glove is too, because whoever's taking the throw knows it's coming at his chest, leading him across the bag. It's like the movies I used to watch in San Antonio, with one of those dances that start with a chorus of pretty girls, then they move back for the man and woman: he is in a tuxedo and she wears a long white dress that rises from her legs when she whirls. The lights go down on the chorus, and one light moves with the man and woman dancing together and apart but always together. Light sparkles on her dress, and their shadows dance on the polished floor. I was a kid sitting in the dark, and I wanted to dance like that, and felt if I could just step into the music like into a river, the drums and horns would take me, and I would know how to move.

That is why Tommy said what he did. And Jesse said he wished Manuel was here too, which he probably did but not really, not at the price of him being back with the Yankees where he was the back-up catcher, while here he is the regular and also has our short left field wall to pull for. Because we couldn't do anything and we started to feel like Spanish was the answer, or the problem, and if just somebody could speak it to Joaquin he'd be all right and he'd put down that shoe and use his eyes again, and take off his jockstrap and socks, and head for the showers, so if only Manuel was with us or one of us had learned Spanish in school.

But the truth is the president or dictator of the Dominican Republic couldn't have talked Joaquin into the showers. Doc Segura gave him three shots before his muscles went limp and he dropped the shoe and collapsed like pants you step out of. We caught him before he hit the floor. The two guys with the ambulance got there after the first shot, and stood on either side of him, behind him so they were out of Doc's way; around the end, before the last shot, they held Joaquin's arms, and when he fell Bobby and I grabbed him too. His eyes were closed. We put him on the stretcher and they covered him up and carried him out and we haven't seen him since, though we get reports on how he's doing in the hospital. He sleeps and they feed him. That was three weeks ago.

Doc Segura had to wait thirty minutes between shots, so the smokers had their cigarettes and cigars going, and guys were passing beers and pizza up from the back, where I had stood with Bruce.

He was still on the bench, drinking a beer, with smoke rising past him to the ceiling. I didn't feel right, drinking a beer in front of Joaquin, and I don't think Bobby did either. Terry is an alcoholic who doesn't drink anymore and goes to meetings, so he didn't count. Finally when someone held a can toward Bobby he didn't shake his head, but got it to his mouth fast while he watched Doc getting the second needle ready, so I reached for one too. Doc swabbed the vein inside Joaquin's left elbow. This time I looked at Joaquin's eyes instead of the needle: he didn't feel it. All my sweat was long since dried, and I had my jacket off except the right sleeve on my arm.

I know Manuel couldn't have helped Joaquin. The guys keep saying it was because he was lonesome. But I think they say that because Joaquin was black and spoke Spanish. And maybe for the same reason an alcoholic who doesn't drink anymore may blame other people's troubles on booze: he's got scary memories of black-outs and sick hangovers and d.t.'s, and he always knows he's just a barstool away from it. I lost a wife in my first year in professional ball, when I was eighteen years old and as dumb about women as I am now. Her name was Leslie. She left me for a married dentist, a guy with kids, in Lafayette, Louisiana, where I was playing my rookie year in the Evangeline League, an old class C league that isn't there anymore. She is back in San Antonio, married to the manager of a department store; she has four kids, and I hardly ever see her, but when I do there are no hard feelings. Leslie said she felt like she was chasing the team bus all season long, down there in Louisiana. I have had girlfriends since, but not the kind you marry.

By the time Joaquin fell I'd had a few beers and some pizza gone cold, and I was very tired. It was after one in the morning and I did not feel like I had pitched a game, and won it too. I felt like I had been working all day on the beef-cattle ranch my daddy is building up for us with the money I send him every payday. That's where I'm going when my arm gives out. He has built a house on it, and I'll live there with him and my mom. In the showers people were quiet. They talked, but you know what I mean. I dressed then told Hammersley I wanted to go into the park for a minute. He said Sure, Billy, and opened the door.

I went up the tunnel to the dugout and stepped onto the grass. It was already damp. I had never seen the park empty at night, and with no lights, and all those empty seats and shadows under the roof over the grandstand, and under the sky the dark seats out in the bleachers in right and centerfield. Boston lit the sky over the screen in left and beyond the bleachers, but it was a dull light, and above the playing field there was no light at all, so I could see stars. For a long time, until I figured everybody was dressed and gone or leaving and Hammersley was waiting to lock up, I stood on the grass by the batting circle and looked up at the stars, thinking of drums and cymbals and horns, and a man and woman dancing.

Dressed Like Summer Leaves

MICKEY DOLAN WAS eleven years old, walking up Main Street on a spring afternoon, wearing green camouflage-colored trousers and tee shirt with a military web belt. The trousers had large pleated pockets at the front of his thighs; they closed with flaps, and his legs touched the spiral notebook in the left one, and the pen and pencil in the right one, where his coins shifted as he walked. He wore athletic socks and running shoes his mother bought him a week ago, after ten days of warm April, when she believed the winter was finally gone. He carried schoolbooks and a looseleaf binder in his left hand, their weight swinging with his steps. He passed a fish market, a discount shoe store that sold new shoes with nearly invisible defects, a flower shop, then an alley, and he was abreast of Timmy's, a red-painted wooden bar, when the door opened and a man came out. The man was in mid-stride but he turned his face and torso to look at Mickey, so that his lead foot came to the sidewalk pointing ahead, leaving him twisted to the right from the waist up. He shifted his foot toward Mickey, brought the other one near it, pulled the door shut, bent at the waist, and then straightened and lifted his arms in the air, his wrists limp, his palms toward the sidewalk.

"Charlie," he said. "Long time no see." Quickly his hands descended and held Mickey's biceps. "Motherfuckers were no bigger than you. Some of them." His hands squeezed, and Mickey tightened his muscles. "Stronger, though. Doesn't matter though, right? If you can creep like a baby. Crawl like a snake. Be a tree; a vine. Quiet as fucking air. Then *zap*: body bags. Short tour. Marine home for Christmas. Nothing but rice too."

The man wore cut-off jeans and old sneakers, white gone gray in streaks and smears, and a yellow tank shirt with nothing written on it. A box of Marlboros rested in his jeans pocket, two-thirds of it showing, and on his belt at his right hip he wore a Buck folding knife in a sheath; he wore it upside down so the flap pointed to the earth. Behind the knife a chain that looked like chrome hung from his belt and circled his hip to the rear, and Mickey knew it was attached to a wallet. The man was red from a new sunburn, and the hair on his arms and legs and above the shirt's low neck was blond, while the hair under his arms was light brown. He had a beard with a thick mustache that showed little of his upper lip: his beard was brown and slowly becoming sun-bleached, like the hair on his head, around a circle of bald red scalp; the hair was thick on the sides and back of his head, and grew close to his ears and beneath them. A pair of reflecting sunglasses with silver frames rested in the hair in front of the bald spot. On his right bicep was a tattoo, and his eyes were blue, a blue that seemed to glare into focus on Mickey, and Mickey knew the source of the glare was the sour odor the man breathed into the warm exhaust-tinged air between them.

"What's up, anyways? No more school?" The man spread his arms, his eyes left Mickey's and moved skyward, then swept the street to Mickey's right and the buildings on its opposite side, then returned, sharper now, as though Mickey were a blurred television picture becoming clear, distinct. "Did July get here?"

"It's April."

"Ah: AWOL. Your old man'll kick your ass, right?"

"I just got out."

"Just got out." The man looked above Mickey again, his blue eyes roving, as though waiting for something to appear in the sky beyond low buildings, in the air above lines of slow cars. For the first time Mickey knew that the man was not tall; he had only seemed to be. His shoulders were broad and sloping, his chest wide and deep so the yellow tank shirt stretched across it, and his biceps swelled when he bent his arms, and sprang tautly when he straightened them; his belly was wide too, and protruded, but his chest was much wider and thicker. Yet he was not as tall as he had appeared stepping from the bar, turning as he strode, and bowing, then standing upright and raising his arms. Mickey's eyes were level with the soft area just beneath the man's Adam's apple, the place that housed so much pain, where Mickey had deeply pushed his finger against Frankie Archembault's windpipe last month when Frankie's headlock had blurred his eyes with tears and his face scraped the cold March earth. It was not a fight; Frankie simply got too rough, then released Mickey and rolled away, red-faced and gasping and rubbing his throat. When Mickey stood facing his father he looked directly at the two lower ribs, above the solar plexus. His father stood near-motionless, his limbs still, quiet, like his voice; the strength Mickey felt from him was in his eyes.

The man had lit a cigarette and was smoking it fast, looking at the cars passing; Mickey watched the side of his face. Below it, on the reddened bicep of his right arm that brought the cigarette to his mouth and down again, was the tattoo, and Mickey stared at it as he might at a dead animal, a road kill of something wild he had never seen alive, a fox or a fisher, with more than curiosity: fascination and a nuance of baseless horror. The Marine Corps globe and anchor were blue, and permanent as the man's flesh. Beneath the globe was an unfurled rectangular banner that appeared to flap gently in a soft breeze; between its borders, written in script that filled the banner, was *Semper Fidelis*. Under the banner were block letters: USMC. The man still gazed across the street, and Mickey stepped around him, between him and the bar, to walk up the street and over the bridge; he would stop and look down at the moving water and imagine salmon swimming upriver before he walked the final two miles, most of it uphill and steep, to the tree-shaded street and his home. But the man turned and held his shoulder. The man did not tightly grip him; it was the man's quick movement that parted Mickey's lips with fear. They stood facing each other, Mickey's back to the door of the bar, and the man looked at his eyes then drew on his cigarette and flicked it up the sidewalk. Mickey watched it land beyond the corner of the bar, on the exit driveway of McDonald's. The hand was rubbing his shoulder.

"You just got out. Ah. So it's not July. Three fucking something o'clock in April. I believe I have missed a very important appointment." He withdrew his left hand from Mickey's shoulder and turned the wrist between their faces. "No watch, see? Can't wear a wristwatch. Get me the most expensive fucking wristwatch in the world, I can't wear it. Agent Orange, man. I'm walking talking drinking fucking fighting Agent Orange. Know what I mean? My cock is lethal. I put on a watch, zap, it stops."

"You were a Marine?"

"Oh yes. Oh yes, Charlie. See?" He turned and flexed his right arm so the tattoo on muscles faced Mickey. "U S M C. Know what that means? Uncle Sam's Misguided Children. So fuck it, Charlie. Come on in."

"Where?"

"Where? The fucking bar, man. Let's go. It's springtime in New England. Crocuses and other shit."

"I can't."

"What do you mean you can't? Charlie goes where Charlie wants to go. Ask anybody that was there." He lowered his face close to Mickey's, so Mickey could see only the mouth in the beard, the nose, the blue eyes that seemed to burn slowly, like a pilot light. His voice was low, conspiratorial: "There's another one in there. From 'Nam. First Air Cav. Pussies. Flying golf carts. Come on. We'll bust his balls."

"I can't go in a bar."

The man straightened, stood erect, his chest out and his stomach pulled in, his fists on his hips. His face moved from left to right, his eyes intent, as though he were speaking to a group, and his voice was firm but without anger or threat, a voice of authority: "Charlie. You are allowed to enter a drinking establishment. Once therein you are allowed to drink non-alcoholic beverages. In this particular establishment there is pizza heated in a microwave. There are also bags of various foods, including potato chips, beer nuts, and nachos. There are also steamed hot dogs. But no fucking rice, Charlie. After you, my man."

The left arm moved quickly as a jab past Mickey's face, and he flinched, then heard the doorknob turn, and the man's right hand touched the side of his waist and turned him to face the door and gently pushed him out of the sun, into the long dark room. First he saw its lights: the yellow and red of a jukebox at the rear wall, and soft yellow lights above and behind the bar. Then he breathed its odors: alcohol and cigarette smoke and the vague and general smell of a closed and occupied room, darkened on a spring afternoon. A man stood behind the bar. He glanced at them, then turned and faced the rear wall. Three men stood at the bar, neither together nor apart; between each of them was room for two more people, yet they looked at each other and talked. The hand was still on Mickey's back, guiding more than pushing, moving him to the near corner of the bar, close to the large window beside the door. Through the glass Mickey looked at the parked and moving cars in the light; he had been only paces from the window when the man had turned and held his shoulder. The pressure on his back stopped when Mickey's chest touched the bar, then the man stepped around its corner, rested his arms on the short leg of its L, his back to the window, so now he looked down the length of the bar at the faces and sides of the three men, and at the bartender's back. There was a long space between Mickey and the first man to his left. He placed his books and binder in a stack on the bar and held its edge and looked at his face in the mirror, and his shirt like green leaves.

"Hey Fletcher," the man said. "I thought you'd hit the deck. When old Charlie came walking in." Mickey looked to his left: the three faces turned to the man and then to him, two looking interested, amused, and the third leaning forward over the bar, looking past the one man separating him from Mickey, looking slowly at Mickey's pants and probably the web belt too and the tee shirt. The man's face was neither angry nor friendly, more like that of a professional ballplayer stepping to the plate or a boxer ducking through the ropes into the ring. He had a brown handlebar mustache and hair that hung to his shoulders and moved, like a girl's, with his head. When his eyes rose from Mickey's clothing to his face, Mickey saw a glimmer of scorn; then the face showed nothing. Fletcher raised his beer mug to the man and, in a deep grating voice, said: "Body count, Duffy."

Then he looked ahead at the bottles behind the bar, finished his half mug with two swallows, and pushed the mug toward the bartender, who turned now and took it and held it slanted under a tap. Mickey watched the rising foam.

Duffy. Somehow knowing the man's name, or at least one of them, the first or last, made him seem less strange. He was Duffy, and he was with men who knew him, and Mickey eased away from his first sight of the man who had stepped onto the sidewalk and held him, a man who had never existed until the moment Mickey drew near the door of Timmy's. Mickey looked down, saw a brass rail, and rested his right foot on it; he pushed his books between him and Duffy, and folded his arms on the bar.

"Hey, Al. You working, or what?"

The bartender was smoking a cigarette. He looked over his shoulder at Duffy.

"Who's the kid?"

"The kid? It's Charlie, man. Fletcher never saw one this close. That's why he's so fucking quiet. Waiting for the choppers to come."

Then Duffy's hand was squeezing Mickey's throat: too suddenly, too tightly. Duffy leaned over the corner between them, his breath on Mickey's face, his eyes close to Mickey's, more threatening than the fingers and thumb pressing the sides of his throat. They seemed to look into his brain, and down into the depths of his heart, and to know him, all eleven years of him, and Mickey felt his being, and whatever strength it had, leaving him as if drawn through his eyes into Duffy's, and down into Duffy's body. The hand left his throat and patted his shoulder and Duffy was grinning.

"For Christ sake, Al, a rum and tonic. And a Coke for Charlie. And something to eat. Chips. And a hot dog. Want a hot dog, Charlie?"

"Mickey."

"What the fuck's a mickey?"

"My name."

"Oh. Jesus: your name."

Mickey watched Al make a rum and tonic and hold a glass of ice under the Coca-Cola tap.

"I never knew a Charlie named Mickey. So how come you're dressed up like a fucking jungle?"

Mickey shrugged. He did not move his eyes from Al, bringing the Coke and Duffy's drink and two paper cocktail napkins and the potato chips. He dropped the napkins in front of Mickey and Duffy, placed the Coke on Mickey's napkin and the potato chips beside it, and then held the drink on Duffy's napkin and said: "Three seventy-five."

"The tab, Al."

Al stood looking at Duffy, and holding the glass. He was taller than Duffy but not as broad, and he seemed to be the oldest man in the bar; but Mickey could not tell whether he was in his forties or fifties or even sixties. Nor could he guess the ages of the other men: he thought he could place them within a decade of their lives, but even about that he was uncertain. College boys seemed old to him. His father was forty-nine, yet his face appeared younger than any of these.

"Hey, Al. If you're going to hold it all fucking day, bring me a straw so I can drink."

"Three seventy-five, Duffy."

"Ah. The gentleman wants cash, Charlie."

He took the chained wallet from his rear pocket, unfolded it, peered in at the bills, and laid four ones on the bar. Then he looked at Al, his unblinking eyes not angry, nearly as calm as his motions and posture and voice, but that light was in them again, and Mickey looked up at the sunglasses on Duffy's hair. Then he watched Al.

"Keep the change, Al. For your courtesy. Your generosity. Your general fucking outstanding attitude."

It seemed that Al had not heard him, and that nothing Mickey saw and felt between the two men was real. Al took the money, went to the cash register against the wall behind the center of the bar, and punched it open, its ringing the only sound in the room. He put the bills in the drawer, slid a quarter up from another one, and dropped it in a beer mug beside the register. It landed softly on dollar bills. Mickey looked at Al's back as he spread mustard on a bun and with tongs took a frankfurter from the steamer, placed it on the bun, and brought it on a napkin to Mickey.

"Duffy." It was Fletcher, the man in the middle. "Don't touch the kid again."

Duffy smiled, nodded at him over his raised glass, then drank. He turned to Mickey, but his eyes were not truly focused on him; they seemed to be listening, waiting for Fletcher.

"Cavalry," he said. "Remember, Charlie Mickey? Fucking guys in blue coming over the hill and kicking shit out of Indians. Twentieth century gets here, they still got horses. No shit. Fucking officers with big boots. Riding crops. No way. Technology, man. Modern fucking war. Bye-bye horsie. Tanks." He stood straight, folded his arms across his chest, and bobbed up and down, his arms rising and falling, and Mickey smiled, seeing Duffy in the turret of a tank, his sunglasses pushed-up goggles. "Which one was your old man in? WW Two or—how did they put it?—the Korean Conflict. Conflict. I have conflict with cunts. Not a million fucking Chinese."

"He wasn't in either of them."

"What the fuck is he? A politician?"

"A landscaper. He's forty-nine. He was too young for those wars."

"Ah."

"He would have gone."

"How do you know? You were out drinking with him or something? When he found out they didn't let first-graders join up?"

Mickey's mouth opened to exclaim surprise, but he did not speak: Duffy was drunk, perhaps even crazy, yet with no sign of calculation in his eyes he had known at once that Mickey's father was six when the Japanese bombed Pearl Harbor.

"He told me."

"He told you."

"That's right."

"And he was too old for 'Nam, right? No wonder he lets you wear that shit."

"I have to go."

"You didn't finish your hot dog. I buy you a hot dog and you don't even taste it."

Mickey lifted the hot dog with both hands, took a large bite, and looked above the bar as he chewed, at a painting high on the center of the wall. A woman lay on a couch, her eyes looking down at the bar. She was from another time, maybe even the last century. She was large and pretty, and he could see her cleavage and the sides of her breasts, and she wore a nightgown that opened up the middle but was closed.

"Duffy."

It was Fletcher, his voice low, perhaps even soft for him; but it came to Mickey like the sound of a steel file on rough wood. Mickey was right about Duffy's eyes; they and his face turned to Fletcher, with the quickness of a man countering a striking fist. Mickey lowered his foot from the bar rail and stood balanced. He looked to his left at Al, his back against a shelf at the rear of the bar, his face as distant as though he were listening to music. Then Mickey glanced at Fletcher and the men Fletcher stood between. Who were these men? Fathers? On a weekday afternoon, a day of work, drinking in a dark bar, the two whose names he had not heard talking past Fletcher about fishing, save when Duffy or Fletcher spoke. He looked at Duffy: his body was relaxed, his hands resting on either side of his drink on the bar. Now his body tautened out of its slump, and he lifted his glass and drank till only the lime wedge and ice touched his teeth; he swung the glass down hard on the bar and said: "Do it again, Al."

But as he pulled out his chained wallet and felt in it for bills and laid two on the bar, he was looking at Fletcher; and when Al brought the drink and took the money to the register and returned with coins, Duffy waved him away, never looking at him, and Al dropped the money into the mug, then moved to his left until he was close to Duffy, and stood with his hands at his sides. He did not lean against the shelf behind him, and he was gazing over Mickey's head. Mickey took a second bite of the hot dog; he could finish it with one more. Chewing the bun and mustard and meat that filled his mouth, he put his right hand on his stack of books. With his tongue he shifted bun and meat to his jaws.

"Fletcher," Duffy said.

Fletcher did not look at him.

"Hey, Fletcher. How many did you kill? Huh? How many kids. From your fucking choppers."

Now Fletcher looked at him. Mickey chewed and swallowed,

and drank the last of his Coke; his mouth and throat were still dry, and he chewed ice.

"You fuckers were better on horseback. Had to look at them." Duffy raised his tattooed arm and swung it in a downward arc, as though slashing with a saber. "Wooosh. Whack. Fuckers killed them anyway. Look a Cheyenne kid in the face, then waste him. I'm talking Washita River, pal. Same shit. Maybe they had balls, though. What do you think, Fletcher? Does it take more balls to kill a kid while you're looking at him?"

Fletcher finished his beer, lowered it quietly to the bar, looked away from Duffy and slowly took a cigarette pack from his shirt pocket, shook one out, and lit it. He left the pack and lighter on the bar. Then he took off his wristwatch, slowly still, pulling the silver expansion band over his left hand. He placed the watch beside his cigarettes and lighter, drew on the cigarette, blew smoke straight over the bar, where he was staring; but Mickey knew from the set of his profiled face that his eyes were like Duffy's earlier: they waited. Duffy took the sunglasses from his hair and folded them, lenses up, on the bar.

"You drinking on time, Fletcher? The old lady got your balls in her purse? Only guys worse than you fuckers were pilots. Air Force the worst of all. Cocksucking bus drivers. Couldn't even see the fucking hootch. Just colors, man. Squares on Mother Earth. Drop their big fucking load, go home, good dinner, get drunk. Piece of ass. If they could get it up. After getting off with their fucking bombs. Then nice bed, clean sheets, roof, walls. Fucking windows. The whole shit. Go to sleep like they spent the day—" He glanced at Mickey, or his face shifted to Mickey's; his eyes were seeing something else. Then his voice was soft: a distant tenderness whose source was not Mickey, and Mickey knew it was not in the bar either. "Landscaping." Mickey put the last third of the hot dog into his mouth, and wished for a Coke to help him with it; he looked at Al, who was still gazing above his head, so intently that Mickey nearly turned to look at the wall behind him. The other two men were silent. They drank, looked into their mugs, drank. When they emptied the mugs they did not ask for more, and Al did not move.

"All those fucking pilots," Duffy said, looking again down the bar at the side of Fletcher's face. "Navy. Marines. All the motherfuckers. Go out for a little drive on a sunny day. Barbecue some kids. Their mothers. Farmers about a hundred years old. Skinny old ladies even older. Fly back to the ship. Wardroom. Pat each other on the ass. Sleep. Fucking children. Fletcher used to be a little boy. Al never was. But *I* was." His arms rose above his head, poised there, his fingers straight, his palms facing Fletcher. Then he shouted, slapping his palms hard on the bar, and Mickey jerked upright: "*Chi*ldren, man. You never smelled a napalmed kid. You never even *saw* one, fucking chopper-bound son of a bitch."

Fletcher turned his body so he faced Duffy.

"Take your shit out of here," he said. "God gave me one asshole. I don't need two."

"Fuck you. You never looked. You never saw shit."

"We came down. We got out. We did the job."

"The *job*. Good word, for a pussy from the Air fucking *Cav*."

"There's a sergeant from the First Air Cav's about to kick your ass from here to the river."

"You better bring in help, pal. That's what you guys were good at. All wars—" He drank, and Mickey watched his uptilted head, his moving throat, till his upper lip stopped the lime, and ice clicked on his teeth. Duffy held the glass in front of him, just above the bar, squeezing it; his fingertips were red. "All fucking wars should be fought on the ground. Man to man. Soldier to soldier. None of this flying shit. I've got dreams. Oh yes, Charlie." But he did not look at Mickey. "I've got them. Because they won't go away." Again, though he looked at Fletcher, that distance was in his eyes, as if he were staring at time itself: the past, the future; and Mickey remembered the tattoo, and looked at the edges of it he could see beyond Duffy's chest: the end of the eagle's left wing, a part of the globe, the hole for line at the anchor's end, and *lis* written on the fluttering banner. He could not see the block letters. "I tell them I'm wasted, gentlemen. The dreams: I tell them to fuck off. They can't live with Agent Orange. They just don't know it yet. But fucking pilots. In clean beds. Sleeping. Like dogs. Like little kids. Girls with the wedding cake. Put a piece under your pillow. Fuckers put dreams under their pillows. Slept on them. Without dreams too. Not nightmares. Charlie Mickey here, he thinks he's had nightmares. Shit. I ate chow with nightmares. Pilots dreamed of pussy.

Railroad tracks on their collars. Gold oak leaves. Silver oak leaves. Silver eagles. Eight hours' sleep on the dreams of burning children."

"Jesus Christ. Al, will you shut off that shithead so we can drink in peace?"

Al neither looked nor moved.

"Duffy," Fletcher said. "What's this Agent Orange shit. At Khe San, for Christ sake. You never got near it."

"Fuck do you know? How far did *you* walk in 'Nam, man? You rode taxis, that's all. Did you sit on your helmet, man? Or did your old lady already have your balls stateside?"

"I hear you didn't do much walking at Khe San."

"We took some hills."

"Yeah? What did you do with them?"

"Gave them back. That's what it was about. You'd know that if you were a grunt."

"I heard you assholes never dug in up there."

"Deep enough to hold water."

"And your shit."

Duffy stepped back once from the bar. He was holding the glass and the ice slid in it, but he held it loosely now, the blood receding from his fingertips.

"You want to smell some grunt shit, Fletcher? Come over here. We'll see what a load of yours smells like."

"That's it," Al said, and moved toward Duffy as he threw the glass and Mickey heard it strike and break and felt a piece of ice miss his face and cool drops hitting it. Fletcher was pressing a hand to his forehead and a thin line of blood dripped from under his fingers to his eyebrow, where it stayed. Then Fletcher was coming, not running, not even walking fast; but coming with his chin lowered, his arms at his sides, and his hands closed to fists. Mickey swept his books toward him, was gripping them to carry, when two hands slapped his chest so hard he would have fallen if the hands had not held his collar. He was aware of Fletcher coming from his left, and Duffy's face, and the moment would not pass, would not become the next one, and the ones afterward, the ones that would get him home. Then Duffy's two fists, bunching the shirt at its collar, jerked downward, and Mickey's chest was bare.

He had sleeves still, and the shirt's back and part of its collar. But the shirt was gone.

"Fucking little asshole. You want jungle? Take your fucking jungle, Charlie."

With both hands Duffy shoved his chest and he went backward, his feet off the floor, then on it, trying to stop his motion, his arms reaching out for balance, waving in the air as he struck the wall, slid down it, and was sitting on the floor. From the pain in his head he saw Duffy and Fletcher. He could see only Fletcher's back, and his arms swinging, and his head jerking when Duffy hit him. Al had gone to the far end of the bar, to Mickey's left, and through the opening there, and was striding, nearly running, past the two men who stood watching Duffy and Fletcher. Mickey tried to stand, to push himself up with the palms of his hands. Beneath the pain moving through his head from the rear of his skull, he felt the faint nausea, the weakened legs, of shock. He turned on his side on the floor, then onto his belly, and bent his legs and with them and his hands and arms he pushed himself up, and stood. He was facing the wall. He turned and saw Al holding Duffy from behind, Al's hands clasped in front of Duffy's chest, and Mickey saw the swelling of muscles in Duffy's twisting, pulling arms, and Al's reddened face and gritted teeth, and Fletcher's back and lowered head and shoulders turning with each blow to Duffy's body and bleeding, cursing face.

His weakness and nausea were gone. He was too near the door to run to it; in two steps he had his hand on its knob and remembered his books and binder. They were on the bar, or they had fallen to the floor when Duffy grabbed him. He opened the door, and in the sunlight he still did not run; yet his breath was deep and quick. Walking slowly toward the bridge, he looked down at his pale chest, and the one long piece of shirt hanging before his right leg, moving with it, blending with the colors of his pants. He would never wear the pants again, and he wished they were torn too. He wanted to walk home that way, like a tattered soldier.

Land Where My Fathers Died

For James Crumley

GEORGE KARAMBELAS

IT WAS A cold night, and I was drunk. I couldn't get a ride at Timmy's when they closed, and I had a long way to walk. It was after one o'clock, and I kept thinking of my warm bed. I could see it in front of me, like it was ahead of me on the sidewalk, like those guys in a desert that see water that isn't there. A mirage, it's called. You can see it sometimes on a highway in summer. I thought about summer.

I lost my car. It was an old Pontiac, eight years old next year, that sucked gas. First the exhaust system went, rusted out, and I paid for that. Then it was a new starter, then the carburetor had to be rebuilt and I paid for all that and was broke. Then the transmission started to go and I said fuck it and sold it for junk. Fuck them at Timmy's. Fuck Steve. Fuck Laurie. Fuck George, they say, let him walk a hundred miles in fifty below just to sleep. Well, fuck them too, I said.

Maybe out loud. I was that drunk. I wished I wasn't. I wished I had gone right home soon as I got all the dishes washed and the pots scrubbed out and hung from the beam. I still would have frozen to death walking home, but I'd be in bed. And Timmy's is on the other side of the river so it was a longer ways to walk and I had to cross the bridge going and coming back, and the bridge is long on foot, and the wind was coming down the river. It's the chill factor. You never know how cold it is. The thermometer outside the window will say nineteen, but then you go outside and the cold comes blowing and it's like twenty below. That's the story: it's nineteen but it's *like* twenty below.

I tried to walk straight, looking down at the sidewalk like it was a board over a big hole, but I was zigging and zagging from one snowbank to another. Once I slipped on ice and landed on my ass. I thought about if I had hit my head I could have stayed there and froze to death. But still I couldn't get sober. I walked through the square about a mile above the river. Even the pizza shop was closed. We got a lot of pizza shops in this little town, mostly Italian, some Greek.

When Steve gave last call at Timmy's I started asking around for a ride. Nobody going my way. Who are they shitting? A night like this you can go out of your way for somebody. Up above the square I was walking past houses. Trees were in the yards in the snow and next to the sidewalk. Face it, George, I said to myself. Nobody's ever gone your way. I didn't like hearing that. I'm twenty-three. I started thinking about people that liked me. I got back to eighth grade, there was this Irish kid, but nobody liked him either. I got very sad walking under the big trees. No girl, not ever, and I don't know why. I look in the mirror and I don't know why. I've been laid, sure, but with sluts. It's a wonder I never caught herpes or something. I saw the light on in Dr. Clark's office. I was walking past it, and it was on my right, the road on my left. Then I stopped because I saw that I was seeing the light through the window but through the door too. Hey, I looked around: up and down the street, no cars, and up and down the sidewalk, of course nobody was out. Who would be but Eskimos and a dumb Greek.

I went up his walk slow and casual, like a dude coming home. There was salt on it. I was doing everything but whistling, a Greek dishwasher coming home to sleep in a doctor's office. It was a one-story brick building set back in the trees, a small office, a one-man operation. This was a neighborhood of big old wooden houses. They were dark. At the two front steps I stopped and looked again. I went up the steps and in the door, breathing hard with the booze. Everything was hard to do. This was the waiting room, and it was dark. Or the lights were off, but I could see the desk by the office door and the chairs along the walls; because the light was coming from the office and that door was open. I could see part of his desk in there, a corner and some of the top. To this day I don't know what I had in mind. I was thinking money, but I think about money all the time. Every day, every night. I think I was hoping for drugs. But I was too drunk for any of it to make any sense and if I hadn't been drunk I would have walked right on by. If I hadn't been drunk maybe somebody would have given me a ride, maybe that's it, maybe I drink too much. But that's not it because in high school I wasn't drunk or not much of the time and it didn't matter. I'd go to the smoking area outside where the faggots made us go even if it was a blizzard and I'd look at the girls shivering around their cigarettes and they'd either look at me like the smoke made them blind or like instead of a mouth I had a boil under my nose. I'd go over to the guys and they'd start busting balls on me. Sometimes it's friendly, it depends on how you say things. Bob the chef busts them on me all the time, but it's friendly; he likes me, and he's an old man. The guys at school weren't friendly. *So George, you going to ever shave, or what? He plucks them. All three, every week.* I'd laugh with them. But I wouldn't say anything back.

I was still not walking straight. I got across the waiting room on a slant toward the door and stepped in and saw a dead man. I knew he was dead when I saw him. I've only seen my grandparents, all four, laid out in the coffins. But I knew he was dead. I think I said something out loud. I remember hearing somebody. It did not get me sober but it got me sober as I could get. He was on his back, dressed up in a suit, and there was blood dried on his mouth. It was open. I've never seen a mouth look so open, looser than some-body sleeping. His eyes were closed. One hand was resting on his belt buckle. He was not a very big man, on the thin side. I had never been to see him, we always went to Papadopoulos, our family, but I knew it was Dr. Clark. I had seen him around town in his Mercedes, and sometimes when I was washing dishes I'd look through the window to the dining room and he'd be there eating lobsters with his scrawny old lady. I started to get out of there when I saw the big pistol on the floor. It was lying right beside his face. I bent over and picked it up and I kept my eyes away from his that were shut. I put it in my coat pocket, a pea coat. A prescription pad was on his desk and I put that in the other pocket. Then I got out of there.

I turned off the light switch by his door, and the office was dark. I had to feel my way across the waiting room. I think I was walking straight then. I had my arms out in front of me and moving, like a breaststroke, like I was swimming through the dark. My hands hit the front door. I opened it a little and looked at the street. A car passed. Then it was empty, and I was gone, shutting the door, and down the steps, holding the metal rail cold under my glove. Down his walk to the sidewalk.

I didn't think about the cold anymore. I didn't feel it. I didn't see my bed either. I saw his face on the floor looking up at the ceiling except his lids were down and there was nobody behind them. I saw his hand covering his belt buckle. The pistol was heavy in my pocket, and I was weaving again. I live in an old house that used to be one family's house, all three stories, and now it is a lot of apartments. I went up to mine on the second floor and pissed, shivering, for a long time. Then I swallowed some anisette from the bottle and drank a beer while I took off my clothes. I put the coat over a chair, and left the gun in it. When I got in bed I could still see him and I was tense and breathing fast, curled up on my side under the covers, and I thought I would not sleep. Next thing I knew the sun was in the room and I had a dry mouth and a headache and I had to piss but I lay there remembering everything and thinking here I was with a dead doctor's script pad and a big pistol I didn't want to see. Then I got up and took it out of the coat pocket. It was an Army .45, and the hammer was cocked. I looked some more. The safety was off.

ARCHIMEDES NIONAKIS

Because it was probably not murder—someone hit Francis Clark on the jaw and apparently his head struck the desk as he fell—and because it seemed to involve bad luck more than volition, I sometimes thought George had done it, but it was a thought I could only hold in the abstract, for a few moments, until I imagined him in the flesh. Then I could not believe it, could not see George Karambelas punching anybody, much less a man with a loaded pistol.

Then I believed the story he had just told me. I could still smell his story as I drove back to town from the prison. My car windows were up, and my clothes smelled of George's cigarette smoke trapped in the counseling room, and also the vanished smoke, and words and breath it seemed, of the others who had sat or paced in that room with its two straight wooden chairs and old wooden desk with an ashtray long overflowed, and butts scattered on the desk top with burns at its edges where live cigarettes had lain, and burns on its top where they had been put out. I did not sit at the desk. I leaned against a wall without windows, and said: "I can't believe how dumb you are."

"Don't say that," he said. "You got to make the jury believe it."

He did try to smile, as he tried to be friendly, but in his circumstance it is hard to do either. I don't mean simply incarceration; or being charged with second-degree murder. George is one of those people who have nothing specific wrong with them, except that they are disliked, and it's difficult to understand why. I don't even know why I don't like him. He is not very bright, but it isn't that. So I stood breathing in that room and told him I would represent him, and that is why: I couldn't bear disliking him for no just reason, and seeing him in that room too, and imagining him in the cell where probably already his cellmates didn't like him either. I did not mention money, any more than I would look for a fish in a tree, but he said he would raise it. He did not go so far as to ask how much he ought to raise. I told him we'd talk about that when the time came. I listened to his foolish story again, and congratulated him again on at least burning the prescription pad, forced my hand into his, and fled.

In my old Volvo, once I opened the window a bit to cold air and got past the weariness I feel when I do something good that I don't want to, I was suddenly glad he had called me. This surprised me, then disturbed me, for at thirty-three I should not be able to surprise myself. But there it was: that part of me I can't silence or even fully please, that will sometimes, while I'm in bed with a woman, leave us and stand dressed in the room, laughing or scowling: the little bastard was active again. I know he's the one who makes me an insomniac, when I'm too tired to read, and have no worries about money or family: I have money because I don't have a family, and I live alone by choice so am not lonely; still he keeps me awake, feeling that I'm worrying. Though I'm not. Except about getting to sleep. Now he hoped for some complicated work. Probably, for him, there had been too many times lately when I would stop what I was doing and look around me at my life—or the little bastard would—and feel it was not enough. Not enough for what? was the question I couldn't answer, except to say it wasn't using enough of me. I run a lot.

In the detectives' office, Dom Schiavoni sat on the secretary's desk. He sat on its edge, profiled to her; in winter clothes he looked even bigger, a V-necked blue sweater pulled tight over his belly and chest, his shoulders looking squeezed into an old dark suit coat. His complexion, in winter, changed from dark to pale olive, so he always looked like a swarthy man who had just had the flu. He introduced me to the secretary, Roberta Ford, a buxom woman in her fifties with fleshy cheeks and probably arms too under the sleeves of her sweater; her hair was red and looked like it had been done by one of my brothers, who had colored it for her too. Dom introduced me, and she said: "Your brother Kosta does my hair."

We came over on the boat when I was five, the youngest; my brothers own their shop and work very hard, from seven in the morning till six or seven at night, every day but Sunday; they tell me they could have women in the chairs at five in the morning if they wanted to start that early. There are many Greeks in beauty parlors in the Merrimack Valley; it was work they could learn quickly and could do in Greek while they were learning English, and it paid well. My brothers put me through school and every day they turn, in seriousness, to the stock-exchange section of the *Boston Globe*.

"You still running?" Dom said.

"Yes."

"You look like it. You going to run the Marathon again?"

I told him yes and that I was representing George. I watched his mouth, waiting for the smile; but there was none in his eyes either. Then he said: "Good."

"Why?"

"Somebody ought to."

"You want coffee?" Roberta said.

I told her I hadn't had breakfast and would take anything.

"This is early for him," Dom said. "Maybe there's a doughnut left." He looked at his watch. "Nine-thirty. What's it feel like?"

"Dawn. You don't think he did it?"

Roberta gave me a Styrofoam cup of coffee and a glazed doughnut.

"I *think* he did it. Problem is, I don't *know* he did it."

Then he told me how it took less than forty-eight hours for the arrest because the receptionist found the doctor when she opened Thursday morning and later in the day did a quick inventory for Schiavoni and told him the gun and a prescription pad were gone. Schiavoni found the receipt for the pistol in a desk drawer, and talked to Mayfield, the narcotics officer. Mayfield started talking to punks, and on Saturday one told him who had bought a .45 Thursday.

"So we went to see the new owner. He never heard of the .45 till I told him the name of the previous owner, then he's giving me the gun, seven rounds of ammo, and the name and address of George Karambelas."

"Who didn't even deny it."

"No."

Roberta shook her head, repeating the no.

"The dumb bastard," Dom said. Roberta nodded.

"Why was Clark in his office at night? And on a Wednesday?"

This town has an old custom: a lot of stores close on Wednesday afternoons, and no doctors work. Neither do I.

"The receptionist doesn't know. Maybe his wife will tell you."
Then he smiled.

"They're separated, right?" I said.

"Why do you say that?" He smiled again.

"Because the receptionist found him."

"Archimedes," and he reached out and laid his big hand on my
shoulder, smiling that mischievous way, and said: "They're not
separated."

"Where was she? In Moscow?"

"About five miles from here."

"So you went Thursday morning and told her why her husband
didn't come home last night?"

"Kind of grabs you, doesn't it?"

"What did she say?"

"She designated a funeral home."

Roberta was nodding.

I drove to the address Dom gave me. It was a clear February day,
with deep snow bright on the ground in the sunlight. The down-
town part of our city, on the riverbank, is ugly, and there's nothing
more to say about that. They tell me this place used to thrive; that
was back when my uncle brought us over and put my brothers to
work in his factory. They made parts for women's shoes: bows,
and an arrangement of straps called vamps; these vamps and bows,
when attached to an arched and high-heeled sole, formed an absolutely functionless shoe. My uncle shipped the bows and vamps
my brothers helped make to another factory in another state, and
there they were attached to soles.

There are neighborhoods of big, old houses that prove someone
was making money, but I don't believe this town ever thrived; I
think people mean the shoe business was good and the factory-
owners made a lot of money and most of the poor were employed
poor. They still are; there are no union factories, and unskilled
workers—many of them Greek and Hispanic and now, since the
war, some Vietnamese—work for minimum wage. Our better
neighborhoods have many old trees, and these places are lovely
when the leaves change colors in the fall. As I drove under them
on the way to Lillian Clark's, there were enough pines to scatter

green against the blue sky, and sometimes the sun glinted from ice on the branches of naked trees. I skirted a frozen lake bordered on one side by a public woods that has a good running road under its trees, following the bank of the lake. I entered countryside: woods, and fields of snow with tufts of brown dead weeds. Dr. Clark had a rural mailbox at the road, at the entrance of a paved driveway that curved up through evergreens. I shifted down and went up it, thinking of the good smell he had had in spring and summer, when a breeze went from the pines into his house. It was not an old one but one he had either built or bought from its first owner: two stories of stones and brown wood and A-shaped peaks enclosing windows. The garage was built onto one side, its door was raised, and inside, in one of the two spaces, was a fucking Porsche. The little bastard got excited by that sculpted-looking piece of steel that could feed a family across town in the tenement streets for five years or more; he liked knowing that the big surprises of pain and death infiltrated so impartially. I told him to show some compassion for Christ sake, and got out and pressed the cold button for the bell.

Lillian Clark had bags under her eyes, and they were not the recent kind that let you know someone's had a bad night. They were permanent knolls on the landscape of her face. She was a thin woman who could have been dissipated in her forties or poised in her fifties for a final decline. There was gray in her brown hair; her eyes were brown and angry, so that I apologized and felt my cheeks flush as I introduced myself and asked if I could speak with her; then I realized the anger was permanent too. Or guessed it, because of the rest of her face, its lines in her cheeks and about her eyes, that appeared set in some epiphany of bitterness. You have seen them, when you spy on people in airport lounges or pedestrians walking toward you: their eyes focus on things, and you wonder what they could be looking at to cause such anger; then you know it is being fed to them from inside their skulls. Her skin was the pallid tan of Dom's, but hers was not genetic; this was a woman of the sun who had probably had a winter vacation a month ago in Florida or the Caribbean. Wherever it is they go. Her voice was soft, though a bit crisp at the edges, and probably that was permanent too, a chord telling the world that was all the control she could muster. In the living room I sat in an armchair that was too deep and soft, so only my toes touched the floor. She sat opposite me; our chairs were half-turned toward a cold fireplace with ashes between the andirons. She drank sherry from a stemmed glass, and flicked a hand, as though backhanding a gnat, toward a bottle of Dry Sack on the table beside her, and asked if I wanted some. There was no question mark in her voice, so the invitation had the tone of a statement like: Your socks don't match. I said no and repeated the condolences I had offered at the door, while she sipped and gazed at the fireplace. I offered to light a fire, and she said: "I can make fires."

I said something about chimney drafts and the trick of holding a torch of burning paper up the chimney to start it drawing, and I began telling her about a bricklayer I knew who built a chimney for a man with a bad reputation for paying bills, and halfway up the chimney he laid a plate of glass across it, but her head jerked toward me, and this time her eyes glared. I liked the story and had believed it when I heard it, though it was one of those I stopped believing the first time I told it; still, I wanted to tell her about the man calling to complain about the smoke backing up in his living room and the bricklayer telling him he would fix it when he got paid for the chimney, in cash, and driving to the man's house and, with the money in his pocket, going up his ladder with a brick in his hand and dropping it down the chimney. But I said: "Can you tell me why your husband was at his office on a Wednesday night?"

"He took Wednesdays off."

"The afternoons?"

"Yes. He went to the hospital in the morning."

She was looking at the fireplace. So did I. I kept seeing George in prison, suspended in dismay, but not one sentence, not one word, came to me.

"Why did he do it?" she said.

I looked at the side of her face, and an attractive streak of gray above her left ear.

"George didn't do it."

"You don't think so?"

"No."

"Would you defend him if he had?"

"No."

"Really? Why?"

"I couldn't enjoy it."

"You couldn't enjoy it."

"No."

Now she did look at my socks, which matched and were folded over the tops of hiking boots. Her eyes moved up my legs, or slacks, and shirt and coat to my face.

"I like you with a mustache."

I was about to ask when she had seen me without one, but caught that in time and said: "He didn't know Dr. Clark."

"He could be angry at him without knowing him."

"Is that why your husband had a gun?"

"Probably."

"Did he see patients on Wednesday nights?"

"That's what he said."

She was looking at my eyes, and I wished she would turn to the fireplace again.

"Because they needed him?" I said. "Because of the afternoons off?"

"Some. He said."

"So why not work on Wednesday afternoons and take the evenings off?"

She was watching my eyes. I had heard or read about recent widows being angry at their husbands for dying. I had not understood it, though I recognized that it must have something to do with grief; but those were widows of husbands who had died of what we call natural causes. Their husbands had not been murdered. Yet there was nothing of sorrow, of memory, in Lillian Clark's eyes.

"For the receptionist?" I said. "So she could have time off? Or did she work on Wednesday nights?"

"You could ask her."

"You don't know, then?"

"I never phoned the office on Wednesday nights."

"Was she a nurse?"

"You mean is she. Francis was killed, not Beverly. Yes, she's a nurse."

"She would have to be there, wouldn't she?"

"Would she?"

"For female patients. Doesn't there have to be a nurse in the examining room?"

"I suppose."

"All this is very strange."

Finally she looked away, back at the fireplace. So did I.

"Did he ever talk about trouble with a patient?"

"Trouble?"

"Someone who might have got angry and hit him. I think it was an accident. His death, I mean."

"Depends on what you call an accident."

"I suppose it does. Are you the executrix of the estate?"

"That's funny."

"What is?"

"My new title. Yes."

"Could I look at his files?"

Looking into the fireplace she called Teresa, with Spanish pronunciation, and my thighs jumped taut. I looked behind me, stretching to see over the back of the chair, at the sounds of footsteps. Teresa was young and too thin.

"Bring my purse down from the bedroom."

She left, and I listened to her climbing stairs and walking above us, and I looked around the room. A model of a yacht was on the mantelpiece. In one corner was a small bookcase with a glass door; the corner was dark, and I could not read the titles. More furniture was behind us and against the walls. The floor was carpeted, and Teresa crossed it now with the purse, then was gone. Lillian took out a key ring, and worked one of them to the top.

"Where's the other car?" I said.

"He had a Mercedes. I gave it to my daughter."

"What was his practice?"

"Internal medicine. Here."

I took the key and thanked her.

"Mrs. Clark?" I stood up, looking down at her face gazing at the fireplace. "Did you call anyone when he didn't come home Wednesday night?"

"I was asleep."

"What about next morning?"

"I slept late. I always do."

"So Detective Schiavoni woke you up?"

"No."

"I don't understand."

She looked at me.

"You don't understand what?"

"Why you didn't know."

"I always woke up alone. He got up at seven."

"You couldn't tell he hadn't slept there?"

"How?" She was still looking at me.

"The blankets. The way the pillows were. Teresa must make a tight bed."

"Why are you upset?"

"I'm not."

"Yes, you are. I suppose I didn't look."

I thanked her, told her I'd bring back the key, and left. In the car I felt I had a hangover: the weariness, the confusion. On the way to my office I bought two meatball subs and four half-pint cartons of milk. My office is small, the waiting room no larger, and the receptionist's desk was empty, its surface bare save for a covered typewriter. I did not have a regular secretary, and was using interns from the small college in town. I gave them work to do and even taught them, and the college paid them with credits. My intern was Paula Reynolds, a lovely girl with healthy skin and long blond hair. I opened the office door. She was lying on the leather couch my brothers gave me. She wore a sweater, and jeans tucked into high boots, and was smoking a French cigarette.

"Jesus," I said, and opened the window behind my desk. A pack of Gitanes was on the floor beside her. Sometimes she does this, shows up with Gauloises or Gitanes, and I accuse her of affectation; but the truth is she spent a year in France before college, and now and then she has the urge. While she finished smoking I told her about my morning, then she took her milk and sandwich to the couch, managed to eat daintily, a good trick with a meatball sub, and she was smoking again as we left the office and I drove us to Dr. Clark's.

He was either a yachtsman or simply loved boats. What had been a model of a yacht, painted white, was on his desk, the bow split and crumpled, the masts snapped in two and held together only by sails; it looked as though a storm had driven it against rocks. I thought of all the concentration he had put into it and the one on his mantelpiece at home. Then I imagined the ocean rushing through the hole with its splinters, unpainted on the inside, and I looked away. On the wall were three color photographs of the same yacht, at anchor. Paula stood beside me, looking down at the yacht, and when I turned our arms brushed, her sweater and my jacket and shirtsleeve padding our muscles and bones. I unbuckled her belt, turned her toward me, and, kissing her, slipped her jeans down her hips. Her pants were pale blue and already moist. We undressed and, as she lay on the floor, she said: Isn't this where—and I said Yes, and was in her.

We dozed for half an hour on the carpet, then dressed and stood at the filing cabinets against one wall. Paula started with the As, on my right, and I crouched to the Zs, three of them, and sat on the floor and read about a man named Zachary who was fifty-eight years old, had seasonal allergies, got an annual physical, and since five years ago, when he had asthmatic bronchitis, had either not been sick or had treated himself at home. Paula went to the reception room to look for an ashtray and came back empty-handed except for her unlit cigarette and said: "Goddamn doctors."

"Just chew it. Then I can breathe."

"Goddamn joggers."

"I'm not a *jog*ger."

"Goddamn runners then. Why don't you put pictures of running shoes on your office wall? And a bronze pair on your desk."

"My bronze pair is between my legs."

Then she was bending over me, her fingers coming like claws at my crotch, and I quickly shut my legs. She put the cigarette between her lips, untied my hiking boot, pulled it off, took it to her end of the cabinets, and set it on top of the As. I put away Zachary and opened Zecchini. Florence Zecchini was not doing well: she

was sixty-three and had high blood pressure, bursitis in the left
shoulder, and every year, from November to April, she contracted
a mélange of viruses.

"The Zs are all old." I watched her flicking ashes into my boot.
"What happened to wastebaskets?"

"It has paper in it. What are we looking for?"

"Are you going to put it out in my boot?"

"The toilet." She went there, through the examining room beside
the files. When she came back, I said: "I don't know. Anything
that'll help George. The poor fuck."

She looked at me over a file. She was still standing, working at
the top drawer.

"You're not a poor fuck," she said.

"Neither are you."

I was thinking about the endless money from her parents, but
her eyes looking at me were brown and lovely, so I did not clarify.

I was in the Ps, still wearing one boot, when the sun shone on
the windows behind Clark's desk and on its glass top, and the bow
of his broken white boat. The sun was very low, and I had missed
my run. When we finished, Paula's smoke lay in the air, and the
sun was behind the houses and trees beyond the windows, a rose
glow beneath the dark sky. In the car I said I would run before
dinner, and Paula told me I was crazy, that I would twist an ankle
or slip on ice or get hit by a car; I said I needed a run after an
afternoon shut up in an office reading files, and she said It wasn't
all reading files, and a drink would do as well. I have never run at
night, for the reasons Paula gave, and I crossed the bridge over the
Merrimack as the last glow of sunset faded to dusk, and stopped
at Timmy's, where we stood at the bar and had two vodka martinis,
and talked with Steve Buckland, the bartender, who has a long
thick reddish-blond beard and is one of the biggest men I've ever
known; he is also a merry one.

We had planned to go to my apartment and cook steaks and
spend a quiet evening; she had her schoolbooks with her, and I was
reading *Anna Karenina*, although I meant to watch a Burt Reynolds
movie on television at eight. I had not told her this because she
might have the discipline to go to the dormitory to study. I was

going to glance at the paper after dinner and say, Oh: *Hustle* is on, then she would watch it with me, tensely for a while, but she would stop worrying about her work, and after the movie, because the television is at the foot of my bed, we would make love, and soon she would fall asleep studying beside me and I would read *Anna Karenina* until two or three, when I would sleep. But we had our third martini at an Italian restaurant south of town, and the young woman tending bar made them so well that we violated the sensible rule, whether we had one or not, about martinis, and drank a fourth. We shared a bottle of chianti with dinner; Paula eats well and does not exercise but is flat-bellied and firm. Of course, as she approaches thirty, six or seven years from now, her flesh will soften, then sag. We each drank Sambuco with three floating coffee beans, and she drank coffee. I didn't dare.

I do not record this drinking as some laurel for hedonism, but because the alcohol gave us a distance from the afternoon, as surely as air travel would have, and during dinner we were able to see clearly what had, in Clark's office, been blurred by names (I knew some of them), and ages, and ailments. We were talking generally about mortality and the distillation of its whisperings that we had confronted in the files, when Paula stopped talking, and stopped listening to me, though she watched me still as she twirled spaghetti in oil and garlic around her fork.

"Jesus," she said. "He was a script doctor."

And there it was, as though rising to the surface of a dream, the truth coming as it so often does in that last hour of drunkenness when all that is unessential falls away and suddenly you see clearly. Soon after that you are truly drunk and may not remember next day what it was that you saw. But we had it now, the truth—or a truth out of all the pneumonia, flu, strep throat, two cases of gout that had made me feel I was in the nineteenth century watching Anna Karenina's eight rings sparkle in candlelight, cancer and heart disease and strokes, an afternoon of illness and injury and their treatment recorded in Francis Clark's scribbled sentences that began with verbs: *Complains of chest pains. Took EKG*—a truth that seemed tangible and shimmering on the table between us, among the odors of wine and garlic and Paula's lipsticked unfiltered Gitanes in the ashtray: a number of girls and young women whose only complaint was fat, and whose treatment was diet and prescriptions. Speed, Paula said. That's what they get, so they won't eat. And downers so they can function. Which did not really mean he was a script doctor, for neither of us could recall whether the patients were fat or simply getting drugs. There was also the matter of his Wednesday nights, and I knew they involved a woman, or women, and believed Paula knew it too, though was too loyal to what her sex has told itself it has become to admit it, and she argued that both my age and my Greek heritage had combined to blind me as surely as the famous Greek motherfucker; that Lillian Clark's bitter and unhappy face and Francis Clark's Wednesday nights did not add up to adultery.

"She may be unhappy for a *to*tally different reason," she said, waving a cool and hardened chunk of garlic bread. "Something that has *not*hing to do with a man."

"Right," I said. "One morning she woke up and looked under the hood of her Porsche and found an engine there instead of God."

"I knew you'd see the truth. You don't know how hard it is to be a rich woman."

"A rich lovely woman."

"Yes."

"A rich lovely sensual woman."

"With a balding Greek for a lover. Yes."

"It runs in my family."

"Why don't I ever meet them?"

"Saturday."

"This Saturday?"

"There's a Greek dance."

"Will you teach me how, before we go?"

"I don't know if WASPs can learn it."

We left the epiphanic phase with Sambuco, and had a second one, and I drove carefully home, turned on the eleven-o'clock news, found that I could not understand it and was drinking a bottle of Moosehead beer; so was Paula; then I remembered bringing them to the bedroom. I turned off the television and lights and we undressed and got into bed and talked for a while, about snow I believe, or rain, and forgot to make love. I woke early, at eight-fifteen, with a hangover, and got the *Boston Globe* from the front steps, and after aspirins and orange juice and a long time in the bathroom with the paper, I ran ten miles and returned sweating and clearheaded to the smells of dripping coffee and the last of Paula's Gitanes.

Beverly Strater lived on the second floor of an apartment building that had been a house, and the front door did not unlock from inside her apartment. About ten years ago, in this town, that would have been customary, but whatever was loose in the land had reached us too, a city of under fifty thousand where old people living in converted factory buildings, renting good apartments for small portions of their incomes, boasted of the buildings' security. Beverly Strater was neither old nor young, and had the look about her of a divorcee whose children had grown: that is, she looked neither barren nor discontented, had a good smile and some lines of merriment in her face, and a briskness to her walk and gestures that seemed to come from energy, not nerves. I had simply climbed the stairs and knocked on her door, and I wished she were not so accessible; I did not think she could afford thieves, and she was certainly not too old to discourage any aesthetic considerations a rapist might have. She dispelled my worries before I mentioned them, as, over tea in her kitchen, she told me about Francis Clark's gun, and that she kept a loaded .38 at her bedside, and took it with her when she went places that would keep her out after dark. Her husband had taught her about guns, and it was his revolver she had now; she had reared three children and gone back to nursing six years ago, after he died. Because of her husband's attitude—and her own—about guns, she had not thought it unusual of Dr. Clark to own one and keep it in his office. Sometimes he left the office after dark, always in the winter months of short days, and she assumed he armed himself before walking to his car.

"It's just the times," she said. "And you see, poor man, he was right."

In winter I am condemned to sit in rooms of smoke. Beverly was filling the kitchen, and her lungs too, and watching her inhale, I shuddered. Or perhaps I shuddered at the image of Clark putting a .45 in his pocket to walk out to his car, and Beverly's seeing that as something of no more significance than wearing a hat or a pair of sunglasses. Yet I liked her. She was one of those women whom, if I had children, I would trust to care for them. I liked her stockiness, which reminded me of my mother, who was at that time visiting Greece, and reminded me also of women in a Greek village, not of a stout American. I have never held a gun, and would be frightened if I did, and as I was about to tell her that, I thought of something else, of the fear and anger I would feel if anyone pointed a gun at me and what I would do if I could get that gun from him, and I said, "It may have got him killed."

"That's true too. My husband always said: Don't ever use it for a bluff. He meant—"

"I know what he meant. Did he ever use it?"

"Oh, Lord, no: he was a mailman. He had a spray for dogs. The gun was to protect our home at night."

There are days, and this was one of them, when I cannot bear the company of my countrymen. I wished Paula were not at classes. My God, you can stay more or less happy doing your work and enjoying the flesh and the company of friends until you get a glimpse of the way people perceive the world. Once in a psychology journal I read an article on suicides in New Hampshire during the decade from 1960 to 1970; there were graphs showing that suicides by women were on the rise; the two authors did not mention it, but I noticed that suicides by both women and men increased each election year. My own notion is that my neighbors to the north were incurably shocked to see the evidence of what the majority of people were not simply content with, but strove for. I often feel the same, and conclude that most of us are not worth the dead trees it takes to wipe our asses one summer. I was feeling this now, watching Beverly's motherly face talking about life as though it were lived in a sod hut in Kansas in 1881 or in a city slum where teenaged criminals routinely sacked apartments.

I asked her about Wednesday nights. She was truly surprised, and she remained so, went from surprise to puzzlement and was still frowning with it when I left. Before doing that, I asked her about the girls and young women on diets. She answered absently, still trying to understand the Wednesday nights: A few, she said. He wasn't a *diet* doctor, but there were a few patients—girls—who came to him with a weight problem. I have noticed that women of the working class call each other girls, as men say "the boys." I asked only one more question, at the door: "Were they really fat?"

"If they weren't, they *thought* they were. It's the same thing, isn't it?"

Paula and I met for lunch in my office, then went to Clark's. Because she does not exercise, she still had a hangover. In front of the filing cabinet, she touched me, but I shook my head, starting to explain, but then said nothing, knowing I was too despondent to give meaningful words to my despondency and my dread, so muted that it was lethargic, as impossible as that sounds. But it was lethargic, my dread, and it made me think of summer and lying on the beach in the sun, so that I wanted to lie on the floor and sleep, for I was beginning to know that in simply trying to save George Karambelas I was going to confront nothing as pure and recognizable as evil but a sorrowful litany of flaws, of failures, of mediocre hopes, and of vanity. We wrote the names and addresses of the twelve, and Paula said That's what Jesus started with, and I said So did Castro, and at the sound of my voice, she said, "Are you all right?"

She stood at Clark's desk, holding the notebook, and looking at me in a way that would have been solemn if it weren't tender too.

"Sure," I said. "Let's start."

We did, in midafternoon, in the low winter sun of that Tuesday. The sun lasted through Wednesday, and that night we lay in the dark and watched snow blowing against the windows and listened to Alicia de Larrocha play Chopin Preludes. We spoke to one woman on Tuesday, three on Wednesday, three on Thursday, and two Friday; then we did not need the other three. Paula rescheduled some of my appointments, mostly for tax returns and wills, work that could wait, though I felt like a gambler when we changed the appointments for wills, and since the gamble did not involve me, I felt a frightening sense of power I did not want. Wednesday morning we brought the key back to Lillian; Paula wanted to see her. But Teresa answered the door and said She is busy, and I gave her the key, looking at her brown eyes and thinking of her making Lillian's bed, and cooking her meals, and cleaning her house.

The first woman was a florist, or she worked in a florist's shop, and she took us to the office at the rear of the store and gave us coffee while the owner stayed in front with his flowers. Ada Cleary was twenty-five years old, one of those women whose days for years have been an agony about the weight of her body, or how much of it she could pinch. She looked at Paula, with polite glances to include me, as she spoke of her eight years of diets. I could not see the results, since I did not know what she had looked like before she had started seeing Clark a month ago. What I saw was a woman in a sweater and skirt, neither fat nor thin, but with wide hips and a protrusion of rump that looked soft enough to sink a fist into; I did not dare look at her legs, though I tried to spy on them but was blocked by the desk she stood behind. Her cheeks, though, were concave, and the flesh beneath her jaw was firm, and her torso looked disproportionate, as though it were accustomed to resting on smaller hips; or, the truth, it had recently been larger. Dr. Clark was very nice, she said, very understanding. And for the first time she was able to say no to food. It was the drugs.

"Speed," Paula said.

"Yes. And I take the others. You know, to get me down."

"Don't you worry about your head?" Paula said.

"I can't. Once I get down to one hundred and six pounds, that's when I'll stop the drugs. And see if I can make it on my own. You know: throw away my clothes, buy some new ones."

"Why one-oh-six?" I said.

"That's what I weighed in high school. Junior year. Before I turned into an elephant."

"What will you do without Clark?" I said.

"Oh, Gawd, find another doctor. I still have some pills left."

"Will he be hard to find?"

"Oh, no. It's like sleeping pills. I've never had trouble sleeping, but a friend of mine does. You just have to shop around. Some are strict, some are—helpful."

"Understanding," I said. "I don't sleep well either."

"Oh? What do you take?"

"Moosehead," Paula said.

"Really? You don't look it."

"Sometimes," I said. "Sometimes I just read."

"He runs a lot," Paula said.

"It's all legal," Ada said. "I mean, wasn't it?"

"Sure," I said. "Good luck with the one-oh-six."

In the car, Paula said: "You shouldn't have looked at her like that."

"Like what?"

"Angry."

"Was I?"

"Weren't you?"

"Yes."

"Why?"

She opened her purse and went through the smoker's elaborate motions, whose rhythm was disrupted by her hurriedly lifting and pushing aside whatever things had found or lost their way into her deep purse, until her hands emerged with the pack and lighter, and with thumb and forefinger she tore open the cellophane, opened the box, removed the top foil, put it and the crumpled cellophane into her purse, and so on. I have never wanted to smoke, but I would enjoy opening those pretty little boxes, as I would enjoy filling a pipe. My brother Kosta carries worry beads, but at work he is too busy to play with them. If he smoked, he would have to pause to give his attention to the cellophane, the cardboard, the foil. I thought of telling him he should stop every half hour to play for five minutes with his beads, and opened my window a few inches. Her cigarette was American.

"Well?" she said.

"Because it's bullshit."

"What is?"

"All that dieting."

"You should feel sorry for her."

"I do."

We passed the college where she lived and, on some nights, slept.

"Describe her," she said.

"Okay."

"Well. Go ahead."

"I mean okay, I get your point."

"Do you really?"

"I don't want to, but I do."

"*You* look at women that way."

"You couldn't let it go, could you?"

We passed the Common, a small park with a white fence and scattered old trees. On Thursday nights in summer an orchestra of old men plays old popular songs and marching tunes, and old people bring their lawn chairs and listen. At other times, young people gather under the trees. In the summer afternoons they are still-lifes, except for an occasional Frisbee game. I have never understood why they cup their hands and lower their heads when smoking dope, since those are the only signs giving them away to anyone passing by. They should pretend to be smoking cigarettes, but then no one cares anyway, until night when the police cruiser disperses them.

"You just had to say it."

"Yes."

"Okay."

At the Square that is not a square but a street and one parking lot in front of commercial places, I parked and we crossed the street and looked in the window of the young Greek's fish market. He waved from behind the counter where he was wrapping and weighing white fillets of fish for a woman taking bills from her wallet and wiping her nose with Kleenex. We waved and went to Timmy's.

"Does it bother you?" I said at the bar.

"Why should it? I'm not fat."

"It bothers me," I said, and big Steve Buckland came and greeted us and took our orders. Steve has a grand belly, but his chest is even larger, by eight or ten inches, and if he didn't have the belly he would look like those body builders who seem involved with their bodies to the point of foolishness, so I don't like looking at them. It gets confusing. We drank beer, then went to my apartment for the steaks we had not cooked the night before.

When I look back on that week, I see a series of female faces and gesturing hands, and I hear their voices, and I remember the constriction I felt, as though I had left the world and its parts I recognized, and was immersed in only one of those parts, and it blinded and deafened me to the others. All I could see was female flesh, all I could hear was female voices: they were intense, as from long anger; they were embittered yet resolute; they were self-effacing, with a forced note of humor; they were lyric in their plaintiveness, abrupt with considered despair; they were hopeful. Their hands held pencils, pens, cigarettes, black coffee, diet drinks, and moved in front of and beneath their faces, hovered and swooped over laps and desks, and darted to the mouth that sucked or chewed, smoked or drank. Their faces, I realized, were the faces of the obsessed. Always, behind their eyes, I could see another life being lived. They spoke to us of Dexedrine balanced by Seconal, Nembutal, or Quāāludes and, before the drugs, water diets, grapefruit diets, carbohydrates, calories, diuretics, laxatives, vomiting—every one of them but Ada had forced herself, until Clark's treatment, to vomit at least three times a week, usually more, so we assumed Ada had too, and I liked her for not disclosing that, for keeping private at least that humiliating detail, and also the other one these women did not spare us: images of frequent and liquid emptying of the bowels, whose imagined sounds and smells destroyed, for me, whatever beauty the women did have (none of them was truly fat), as well as that ideal of weight and proportion they strove for. Yet, while they turned their bodies, before my eyes, into bowels, intestines, adipose, digestive juices, piss, shit, and vomit, there was that other life visible in the light of their eyes. Perhaps they strode across the room of their consciousness, graceful, svelte; or sat naked, their stomachs flat, unwrinkled, the skin as taut as the soles of their feet; or, with slender arms, whose only curves were those of athletic muscles, whose flesh did not shake or hang, they reached for steaming bowls of food and piled it on their plates.

That week, except for the martini and Sambuco night, I kept my usual discipline and drank only a few Mooseheads in the evening. So I was sober all those nights after our talks with the women, and I lay awake long after Paula slept, and the little bastard spoke to me of flesh, of food, of dresses, of Lillian's Porsche and my brothers bent over bows and vamps, and I tried to shut him up with the word *vanity*, but he was persistent. *It always connects*, he said. *Everything connects. You have only to look.* I got up to drink milk in the dark living room; I rolled from side to side on the bed and lay still, listening to Paula breathing, and I thought of my brothers fleeing the shoe factory and the future my uncle had planned for them: to learn English while they learned the work of every room and bench in the factory, from the designer in the basement, whose ideas were stolen from Italian shoes bought or photographed in Italy by my uncle, or clipped from magazines, to the cutting room, the stitching room, and so forth, to the room where women inspected and boxed and shipped the pieces of leather that would be the tops of shoes, and then perhaps my brothers would become foremen, certainly not partners, for my uncle had his own sons (has: they now own the factory), though maybe he would have left them a share. Fled to beautician school, then borrowed money and opened a shop and married Greek women, lovely Greek women who bore children who are respectful, beautiful, and well behaved, not at all like American children, though they speak English without the accents of their parents. Anyone visiting my brothers' houses will be given a drink and food, and always there are feta cheese and olives, and my brothers' wives keep stuffed grapeleaves and spinach pies in the freezer. They proudly sent me through school, and now, with love and less pride, they look at my life, and sometimes they ask me, as the little bastard did those nights of the week of the dieting women, why I am, at thirty-three, still living in a three-room apartment (including the kitchen, with the table where I eat) and going to work at ten in the morning and taking Wednesday afternoons off and spending so much time running and fucking young girls. They are not opposed to running but that I do it during my long lunch break and so return late for the afternoon's work; nor are they opposed to the young girls, but insist that I could have them and marriage and a family. I have no answers. But when they tell me I'm thirty-three, I am for moments, even minutes, frightened. It is strange: no one is Christian anymore, but every man I've known reach the age of thirty-three has been afraid that he will not see thirty-four, as if none of us can forget that the most famous death of our culture occurred at thirty-three. I do tell them I don't need more money, but they say I do, I should be investing in stock, in bonds, and buying a house, and I shiver at this and grow silent until they laugh and clap my shoulder and hug me, and I am the baby brother again, whom they care for and indulge.

The little bastard is not so gentle, and those nights he demanded answers and got none, and he kept saying, *It all connects; it all connects*, as I tried to sleep and tried to read, but *Anna Karenina* took me back to, rather than away from, the women; for if she had lived now and had believed she was fat because her stomach creased, because she could pinch flesh over her ribs, because she could not wear her size eight or ten, she would have been among them, taking pills and getting through the day on black coffee and cigarettes, nibbling food while her face tautened and her heart beat faster, creeping down to the kitchen at night to eat a half-gallon of ice cream, then rushing in remorse to the bathroom to jam fingers down her throat and vomit the colors of that food children and dieting women so love, if I can take as a microcosm the women we interviewed, for each of them confessed ice cream as her secret wickedness. These images of shitting and vomiting induced by laxatives and fingers interrupted me whenever, that week, I touched Paula: to teach her a Greek dance in my living room, standing side by side, hands on each other's shoulders, as I counted one-two one-two; to make love with her before she slept and I lay staring opposite the bed, at the dark window, its glass fogged and moist.

We simply happened, on Friday, to be free at two-thirty, so we drove to the public high school, whose crowded halls and rooms I had endured for four years. I parked at the front of the building. They would all come out there, to the waiting buses in line ahead of us, to the cars in the lot. A large statue of *The Thinker* was on the schoolground, between us and the building. A bell rang loudly, and as they came out, some singly, most in hurried groups, lighting cigarettes, Paula got out of the car, stopped several of them until one boy turned back to the grounds and pointed at a girl alone, lighting a cigarette in the lee of *The Thinker*. Paula went to her, and I watched them talking. Then they came to the car. I watched Paula talking, smiling; when they got closer I could see that the girl was doing neither, and as she slid into the back seat and looked at me, I thought she wouldn't, not in this car, not with us.

"Who's your father?" I said.

"Jake."

"Jake? I know Jake."

KAREN ARAKELIAN

They said they would take me home, but could we go by his office first and talk where it was comfortable so him and the girl didn't have to stay twisted around to look at me. I knew who he was, I had seen him a lot in town, but he didn't recognize me, because I kept growing up while he stayed the same. Except he had lost more hair. He drove, and I just watched his bald head and the hair at the back and sides and smoked two cigarettes. I didn't say anything, and I didn't know if I would or not in his office; I wouldn't know till it was over. But I felt like it was all over and nobody would understand what it's like when they're all so thin. Everybody, even Heidi, even though she's always talking about how fat she is, but I know it's so we'll look at how thin she is and be jealous. And we are. Anyways I am.

I think it was money. I even thought of shoplifting and trying to sell things, but after I figured out how I could do it and where, and that took hours and hours, for days and nights, a lot of time thinking about the different stores and what they had in them and where the clerks were. I even went to some of them and looked around. Then after I planned how to do it and what to take, I realized there was no one to sell it to. Because if they could afford to buy the stuff, then they didn't have to buy it cheaper from me, and if they were my friends, or people like them, they couldn't buy anything anyways.

I was relieved, but I was at the bottom again, like the times when I wanted to be dead, because the pills were working but I couldn't afford a second prescription. I had saved for the first one, and for the first visit to Francis too, and there were no jobs, not unless I quit school and worked full time, which I would do, but my parents would never let me. All of us were supposed to go to college, my Dad was very proud about that, and I could see why: he had worked so hard at that shitty place, and his father had come over from Armenia to get away from the Turks. I have heard those stories, about them killing my great-grandparents, and other stories, and I hate fucking Turks. Everyone else went to college, and I'm the youngest. So I couldn't get a job.

I went to Francis for my second appointment in January, when school had just started and my Christmas job at the department store was over and I was down to my last two days of pills. He weighed me; then I started crying, and he told me to get dressed and he sent the nurse out. When I was dressed he sat me down in his office and said, "You lost seven pounds. Why did you cry?"

So I told him, and I see now that's when he knew my parents didn't know I was going to him, didn't know about the pills and the vomiting. You know how they are, the doctors: they handle you so fast they hardly look at you, and even if they do, even if they touch you with their stethoscope and their fingers, you feel like they haven't. But he was definitely looking at me, and I couldn't believe it: there it was in his face; he wanted me, the first time almost anybody ever looked at me like that, anybody but punks in the halls and at parties, the first time ever that the guy was a grown man. An old one too. So I looked back. And saw that he was old but not too old. He was probably fifty or more, but he was distinguished-looking; he had a nice haircut, not too short, and blow-dried hair, dark brown with some gray at the sides and temples; and he was tall and trim, athletic-looking, probably racquetball and tennis. I knew he sailed his boat. The lines in his face must have come from the boat; they looked like outdoor lines. I watched him watching me; then I took out a cigarette, which I'd always been afraid to do in a doctor's office, and I lit it and he didn't say anything. After a while he got up and gave me his Styrofoam cup for an ashtray. A few drops of coffee were in the bottom. He drank it with cream. Then he said: "I can help you."

He was standing right in front of me, his legs nearly touching my knees, and I moved my cigarette out to the side so the smoke wouldn't go up to his face.

"Please do," I said.

"Come here tomorrow night at eight."

Tomorrow was Wednesday. I said I would. He kept standing there. I finished my cigarette, blowing the smoke off to my side and watching him talk to me. We would have to be careful, he said. He could get into very bad trouble. But he could give me the pills. But I mustn't ever say a word. I nodded. Then, I don't know why, I knew he was hard. When I put out my cigarette I glanced at it. His pants stretched across its top, and it was like it was trying to push through the pants and touch my eyes.

On Wednesday night it was very big, and I knew I had never really fucked before. I had done it in the yard and in cars at parties, when I was loaded on drugs and beer. But this was slow getting undressed, and his hands weren't a doctor's anymore, they were slow and gentle and everything took a long time. He liked eating me and he stayed down there till I came; then he sat on the floor beside the couch and touched me till I was ready again. Then he put on a rubber, and for a long slow time he was in me and I came again and finally he did: when it happened to him he groaned and shuddered and cried out in a high soft voice like a girl. That night he gave me birth-control pills too.

So I had all these pills to take, and I hid them in my underwear drawer where I keep my cigarettes and grass, and I should have kept them all in my purse, but I'm so careless about my purse—I keep dropping it on the kitchen table with my books, or leaving it in the living room, on top of the television or on the couch—that I was always afraid, when it was just grass and cigarettes, that my mother or father would pick it up wrong, just to move it, and everything would fall out on the table or floor: my Newports and my dope, and then it was speed and downs and the birth-control pills, so everything was under my pants. Still I should have been safe. I do my own laundry and fold it in the basement and put it away.

But that night Heidi was over and we were up in my room, and I was putting away my clothes when Dad knocked on the door. I said come in. He opened the door and stood in the doorway a while, talking to us. He always liked to talk to us kids and our friends. That night we talked about school, and he said we had to work hard and try to get scholarships but that he'd see to it I went to any place I could get into. He could always get money, he said, and I was the last one, so it was easier. Then he was talking about when he went to the high school and the trouble he and the guys got into, getting wise with old Mrs. Fletcher (she still teaches English, even though we think she's senile the way she keeps reciting "Snow-Bound" every year on the first day it snows because Whittier was born here and lived here), and he and his buddies would get sent to the principal; and talking Armenian in French class; and sneaking fishing rods out of the house in the morning and walking down to the bus stop with the rods in two parts down their pants legs, so they walked stiff-legged, and when they were around the corner they took out the rods and went to the pond—and it was all so tame and old-fashioned I felt sorry for him.

I've told him there are guards in the halls and patrolling the lavs for pushers, and he knows, because every kid in the family has told him, about kids smoking dope and drinking on the bus at seven in the morning, but it's like to him it's something that's going on, but it's out *there* somewhere, with the Puerto Ricans and Italians, but it's not here, in this nice house he's buying every month, like we have our own world here. And Goddamn me, that's when I put the panties in my drawer, while he was laughing about him and his buddies growing up. He had moved into the room, by then, and was standing on the rug under the ceiling light, and what I didn't think of is how tall he is. If I were standing there, I could not see into the back of my drawer. I can't even see into it when I'm standing beside it; I have to sort of raise up and look toward the back. But he could look straight down in it. Not that he was. He was talking to us, Heidi sitting on the bed and me standing between the bed and the chest of drawers, and I suppose his eyes just naturally followed my hands as they took clothes from the bed and put them in the drawers, and when I put a stack of pants in the top drawer, all he did was glance that way, and what he saw wasn't the cellophane of grass or the two bottles of pills or the birth control pills, but the Goddamn turquoise of the Newport pack, and he stopped talking and I saw his face change; he said "Uh-oh," and I shoved the drawer closed.

"Karen," he said, and I looked at Heidi. She said later she thought it was the grass. She didn't know about the pills, none of them, and she still doesn't.

"It's for me," Heidi said. Her face was red, and her mouth and eyes were scared-looking, and I will never forget what she did for me, or tried to. Because she knows my Dad has a temper, and telling him you smoke dope is like telling some of these other parents you're on heroin. "Karen doesn't smoke it," she said. She looked like she was about to cry.

Then he knew. He lives at home like he doesn't know anything but the leather factory—he's a foreman there—but he is not dumb. I wish for him and me both, and Mom, and Francis, that he was. Because then he said: "You better go on home now, Heidi."

She got her parka and was gone, looking at the floor as she walked past him; at the door she looked back, and her face was still red and her eyes were bright and wet. Then she went down the hall and I heard her on the stairs and my mom calling good night and Heidi said it too, and I could tell it was over her shoulder as she went out the door. I heard it, and then the storm door, and was looking at Dad's shoes.

"Open it," he said.

I shook my head. If I spoke I would blubber. He turned his head and shouted, "Marsha!"

Mom didn't answer. She came up the stairs, her footsteps heavy like running, but she was only climbing fast. She stood at the door a moment looking at me and at Dad's back; then she came in and stood beside him.

"She's smoking dope," he said. "Cigarettes too. Show your mother the drawer, Karen."

Then I was lying on the bed, face-down, like I had fainted, because I didn't remember deciding to do it or getting there: one second I was standing looking at them, then I was crying into the bedspread, and I knew from the footsteps and the slow way the drawer opened that it was Mom who did it. Then she was crying over me, hugging me from behind, her hands squeezed between my shoulders and the bed, and Dad was talking loud but not yelling yet, and I started talking into all that, babbling I guess, but it wasn't about Francis and me. I said that too, but it was like a small detail when you're describing a wreck you were in, telling the police, and Francis and me were just the rain or the car that stopped to help: sometimes I screamed, but mostly I moaned and cried about vomiting my dinner and hiding that from them and laxatives and having to go at school and holding it and holding it till the bell, then hurrying to the lav and the sick sounds I made in the stall with the girls smoking just on the other side of it and saying *gross gross*, and my fat ugly legs and my fat ugly bottom and my fat ugly face and my fat ugly floppy boobs and how I wanted to be dead I was so fat and ugly, and some time in there my dad stopped talking, stopped making any sound at all, except once when he said, like he was going to cry too, like Mom was the whole time: "Oh, my God."

ARCHIMEDES NIONAKIS

I said it too. I didn't say much more as I stood at the window looking from Karen to the twilit traffic to Karen again while she talked and wept and Paula's eyes brimmed over and she wiped her cheeks. Then Paula took her to the bathroom behind the waiting room, and they worked on their faces and came out cleansed of tears and made-up again, walking arm in arm. Karen was plump. But, like all those others—and I know all is hyperbolic for only eight women, nine with Karen, but on that Friday afternoon their number seemed legion—she was not fat.

Looking out my window at people driving home from work in the lingering sunset, the snow having stopped Thursday morning and the sky cleared overnight, I listened to Karen and thought of my brothers, perhaps the happiest Americans I know. I barely remember my father—I am not certain whether I recall him or merely have images from stories my brothers and mother have told—but my brothers remember him and the village where we lived. My father owned a small café and was also the mayor of the town, so when the Communist guerrillas came they took him with them, to the hills. They all knew him, and they said We have to take you because you are the mayor. Some months later one of them came through town and stopped at our house to tell my mother her husband was well. Kosta was ten, and my mother sent him with the man and a knapsack of food and wine, and they walked for two days to the camp in the mountains, where Kosta spent a day and a night with my father, who showed him to everyone in the camp and boasted of his son who had come to visit. It was, Kosta says, a gentle captivity. They treated my father well, and he could do whatever he pleased except escape. Kosta walked back alone, stopping at houses along the way. Later a guerrilla came to tell my mother that my father had died, probably of pneumonia, and they had properly buried him, with a marker, in the hills. She managed the café and cared for me, playing among the tables, and worried about her older sons and wrote to her brother in America to sponsor us.

So my brothers have built a business and houses, and when I go visit them or, more important, when, unobserved, I see them driving in town, and I watch from the sidewalk, I know they are happy, as I do when I go to their shop and wait for one of them to trim what is left of my hair. They laugh and talk; for eleven or twelve hours a day, six days a week, they do this, and they make a lot of money from those women, as though, immigrants that they are, they had seen right away in the shoe factory where the heart of the nation was and left that bleak building and women's feet and moved up to their own building, and later their homes, paid for by women's hair. And remained untouched, unscathed: swam and skied and played tennis with their wives and children, indeed lived athletic lives as naturally as animals and never considered the burning of fat or the prolonging of life. As I run, not for my waist or longevity, but to maintain some proportion of my *homo duplex*, to keep some balance between the self I recognize and the little bastard who recognizes nothing as familiar, a quotidian foreigner in the land. My brothers watched with amusement, if even that, as their hair fell out. They celebrate all Greek holidays, as I do with them, and on Greek Easter we cook a lamb on a spit; they take their families to the Greek church, and I do not know whether they believe in God as much as they believe a father should take his family to church. They visit Greece, where now my father's bones lie in a cemetery in our village, and I go there too, having no memories save those of a tourist who speaks the language and shares the blood, so that I have no desire for a Greek household as my brothers have made with their marriages here, nor do I have a desire for an American one. So this year in my apartment I have Paula, and I have a law practice that is only an avocation, and my only vocation is running each year in Boston the long run from my father's country.

Still Karen talked, seated at my desk, leaning over it, her hands outstretched, held and stroked by Paula's. I looked at Paula sitting in the chair she had pulled up to a corner of the desk, and I thought

I could tell my brothers now; it was clear to me, and I could explain it to them, could show them why I would not, could not, work twelve or eight or even six hours a day five or six days a week for any life this nation offered. I had not fled a village where I would roam without education till I died. I had simply been a five-year-old boy placed on a ship. I looked out the window again and thought of Lillian Clark and those terrible eyes and the Puerto Rican girl she had to free her of her work, so that she had nothing at all to do, while in the garage the steel of the Porsche drew into itself the February cold. I spun from the window in a moment of near glee, so that Karen stopped and sniffed and looked at me, wiping her eyes. But I stopped myself and turned back to the window. I had been about to tell her I was glad Jake had done it.

She did not mention once, that entire time, the killing of Francis Clark. Nor did I ask her to. When she finished I told her we would take her home and saw at once in her eyes what I knew as soon as I had spoken: we could not do that, we could not enter or even drive to the front of Jake's home, and I felt affection and respect like love for her then, saw her as a sixteen-year-old daughter who not only loved Jake but understood him too. She would have done everything again so she could clothe herself in smaller and smaller pants and skirts and dresses and blouses, but she would have done it with more care. And I remembered from somewhere, someone, in my boyhood: *Don't shit where you eat.* It was the way my brothers ran their households, and perhaps one of them had said it to me. I told Karen that Paula would drive her to her streetcorner and I would phone her father. They both nodded and went to the bathroom. When they came out, I held Karen's parka for her and told Paula I would see her at my apartment.

I sat at the desk in the smoky and shadowed room—we had not turned on a light—then I looked up Jake's number, closed the book, gazed at the window and the slow cars, forgot the number, and opened the book again. His street was not far away, and I wanted to give him time to leave before Karen walked into the house. Marsha answered, and I heard the quaver of guilt in my voice and heard it again when Jake took the phone, and beneath the warmth in his voice I heard what I knew I would see in his eyes. I asked him if we could have a talk.

"Sure, Archimedes, sure. I'm on the way."

I waited outside, in the waning light now, and watched every car coming from his direction. His was large, and American, and I peered at him through the window, then got in. He drove us to the ocean. I do not know why. Perhaps it was for the expanse of it, or some instinct sent him to the shore. But I do not want to impose on Jake my own musing of that day: perhaps he wanted a bar where no one knew us. He drove for half an hour, and we talked about my brothers and his and his sisters and his work at the factory. We did not mention my work or Karen or Marsha or his grown children. Now and then I looked at his face, lit by the dashboard, and his eyes watching cars and trucks, while they stared at his new life.

He stopped at a restaurant across the road from the ocean; on the beach side of the road, a seawall blocked our view of the water, but night had come, and we could only have seen the breakers' white foam. The empty tables in the restaurant were set for dinner, their glass-encased candles burning over red tablecloths; we went through a door into the darkened lounge and stood for a few moments until we could see, then moved to a booth at the wall, across the room from the bar. The other drinkers were at the bar, four men, separate, drinking quietly. The bartender, a young woman, came for the order. Jake said a shot of CC and a draft, so I did too and had money on the table when she came back, but he covered it with his hand, said, No, Archimedes, and paid her and tipped a dollar. He raised his shot glass to me, and I touched it with mine. He drank his in one motion; I swallowed some and said, "I'm defending George Karambelas."

"Yes."

"I've just talked to Karen."

"Ah."

He drank from the mug of draft and called to the bar: "Dear? Two more shots, please."

So I drank the rest of my whiskey, and we watched her cross the floor with the bottle and pour, and he gave her money again before I saw it in his hand, but I said: My round, Jake, and gave her my ten and told her to keep one. We watched her until she was behind the bar again, then touched glasses, and I sipped and looked at his wide neck as he drank. Then I said: "I've been wondering about the boat."

"The boat?"

"That model. How did it break?"

"I broke it. With my fist, on the desk."

"Why?"

"How do you think he paid for it, Archimedes? You think he was a good man? An honest man? A good *doc*tor?"

"No."

"That's why I broke it."

"Then what?"

"He was sitting behind his desk when I broke it. He was waiting for—you know what he was waiting for."

"Yes."

He turned toward the bar, lifting his glass.

"No," I said. "Finish first. Please."

"Okay. That's when he took out the gun. From his drawer. He took it out and he worked it, so he had a bullet in there, in the barrel, and it was cocked. You know something? I looked at that big hole in the barrel, pointed at me, and I looked at that son of a bitch's face, and I wasn't scared of that gun. I think because if I died I didn't care. I can't tell you how bad I felt. You don't know; I can't say it."

"I know."

I took our shot glasses to the bar and she filled them and he said loudly, to my back: "Archi*mede*s. That's my round."

"I'll run a tab," she said. I noticed then that she wore glasses, and in the light behind the bar was pretty, and I wanted to be home with Paula, only to lie beside her, and to sleep. I spilled whiskey on both hands going back to the booth.

"She's keeping a tab," I said.

Jake nodded, and raised his glass to mine, and I smelled more whiskey than I drank.

"He told me to leave. How do you like that? He's doing that to my daughter and giving her those pills, and he says to me, leave. Go home. So I didn't move. I came to talk to that son of a bitch —"

"He was certainly that, Jake."

"Yes. And you know how they are, those rich doctors, all the rich people, they're used to saying leave, go home, and everybody goes. So what's he going to do, Archimedes? Shoot me? Of course not. He's got the gun and he's behind his desk, but *still* he has to listen. Because I'm talking to him, Archimedes; I'm telling him things. So he gets mad. *Him.* And he comes around the desk with that gun, and I tell him I'll shove that thing up his ass. Then I hit him. But, Goddammit, he hit his head. On the corner of his desk there, when he went down. Just that once. I hit him just that once, and the son of a bitch cracked his head. I can't feel bad. For him. But let me tell you, since that night nobody talks in my house. Marsha and Karen, they just go around sad. And quiet. Jesus, it's quiet. We talk, you know; we say this and that, hello, good morning, you want some more rice? But, oh Jesus, it's quiet, and me too. I've just been waiting. You see, when they blamed it on George, I knew I had to go tell them. Every night, I'd say to myself: Tomorrow, Jake. After work, tomorrow, you go down to the station. Then I'd go to work next day, and when five o'clock came I'd drive home. I couldn't leave them. My family. I don't mind being punished. You kill somebody, you go to jail, even if he's a son of a bitch. But every day I couldn't leave my family."

"Monday," I said.

"What about Monday?"

"Let's do it Monday. That'll give you two days to raise bail."

He drank the rest of his beer, then leaned over the table.

"How much?"

"Probably five thousand for the bondsman."

"I can get it."

"I could ask my brothers," I said. "You might need ten, but I doubt it."

"No. I have some family. And I have friends."

He slid out of the booth, stood at the table's end, held two mugs in one hand, the glasses in the other.

"Well," he said. "Okay. Yes: Monday."

He went to the bar, tall and wide and walking steadily, and I wanted to tell him not to bring me another shot, but I could not keep that distance from him, though my legs under the table felt weak, as if they alone, of my body, were drunk. Then he paid her, so this was our last drink, and I imagined Paula in the warm bedroom, lying on the bed reading her philosophy book, glancing at her watch. When Jake sat across from me, we raised the glasses, and I said, To Monday; then we touched them and I drank mine in one long swallow, exhaled, and drank some beer.

"You said let's," he said.

"What?"

" 'Let's do it Monday.' What did you mean?"

"I don't charge much," I said. "I don't charge anything at all, for a good Armenian."

"Really? You? You want to be my lawyer?"

"Jake, you'll never see the inside of a prison."

"*No.*"

"I'm sure of it."

"Really?"

"Really."

"What about George?"

"He won't be my client anymore."

"But this weekend. He stays in jail?"

"Only till Monday. What the hell: he shouldn't drink so much."

His smile came slowly and then was laughter that rose and fell and rose again as we walked out of the dark lounge, to the parking lot and the smack of breakers beyond the seawall and into his car, where pulling down his seat belt, he turned to me and said, "Come to the house and have dinner."

"Another time," I said. "I've got a woman waiting at home."

He squeezed my shoulder, reached across me and pulled my seat belt over my chest and snapped it locked, then started the car and turned on its headlights and slowly drove us home.

Molly

for George Gibson

ONE

WHEN CLAIRE'S HUSBAND left her and their daughter, she
was twenty-five years old and Molly was three. By the time she
was thirty Claire knew other men like Norman, knew them because
their sad wives were her friends. These men were absolutely com-
petent in their work, even excellent, better than others because
more committed or obsessed. Or possessed. But they and Norman
could not be husbands and fathers, unless their wives and children
wanted little more than nothing, or little more than what money
gave them. So Norman had left to be free, to work as an anthropologist all the way across the country in California, as if he needed
that distance between him and Massachusetts to make final his leaving. Every month he sent Claire a check drawn on the Wells Fargo
Bank in Pacifica. After receiving the third check, she divorced him.

Norman was a tall, angular man who appeared clumsy: a coffee cup in his large and bony hands seemed to be in its last moments before fragmentation; a car in his control looked alive, like a horse that senses his rider is a novice and is deciding whether to be gentle and patient, or a rascal. But he was not clumsy. He moved that way, looked that way even at rest in a chair, because he seemed to live always in a world that was not physical. Or nearly always. At his long table in his large cluttered den he studied artifacts and catalogued them, and his hands and face then, his sloping shoulders and long arms, reminded her of a pianist's. To him, his den was not cluttered: it was perfectly in order; but that order was for Claire an accumulation of objects that she knew were part of her own history in America and with Norman but now, unearthed and collected, had no connection with the world she lived in.

She prepared meals that he ate as a pet dog eats its dry food, out of hunger while knowing there is better food he would gobble if only he could get it. But for Norman there was no better food. He did not smoke, and before dinner he drank whatever she did, and he took his alcohol as he did his food: quickly, and without visible pleasure or lack of it, and always moderately. Some evenings, with what she believed at the time was mischievous curiosity, she mixed herself a bloody mary or salty dog and gave him only the seasoned tomato juice or salted grapefruit juice, and he drank these, fooled and never knowing it. Then she realized he would not care if he did know it, and with scorn but fear too she saw him not as a fool but as a creature who needed almost nothing that she did. After that she nightly gave him juice and doubled the vodka in her own drinks, wanting to drink his portion as she sat across the living room from him, and Molly played on the floor between them and Claire drank until she was drunk: a drunkenness she masked so well that he could neither see nor hear it. She sat talking as though sober and smelling the food on the stove and in the oven and wishing he would suddenly die, drinking grapefruit juice in his large chair where he could not look comfortable, where his long arms and legs shifted and jutted out and would not rest in the chair's sturdy depth.

He touched and held Molly, and spoke to her, as absently as he ate and drank and drove and touched everything that was part of their lives. Before she began wishing for his death, she had at times felt compassion for him as she watched him with Molly, saw him as though deprived of his sense of touch and so removed from the world and condemned to move in it on a chair with motor and wheels. Also, during that time, she often read in his den while he worked at night, after his workday was over, and he had drunk his two drinks and eaten his dinner. She sat in a chair across the room from him, facing his profile at the table, and sometimes she lowered the book to her lap and with yearning sorrow that dampened her eyes she watched him fondle the old bottles and potsherds and crusted iron, the only things she ever saw him fondle, and she wanted his hands like that on her flesh. This was early enough in the marriage for her sorrow to include him, for her to feel that his steadfast lack of proportion was a curse on him too, and gave him pain he could neither voice nor heal. And then her sorrow included hope too: that as he grew older, toward thirty, and attained some of the achievement he wanted, he would change, would become a whole man whose pleasures as husband and father were two-thirds of his fulfillment instead of the third or fourth or even less they were now.

On one of those evenings she admitted they were less. She did not admit this so much as she was finally no longer able to deny it: the truth of it rose in her and she fought it, tensed her muscles against it; then she tired and with a sigh he did not hear at his table, she surrendered to it. She and Molly could vanish tonight, and his life would move on, move in the direction he believed was forward. This man, whose only physical appetite was sexual, who left his desk for bed and her body and excited her with the extremity of his only passion away from his work, who plunged and panted and gasped and groaned, was nothing more than an anthropologist who was beyond hardworking, who was even a bit mad, and after his work he was a good fuck. Soon she started serving him juice before dinner and watched him from her secret and vengeful drunkenness, and spoke to him, made the sounds of marital exchange that she had once loved, those words whose function was not so much to inform but to assure, to celebrate even, the communion between a woman and a man; and she looked at him dangling in his chair and wished he were dead.

So he had left her and Molly long before he took his body and artifacts and other possessions with him, took them from Massachusetts to California. Always he sent the monthly check, inside a folded and blank page of white stationery. She assumed the checks would stop arriving on the first of each month when he realized that Molly was eighteen or twenty-one, whatever age he had in mind. Or perhaps the money was for her, and it would keep coming until he died or she did, and if she died first whoever did such things would find him through his bank (there was no return address on his envelopes) and tell him it was over now, he could stop. He might have married out there, but she could not imagine it. Because he had left to be free, and for him freedom was selfishness, while for her it was being able to live each day without violating her conscience. She came to believe this after he left, when for the first time in her life without parents or a husband, and so without another adult between her and the world, she had needed a conscience, a place in her spirit where she could stand with strength, and say yes or no. When Molly was nine, Claire told her: "I grew up when he left."

This was during their time before dinner, when each evening they sat in the living room of the house Norman had left, and during Claire's cocktail hour they talked.

"I had to learn to sell real estate, then I had to sell it. And I learned something else. This was during Vietnam. That it wasn't just the Pentagon and the President and Congress that lied. And were cowards. And were evil. Doing terrible things and calling them something else. It was people everywhere, little people. They made money and maybe thought they had power but whether they lived or died wouldn't make any difference. Not to the world. They were people with jobs. It's how they got the jobs and made money. They're cowardly with their bosses and they call it being shrewd. Smart. They call lying 'business.' They always call something by another name. I think it's because people know. They know what's right and what's wrong. And they want to be good. So when they do something evil they say it was something good. It was justified. I've never heard anyone say, 'I did this terrible thing to somebody and I loved it.' Except a boy I knew who'd been to Vietnam. But that's different, and we can't understand it. So it wasn't just Johnson and Nixon and Kissinger and all the rest of them. The country was at war over there, and it was a war here too, of beliefs, and every

day it was with me. A confrontation—a fight—between good and
evil, truth and lies. People marching in the streets. And there I
was with my little life. Working with real-estate agents, and law-
yers, and banks—Jesus: *banks*—and architects and building con-
tractors. And I think everything would have been blurred. For me,
anyway, if it weren't for the war. I think I would have figured,
this is the way the world is. And maybe that's how these people
got that way when they were young. Maybe they just figured this
was it: lying and fucking over people. And they either had to do
it or go live in the desert on locusts and honey. But the war gave
me a—moral energy, maybe. Or maybe it just woke me up. Because
everything connected in the war. You could hardly buy anything
without supporting some corporation that made money on killing
people. And your taxes. And the money you earned: you never
knew where it came from. What stocks. What profits. So there was
always blood on it. None of this got to Norman. He almost cried
at the My Lai pictures. The ones I showed you. I never saw him
cry but that night he looked like he would. Then he went upstairs
to work. And I sat downstairs with the *Life* magazine. The same
one we threw away last year. I was pregnant with you. And I sat
there and knew we did not live alone anymore, me and you inside
of me. I was part of the war. So I was part of everything. I had
paid for bullets, and I started imagining money I had spent working
itself through the economy. From the counter at the store to the
people who made what I bought and made bullets too, and I saw
my money finally buying bullets for Calley's gun. And I saw my
money spent on those bullets coming back to us—you and me—
in Norman's paycheck. I didn't do anything. I didn't stop buying,
or paying taxes, or go to jail or march in the streets. But by the
time Norman left I had at least learned something. So I'm glad I
went to work late in my life. I didn't connect it right away with
the war. But I do now. I've never done anything at work I'm
ashamed of. I'm ashamed of a lot of things I've done as your mother.
But I'll keep learning how to do that, all my life. I don't lie to my
clients."

A year after Norman left, when it was clear that he would not
be a father for Molly, she changed their names from Thornton back
to Cousteau. It did not feel like a change. Even early in the marriage,

when she wanted his name, it was strange on her tongue and in her ears; at times she felt pride and love, yes, but she also felt separated from the name, as though it were an acquired title that did not touch all the depths of Claire Cousteau. By that time she was working and Molly was with sitters during the day, so after work Claire gave her the attention she would have shared with a man, if she had been with Molly all day, and if she had had a man. Now her companion for cocktail hour and dinner was Molly. And Claire did not go out in the evenings before she and Molly had eaten dinner together and Molly was asleep. At work Claire missed her, and called home and spoke to the sitter and then to Molly: the pleased and confused child holding the phone to her face, repeating Claire's greetings and the promptings from the sitter: *We played in the snow; I ate pea soup.* After work she drove home to a daughter whose company she dearly wanted.

By the time Molly was nine she was a sensitive and eager listener who understood everything, it seemed, that Claire told her of work, of what she had learned and was learning about people, how much of themselves they would give away for money or simply to avoid standing their ground, even when the issue was trifling and the consequence they feared was only embarrassment. You could see in their eyes the cages they had built between their lives and their beliefs.

"It's what makes people age," she said to Molly. "I'm sure of it. Not wrinkles, or gray hair, or getting flabby or dull. It's that compromise, over and over for years. That's what you see in those tired old faces. You and I—only our skin and hair will age."

Molly was able to connect her own moral landscape with Claire's: the disloyalty of children at school, and their fear of teachers and other children, and their willingness to do anything, say anything, so they would not seem foolish, or separate from the others. Molly could listen to Claire talking about a man she was seeing: what Claire liked about him, what she was uncertain about, what she found amusing, and Molly could talk about him, and on these evenings the two of them were like roommates as they recounted and mimed the comic flaws of Claire's lovers.

She never had more than one at a time. In her affairs she obeyed a pattern she had lived with before marriage and was comfortable with as a divorced woman: a series of dates, a ritual of drinking and eating and talking and touching and kissing that allowed her to believe that she and the man were learning to know each other rather than simply increasing their excitement by conducting fore-play while clothed in restaurants and movie theaters and bars. Norman had been her first lover, and from her marriage she had learned that the desire to know another, and to be known by him, was futile. But she could live with the illusion of it. She believed there was nothing harmful in living a lie if you knew you were. It was, in fact, good. For how else could you live, except to will yourself into an alteration of the truth you were dealt at birth?

When Molly was twelve, her curiosity about sex became concrete and personal. Until then, beginning years earlier, Claire had given her long answers to her questions about procreation, pregnancy, menstruation, childbirth, nursing, and these lessons had seemed to Claire abstract and general, like their talks about death. Now Molly knew girls only a year or two older who kissed and let boys touch them and even touched the boys. Some old instinct urged Claire to lie: to tell Molly it was wrong. But she knew the emotions of that instinct were fear and a desire to protect Molly, and she resisted them because the truth was that girls no longer had to worry about either pregnancy or bad reputations, they were as free as boys now, and so there was little to fear, little need to protect Molly. The world she was growing into held in waiting far more complex and dangerous threats to her young spirit. And women, even girls, had always been more sane about sex than men, than boys: women's instincts were sound, and saved most of them from the damages of promiscuity or guilt.

She forced herself to look across the dinner table at Molly's eyes: at their curiosity, their fascination. And gratitude too, for being able to talk to her mother, with the confidence that her mother would tell her the truth. So Claire felt blessed, sitting in candlelight, pleasantly well-fed, drinking wine; and oblivious of their soiled plates on the table and the pots waiting in the kitchen to be emptied and cleaned, she sank warmly into the deep pleasure of motherhood. She said that she discovered after Norman left—always she called him Norman when she spoke to Molly—that you had to find some answers for yourself. And after a long and painful and frightening time—about six months, while men invited her on dates and she said no—she decided she did not have to either marry again or be doomed to loneliness only because as a young woman she had loved, then married, a man who believed he wanted marriage and children and learned too late that he did not. But as soon as she said the word loneliness, it jarred her. She said to Molly: "No. I didn't mean loneliness."

She believed she said this so Molly would not feel that Claire could live with her and still be lonely. Then she knew that wasn't the reason either, and for the first time since divorce she went beyond that word she had used for years as a name for her desires. Now she felt as though she were actually removing the word from her tongue, or from the air between her and Molly, and holding it before the candles' flames, turning it in her hands, squeezing and probing it, finding that it was not the truth, was not even close to it.

"No," she said to Molly. "I was never lonely. Not after Norman left. I was lonely when he was here, around the end of him being here. Because there were three of us, and we had a home. But the truth is there were only two of us, and we had a house and a two-legged pet I fed. Not a domestic animal, though. Norman was never domestic, except like an ashtray is, or a vegetable bin. Something that's in a house, and only receives. Maybe he was a Goddamn Christmas tree. When he left us I wasn't lonely. I wanted a man. It's—" She looked over the candle flames at their moving light on Molly's eyes. Molly had dark skin, like Claire's, and her black hair too, as though pallid Norman had truly left his daughter without a trace. "It's wanting to be wanted. Listened to. Really listened to. The way a man listens when he's attracted to you. Soon you'll know what I mean. You say something—anything, the stuff people are always saying to each other, and none of it's important. Except that it's you saying it to someone you care about, and who cares about you. *I never remember my dreams. I need a new raincoat.* It's the way a man listens. The way he looks at you when you talk. You're not talking about a raincoat anymore. It's as though you're showing him everything you remember about yourself: the girls you used to jump rope with, the tree you lay under as a child and daydreamed, your first crush on a boy in second grade. And the way a man will notice you. The gestures you make all day, every day. The way you push your hair back from your face. Or knit your brows or tighten your lips when you're trying to remember something. Your different smiles. When you do one of these, you can see it in their faces—it's a sudden look of appreciation. Or satisfaction. That they anticipated what you'd do. They notice everything, so you dress for them, you bathe for them, put on perfume and make-up for them. They do their own version of that for us too. And you feel known. Then you're not just one person among everyone. You're one woman among all women. You're you. That's what it feels like to be loved. And when you're not loved you become worse than part of a crowd. It's like you don't have a body anymore. You become abstract: just your voice inside you talking to yourself, and you feel like you don't even occupy the space you're standing in, like you're weightless. You're standing on a spot on the earth, but your feet are like air. *You* give me weight," she said to Molly, the child's face intense still, curious still, fascinated and grateful still, with a shade of fear too in her eyes: but always you had to tell your children something that brought that fear to their eyes, that awakening to what waited for them. "And I hope I give it to you." Molly nodded twice, three times. "And you need it from your friends too, your teachers, right?" Again the nod: a quick motion of agreement that asked Claire for more of this knowledge, this disclosure in candlelight and her mother's cigarette smoke, and the scents of melting wax and her mother's Burgundy. "And I need it from my woman friends. And from a man. From a man it's not really love. Not true love. But it has all the feelings of it."

"Why isn't it love?"

"Because love is a vocation."

"A what?"

"Work. Work that you love. That you must do to be whole. That you devote your life to. They don't teach it in school, but they should. I learned it with Norman. We got married thinking marriage was the happy ending, like in the movies; we had to learn it was the beginning of a vocation. He never did. He didn't want to. So with men—for me, anyway—it's not love. But it's close enough. And there's the pleasure."

For this she needed a cigarette, and as she lit it she glanced at

Molly and saw in her daughter's face, watching Claire inhale and blow out smoke, an expression of desire, and she knew that Molly wanted to smoke and was twelve years old but would do it anyway; remembering now her own girlhood, watching her parents and their friends smoking and waiting for the time, only a little longer but so long in childhood, when she would have the courage to steal and smoke one, the knowledge that she had to wait based not simply on fear of being caught when she was so young that her parents' anger would be even worse, but also on an instinct in her very flesh that told her you spared your body certain pleasures, and smoking was one of them, until you were older. Her recognition of Molly's yearning disrupted the excitement and reward of talking to her daughter about love, and although Claire was silent she felt she was stammering. She rose and went to the kitchen for a demitasse, and in that movement performed only to regain the rhythm of their talk she at once saw clearly, even as she poured coffee into her small cup, that the look of desire she had caught in Molly's face was not a break from that rhythm at all, but was part of it. Remembering again herself as a girl, waiting for the time, the day, the moment when there would be an open pack in an empty room and she would take a cigarette into the woods behind their home. It had nothing to do with wanting to look grown up, as adults liked to say, perhaps needed to say. It was being a child, and children perceived everything in their homes, so Claire had seen, then wanted, the sensation smoking gave her parents. When she returned to the table to sit and face Molly she was afraid again, as she had been earlier when she overcame the urge to lie about men and women, and men and herself. But she was more afraid of yielding to her fear than of what she meant to tell Molly.

"I'm going to tell you something else, and thank God you'll hear it first from me. Or at least completely from me. I can't tell you not to share this with your friends. But I'm going to ask you. I'm going to ask you please not to. Because this is for families. For you and me. And your friends should hear it and talk about it at home. We've no right to violate that. Each girl has her own timing for this, and you've got no way of knowing what a girl should know, and when. Okay?"

The nod again, the young eyes oblivious now of Claire's smoking, as though knowing what Claire was about to say and already intent on that; the same desire, though, was in her face, and the shyness, and Claire did not know whether to see this as a sign of the deep and trusting comfort between them, or a sign that already she had said too much; and, entrapped by herself, was about to say far, far too much.

"It's the pleasure too," she said. "With a man. Making love with a man. You know how his seed gets into a woman. You looked worried, afraid, when we talked about that. Because you could only imagine pain. That part of his body going into you. But now you know girls who are experimenting. Touching boys there. Letting boys touch their vaginas. Maybe put in their fingers?"

This time Molly's nod was slow, and she blushed.

"They don't talk about pain, do they? Those girls."

"No."

"Only the first time. When the hymen breaks. When a man— or a boy—breaks it with his penis. But it's worth it. It's one of the most wonderful pleasures we can have. Maybe the most intense. Surely the most intense. Making love with a man you care for. It's everything I was talking about before, the way you feel like you, yourself alone among everyone else, and you feel it with your body *and* your heart. Damnit, I'm not going to lie to you. Mostly it's the body. The man's orgasm is his deepest pleasure, and that's when he ejaculates his seed. Our orgasm is even more intense, it lasts longer, and it's better than theirs." She paused, looking at Molly's puzzled, quizzical eyes. "Climax," she said. "Coming. Orgasm is coming."

"Oh. I thought it was—" She looked at her plate, then back at Claire's eyes, blushing again.

"What?"

"Getting pregnant."

"No. It's the completion of lovemaking. And when your body matures, you need it. Not *all* the time. It's not the most important thing in our lives. It's a very small part. But I need it. And that's what I thought and thought about when Norman left. There's masturbation, but it's not the same. It's like seeing only the end of a movie. So I decided back then that I could make love with a man—not any man, not *just* for the body, but a man I felt something for. Respected. Cared about. Could be myself with. And *feel* I was myself with. I hadn't listened to some snake and talked somebody into eating an apple. I was too young to know better, so I married a snake and he crawled away, to California. And left me to get banished like Eve. It wasn't right. Your generation won't go through all that worrying. But it was different for me. Being a young mother. I had to think things through, be sure I was right." Like a narrow beam of white light through a cloud of colors and images in her mind, a discovery came to her: she had either drunk too much, or had become too excited by talking like this to Molly; but something was spurring her to a volubility beyond Molly's reach, beyond her age and experience, and so beyond her ability to comprehend with comfort, with confidence. Then with a heedless shrug or a brave leap of her heart she ignored the light and opened her mind again to the flow of images from her memory and her ideas that she wanted to form into sound, into words.

"Good Lord," she said.

"What?"

"The grape. I'm talking too much. Listen: here's what I want you to know. Since sometime in the first year Norman left, I've had lovers." Molly's body showed nothing, was still, even relaxed; her eyes looking into Claire's were patient and calm. Claire sighed, audibly, louder than she needed to: a sign to Molly that a gift had passed between them, through the fire of the candles. "They've been nice men, good men. I don't hang out in bars and—" Molly quickly shook her head. "Thank you. As long as you don't think I go around looking for them. It's a pleasure I need sometimes." Then she smiled, and then her shoulders and abdomen shook with laughter that she tried to keep behind her closed lips, but it forced open her mouth, and she sat laughing, and as her face rose and fell with it she saw, through the tears in her eyes, Molly's smile. The smile was not forced, yet could not become laughter either. "Woo," Claire said. "Sorry. I just remembered a man who had been in the Navy. On a ship. He told me one night after they'd been at sea for a good while, they anchored off some island. Okinawa. Whatever. Their first night ashore. So you know what they did, besides get drunk. They went by a small boat from the ship to the island and back. They were coming back to the ship at midnight, and an old sailor looked around at all the drunk young men and said: 'Sex is the one thing you can get behind on the most, and catch up on the quickest'—" Then she was laughing again, her legs tightening with it, her torso and head swaying to and fro with it; and across the table Molly was laughing too, doubling over her cold dinner plate; and Claire knew their talk had ended, in this crescendo of laughter, and she gave herself to it until it ended too, then stood and gathered up dishes and carried them to the sink. Then Molly was beside her with glasses and a serving bowl, and she felt Molly's body touching her thigh and hip and ribs, and she placed a hand on Molly's long soft hair; then she gently pressed Molly's head against her side, and she said: "When you're ready—in high school, college, whenever—we'll get you a diaphragm."

She did not have a lover then, but two months later she did, and after twice going to his apartment and then coming home to Molly and the sitter, she told Molly about him. This was in winter at their cocktail hour, Molly with her cup of tea and Claire with the second martini she allowed herself before dinner.

"He's a nice man. Divorced. Or just separated now, getting divorced. I sold him their house three years ago. Now she has it. Some couples do that, you know: their marriage is going under, so they make a leap: buy a new house, or have a baby. It's sad. I had a hunch, when I was showing them houses. There was a sadness about them. And a shyness between them. A fragile commitment to stake their marriage on doing something new together. Now she has the house and the kids and the poor guy—Stephen, his name is Stephen—has the mortgage payments and a little apartment above a dentist's office. He pays rent to the dentist. Are you all right?"

"Sure."

"Hearing this, I mean. Knowing it's where I was last night. I go to his apartment."

"I don't mind."

Molly was twelve still, in the seventh grade; next summer she would be thirteen, and her body was shaping itself toward those numbers, her waist lengthening, becoming distinct and slender, and her breasts giving her sweater two small contours of fertile hope. She wore the subdued lipstick, a delicate deepening of her lips' color, that Claire allowed her for school and parties. On these winter days, when she came in from the cold, with her cheeks reddened, the lipstick looked from across a room like the true coloring of her mouth.

"Would you like to meet him? Have him come here for dinner?"

"Yes."

"What if he stayed?"

"I don't mind."

"To sleep with me."

"I know."

"Are you sure? You wouldn't be embarrassed? Or something else? When you went up to bed and—"

"Mom. It's okay."

"Or at breakfast? Think about it. I'm very serious about this. *It's* not serious, me and Stephen. But our home is. It's more important than me and Stephen, and how you feel about your home is more important. So tell me the absolute truth. Because, Molly, if there's ever anything but the absolute truth between us, then we've failed. And the failure is mine."

Molly had different smiles: some private, some distracted, some childish, some courteous, and she had one that for years had warmed Claire, as though it came to her on wings over whatever space lay between her and her daughter, and touched her; it was the smile of an old and intimate friend who loved you, trusted you, and did not have to forgive you. She was smiling that way now. For moments she did not speak. Then she said: "I better make you a third one tonight. You're like me in the principal's office."

"Do you know how?"

Molly crossed the room, took Claire's glass.

"It's gin and vermouth, right?"

"Not much vermouth. And four olives."

"Two ounces of gin. A few drops of vermouth. Stir."

Claire watched her walk into the kitchen, listened to her tossing ice from the glass into the sink, then working with the ice tray and dropping new cubes into the glass. She lit a cigarette and leaned back in her chair and closed her eyes. Her body felt relieved, as though she had just completed a task. She opened her eyes to a tinkling martini. Then Molly sat across from her on the couch and sipped her tea and frowned because it had cooled.

"Why were you at the principal's office?"

"Smoking."

Claire straightened, her arms rigid in front of her, and cold martini dropped onto her fingers.

"*Dope?*"

"Yuk. I'll never smoke that stuff."

Claire eased back into the chair, and lowered her arms.

"Molly, don't smoke."

"We just passed one around. I didn't even in*hale*."

"Whose was it?"

"Belinda's."

"Do you smoke?"

"*Mom.*" Molly lifted her purse from the cushion beside her, the purse filled, bulging. "Want to look?"

"No. No, of course I don't."

"I took a drag and Conway came in. The French teacher. They've got their own lavs. She just likes to catch people. What kind of grown-ups like to do that anyway?"

"Lord knows, sweetie. Not me, anyway. But please don't start, and get hooked."

Molly's smile now was sly, teasing, and they both looked at Claire's cigarette poised over the ashtray, her finger raised to tap ashes.

"Okay," Claire said. "Hell with spaghetti. Want to go out for dinner?"

The dinners, the evenings, and the breakfasts with Stephen were more comfortable than she had expected them to be; were even as comfortable as she had hoped they would be. On the first night, two nights after Claire had talked to Molly, Stephen came to dinner, and Claire was shy. She heard it in her voice too, and felt it in her cheeks, and glimpsed it in Molly's watching eyes. Molly watched them both as the three of them sat in the living room before dinner, and at dinner, and afterward as they lingered at the dining-room table, then as all of them cleared it and filled the dishwasher. But mostly she watched Claire, and Claire remembered Molly years ago watching her put on make-up. For in Molly's eyes now there was that same look of an astute apprentice. And there was a nuance too of collusion, the look of a female roommate who shares dinner with you and your lover before going to a movie, or to her room for the evening. When the kitchen surfaces were clean and the dishes were in the dishwasher, they went to the living room, and as Claire finished her coffee and offered Stephen more cognac, she realized that she did not control the evening; Molly did. For Claire did not have the courage to send her to bed. So, sitting with Stephen on the couch, she kept talking, including Molly, and hearing her own discomfort in her voice, feeling it warming her face. At ten o'clock Molly stood and said goodnight and came to the couch and kissed her. She shook Stephen's hand as he rose and told her goodnight. Then she left them.

Claire did not want to make love, did not want to climb the stairs with Stephen and take him into her bed where she had slept alone since Norman left. On the couch they kissed and touched until the second floor of the house was quiet. Still she kept Stephen on the couch until her passion overcame her; or nearly did; and she led him creeping up the carpeted stairs and down the carpeted hall and into her bedroom, and behind them she eased the door shut, and slowly turned the knob. She had not made love for so long in this bed that she could not remember whether it was audible or silent. It was silent, as silent as the one down the hall, behind the closed door: her daughter's bed she listened for as Molly slept on it or lay awake listening too, imagining, in the darkened knowledge of her bedroom. Then Claire's body surprised her, left her alone with her caution; yet as she came she clamped her teeth on her voice, panted through her nostrils, then held Stephen to her breasts, and kissed him. At early breakfast, feeding Stephen and Molly before the school bus came to the driveway, she was no longer shy.

That summer Molly celebrated her thirteenth birthday. She and Claire planned a party: after dinner, friends to come for snacks and music, maybe dancing if the boys could be coaxed. Claire and Molly ate dinner in the evening sunlight, the two candles between them: always at dinner Claire burned candles. When they finished dinner Claire went to the kitchen for her coffee and returned to sit with Molly. She lit a cigarette. Then Molly reached across the table for the pack, took a cigarette, tapped it, smiling at Claire; and as Claire watched, with the old cooling fear rising from her calves to her heart, Molly placed the cigarette between her lips, pulled a candle closer, leaned toward it, and drew from its flame—and oh not like an experimenting child with lips curled clumsily inward but with her lips delicately pursed, then she leaned back from the candle, and two fingers gracefully took the cigarette from her mouth and held it beside her cheek as she inhaled.

"Very sexy," Claire said, and heard the bitterness, the angry sense of betrayal in her voice, before she knew it was in her heart too. Molly smiled. Then Claire's bitterness was gone, and the fear too: it was sadness now, and resignation to it.

"Oh shit," she said. "You told me you wouldn't."

"No I didn't. You asked me not to."

"That's true. Well. I guess I can't tell you not to, while I'm sitting here smoking."

"You could. I could keep hiding it."

"How long have you hidden it?"

"Just this summer."

"Why didn't you tell me? When you started."

"I don't know. I guess because I wasn't a teenager yet."

"Jesus."

"What?"

"I don't know." She watched Molly smoke. "I started at thirteen. But it was before the Surgeon General's report."

"Thirteen?"

"It was different. We did it in attics. In basements. We chewed gum so our parents wouldn't know. Cleaned our fingers with lemon juice."

"Would you rather that?"

"No. Aren't you even a little afraid of cancer?"

"No. Are you?"

"I don't think about it. Are you just smoking to look sexy?"

Molly shrugged. "I like it."

Claire did not want to see the cigarette moving again to Molly's lips, but she forced herself to watch. Then she said: "Oh shit. You don't look thirteen anymore."

She pretended not to see Molly's hand coming across the table to touch hers, and she quickly rose with her plate and glass, and her cigarette like steel between her fingers, and hurried to the kitchen before her eyes brimmed and tears trickled on her cheeks.

With a dishcloth she dried her face, and when Molly came in with her cigarette and plate and glass, Claire took the plate and glass from her, put them in the sink, and hugged Molly tightly, and rubbed her back, and stroked her hair.

And that was it, the reason for her sorrow; she realized this more deeply at the party that night: Molly did not look thirteen anymore. And it seemed to Claire that all she had shared with Molly until now had been mere words spoken to a child who was still little Molly, lovely Molly, her little girl she loved so much, and wanted to teach as well. Now a simple burning white cylinder between Molly's fingers and lips gave Claire a sense of dread she did not understand. But there it was, each time she looked in on the party of girls and boys in the living room, most of the girls smoking, only two of the boys, and she knew that Molly was the only child who could smoke at home, with her mother, and so now the others could smoke here too. Why so many of the girls, and so few boys? It was becoming a female vice.

She told herself that the dread and sorrow she felt were irrational. Hadn't Molly said she would never smoke dope? She was an intelligent girl, wise enough to see and scornfully avoid the stoned and perhaps forever ruined lives of the classmates she had talked about with Claire. But when the party ended and she and Molly picked up the soft-drink bottles, and emptied ashtrays, and vacuumed pieces and crumbs of cake and cookies and potato chips, and filled the dishwasher with glasses and plates, and bowls for dips, and the cake plate, and wistfully dropped the thirteen candles into the garbage, she felt that Molly working beside her was more like a grown daughter visiting home than the girl she had come home to from work, and had, with love and pride, watched grow: her young body assuming grace, her mind becoming perceptive and singular, moving toward a character all her own in its intellectual and moral solidity. But she knew that, with time, this sad distance would pass. A night and a day. Two or three days. And she was able, without willing it, to smile at Molly when their cleaning was done and they stood in the kitchen, in the sound of the dishwasher, and to hand Molly a clay ashtray for her room. And at the top of the stairs, when they kissed goodnight, and Molly went down the hall, with the ashtray and her Marlboros and red disposable lighter, and opened her bedroom door, Claire said: "Don't smoke in bed, sweetie. We could do without a fire."

Molly turned and blew her a kiss. Then Claire went to bed and lay awake and tried to clear her mind, to empty it so it could receive, and finally when nothing came she turned on the bedside lamp and got out of bed and crouched before a bookshelf at one wall. It held her books from college, and among the Fs she found the novel she had read twice more since graduation, and brought it to her bed. It was *The Good Soldier* by Ford Madox Ford. She knew the passage was near the end of the book, and that she had long ago underlined it in ink, and she found it and read it: *Is there then any terrestrial paradise where, amidst the whispering of the olive-leaves, people can be with whom they like and have what they like and take their ease in shadows and in coolness?*

TWO

Belinda was blond and her cheeks were pink, her blue eyes glistening, and she was laughing and calling to Molly that she was smoking two cigarettes. Belinda was three feet away, across the long coffee table, sitting on the couch, laughing and pointing at her, and Molly looked at the cigarette between her fingers and then down at the one resting in the ashtray on the table, both of them just lit, and she shrugged and smiled but did not miss a note. She was in love with her voice. Like a precious discovery she had not been looking for, it rose from her diaphragm to her cheekbones, and they tingled; her mouth opened widely and the sound from it was beautiful. She was fifteen and she had sung in the chorale at school. She had sung alone at home, or with her mother, but softly. She had sung loudly with her friends. She had never sung loudly, alone, in front of anyone; and now, though she could hear rock music from the record player across the large basement room, her voice was louder and there were twenty people in the room, and on the couch with Belinda were Dotty and Wanda and Belinda's brother Bruce, a senior, and others were gathering around her: senior girls and boys, and her sophomore friends. And she knew the songs. She had not known she knew them. She spread her

hands outward from her uplifted face, her eyes leaving their faces
to focus on the top of the wall, where it joined the ceiling, to focus
there on the images of the song: the sad lady alone in her apartment
high above a city, holding a drink in a stemmed glass, staring across
the darkened room at the window, and beyond it at the lights
blinking like a heartbeat:

> "Maybe I won't find someone
> As lovely as youuu
> I should care
> And I dooooo—"

They shouted and clapped and without a pause, her eyes closed
now, she swayed and sang:

> "I used to visit all the very gay places
> Those come what may places
> Where one relaxes on the axis of the wheel of life
> To get the feel of life
> from jazz and cocktails—"

She was in their center, yet somewhere above them; beyond her
closed eyes she felt their bodies, but as a snake senses body heat;
and she felt their spirits drawn into hers, and hers leaving her body,
moving in song out of her mouth:

> "I know that if
> I took even one sniff—"

She opened her eyes to their laughter, flipped a hand downward
and gestured with upturned palm at the mirror on the table, the
razor blade, the straws—

> "It would bore me
> Terrif-ically too—"

She did not want to stop and she could not stop; she danced
backward away from the table and couch, spun into the center of
the room, spreading her arms. Someone put a can of Budweiser in
her hand.

> "—just one of those fabulous flights
> a trip to the moon on gossamer wings—"

She looked at the can, frowned with disdain, held it out and
someone took it and gave her a bottle of Dos Equis. She nodded,
drank from it, and sang. Bruce was holding her; tall Bruce. He was
at her side, his arm around her waist, moving with her, his body

with hers, swaying with her melody, his feet moving with hers and her rhythm. She sang "Something Cool" and "Laura" and "Autumn Leaves" and "Moonlight in Vermont." And she kept singing: these songs she had heard on the evenings and nights and weekend mornings and afternoons of her childhood, and she saw her mother's pretty face with the faces in the songs, for all the songs had faces, and Molly's was in them too. Her body was weightless as music and had boundless energy; and everything—the summer night, the party, the people there and herself there, Molly in the basement room and on the earth and in her breath of eternity—was as clear and lovely as a long high note on a trumpet.

She stopped when the songs did. They simply stopped rising inside her. She was not tired. And she did not care whether people had heard too much of her; she did not even consider it. She ended with "It Could Happen to You" and took a cold Dos Equis from an extended hand, a girl's hand, a senior's, and moved with Bruce, his arm at her waist, her body weightless still, her heart racing, through applause and shouts of surprise and delight, to the coffee table, to Belinda beaming at her from the couch, pretty Belinda holding out her arms, standing now, and coming around the coffee table, losing her balance and snatching it back with a quick shift of feet, Belinda hugging her tightly, prying Bruce away, saying at her ear: "God *damn*, Molly."

Belinda moved back, looked at her eyes, kissed her lips.

"You're beautiful. Where did you get those *songs*?"

"My mother's songbook."

"Songbook?" Bruce said. His hand was on her hip, his arm resting across the back of her waist.

"You know. Her records."

"She's a great mom," Belinda said to Bruce.

Wanda and Dotty appeared from behind her. They stood on either side of Belinda. They wanted to know where Molly learned all those songs, and how come they never knew she could sing like that. Wanda was drunk, and the color was leaving her face; she weaved and stared and drank from her bottle of beer, and Molly knew she would be in the bathroom soon, on her knees, hugging the bowl, riding the porcelain bus. Dotty said she had heard that

Janis Joplin got started at a party, just like this; Janis hadn't known till then she was such a good singer.

"Me and Southern Comfort," Molly said.

"Smack and death," Bruce said.

"Somebody change the subject," Belinda said.

"Dos Equis," Molly said, and turned away from Bruce to get one, but he said he would, and he left for the ice chest across the room. Time stopped, or sped. She was leaning against a wall with Dotty, and Bruce stood facing them, talking, and Molly saw that he only remembered now and then to look at Dotty; and Wanda had been in the bathroom since she first hurried there a cigarette ago, or two, or an hour. A girl kneeled at the coffee table, bent over the mirror, holding a straw in her nostril and bending farther, following the straw as the white line vanished into it.

"Vanished," Molly said.

"What?" Bruce said.

Molly shrugged. Somehow she knew people were upstairs, in bedrooms. She remembered a girl and boy going up the stairs. Then another girl and boy. And others. In her mind she saw them as clearly as if she were watching them now, across the room, holding each other and climbing the stairs, their faces flushed, their eyes bright and glazed. But she could not place them among her images of the party, could not establish a sequence. The entire night seemed to be in the present, moving in concentric circles. But she felt them up there in the many bedrooms of this house and on the sunporch couch and living-room couch, her spirit cringing yet fascinated as she watched them, her spirit up there in the enchanted forest where demons made vicious love, their faces neither soothed nor ecstatic: they hissed through clamped teeth, and their eyes shone with the vengeful and raging hate of lust. Belinda came from dancing, sweat dripping on her face, as Molly heard her mother's moans through the wall and down the hall to her bedroom door and through it to her ears, her face on her satin-covered pillow; saw her mother's face next morning, lovelier in a different way, private but not secret, as though her cheeks and eyes were nourished by lovemaking, as a flower by the sun. Her lovers' faces looked only comfortable, contented. Belinda said, "My parents should stay in Maine all week. Think of it. Think of the party we'd have."

"Is Wanda still throwing up?" Molly said.

"Wanda? Is she sick?"

Bruce pointed at the end of the room where it became L-shaped; in that leg with the ping-pong table was the bathroom. Belinda said she would go check on her and Molly said Maybe she's upstairs and Bruce smiled and shook his head and said he didn't think so.

"A lot of people upstairs," Molly said to Belinda.

"Wicked," Belinda said, and left them, walked between clustered people, walked slowly, swaying when she had to change direction to skirt a dancing couple or a group standing and drinking. It was strange for Molly to be so drunk yet to see clearly how drunk Belinda was, how much effort she expended on controlling the balance of each step.

"Let's go upstairs," she said to Bruce, and felt in her purse for cigarettes. He leaned to kiss her but she lowered her face, looked into the open box: two cigarettes. "I can't believe this. I came with one open pack and another whole one and I still ran out and Belinda gave me these. Look. I must have smoked fifty cigarettes."

"It's the cocaine."

"What is?"

"You smoke a lot. And you can drink all night."

"No more of that shit."

"You sang too."

"Yes. I sang." He took the cigarette from her and lit it and put it between her lips. "Come on," she said.

She took his hand and, bumped by dancers, led him through the room; she climbed the stairs, pulling him behind her. They would always follow you. She knew that. Their cocks got hard and their faces looked helpless, no matter how they tried to disguise it, and they would follow you anywhere. She had never let any of them follow her to nakedness. No. And she was not a tease. She simply had not let any of them follow her to where they thought they were leading. She emerged from the stairs into the dark kitchen and turned into the living room, dark too; Bruce was beside her now, holding her hand between them. She went down a hall to the stairs, and stopped. Her fingers flicked ashes before she could tell it not to, and with the sole of her shoe she rubbed the carpet and hoped her foot had found the ashes.

"You guys are so rich," she said.

"It doesn't matter."

"I know. Let's go to the woods."

"What woods?"

"Upstairs."

He moved to her front to kiss her, but she stepped around him and pulled him up the stairs. At their top she looked down the dark hall past closed doors. She looked at him and raised a forefinger to her lips and whispered: "They're so quiet." She looked down the hall. "My mother's not. Probably she thinks she is."

"What are we doing?"

"Ssshhh. Whisper."

Holding his hand, she moved down the carpeted hall. The music in the basement room was faint, and she did not know whether she heard its repetitive bass or felt it through the soles of her sneakers. She stopped at the first door and heard nothing but the music and her clandestine breathing, and Bruce's, faster and louder beside her. She went to the next door and flicked ashes again and when she realized it, her foot moved over the carpet. She followed the hall, turning into another wing, past doors closed to silent rooms, and stopped at the master bedroom at the end of the hall. Behind it the mattress was moving, and Bruce whispered: "It's Goldilocks." She wanted to hear a girl's voice from the bed.

"Your parents' room. They shouldn't do it in there."

"Why not? No: I guess you're right."

She caught his wrist as he lifted his arm to knock on the door. She pulled him away, and all down the hall to its corner she listened behind her for a girl's voice. She imagined hissing, in there on the huge bed. She turned into the first wing, hurrying, pulling him; the heat of her cigarette was near her fingers. One of the doors was open now, and she glanced through it at the dark and the bed's silhouette and smelled marijuana smoke. At the top of the stairs she drew him beside her for the descent. She said aloud: "Get me to an ashtray."

Now he led: into the empty living room with its large windows, and he leaned away from her, then an ashtray was in her hand. Her fingers burned as she put out the cigarette. He took the ashtray and put it on a lamp table beside them. Then he was holding her, kissing her with his open mouth, his tongue, and he was hard against her pelvis. Slowly she was moving backward with the pressure of his weight, and when her calves touched the couch she lay on it and held and kissed him as he moved on top of her and mimed lovemaking between her legs that she spread and then lifted around his waist, her sneakers crossed above him. She had done this before and she would do it now with him, let him come against her in his jeans, listen to the soft cries and groans from her throat and receive his weight as he collapsed on her. But he stopped and shifted and was beside her; with closed eyes she saw herself singing, saw the mirror and the line and the straw from her nostril, and Belinda hugging her, and the smoke of fifty cigarettes pluming from her lips, and Wanda's face so pale just before she pushed herself from the wall and into the crowd between her and the bathroom; Bruce unbuttoned her jeans and carefully, slowly, eased down the zipper; she raised her hips and he slid the jeans down to her ankles, then he was off the couch, squatting, working at the laces of her sneakers and taking them off, one at a time, a hand holding her heel; then he pulled off her jeans and laid them on the floor. She waited for his hands to move up her legs for her pants, waited to twist away from them, and to close her thighs. But he rose and, standing on one leg at a time, pulled off his sneakers; then he unbuckled and unzipped and pushed his jeans down his hips and stepped out of them. His erection was white cotton. He pulled his tee shirt over his head. When his hands touched the waistband of his jockey shorts she turned toward the floor and found her purse on it and lit her last cigarette. She reached to the coffee table for an ashtray and lay on her back again and placed the ashtray on her skin and the front of her bikini pants. She remembered they were pale blue. He lay on his side, at the edge of the couch, the cock pressing her left thigh. She held her cigarette to his lips, then said:

"Can we just lie here?"

"Sure."

But when they finished smoking he moved the ashtray to the floor and kissed her. For a long time he kissed her in the dark and the distant music and low beat from the basement and once the steps and voices of a couple descending the stairs and in the hall and through the dining room and kitchen, music rising through the basement door as they opened it, then they closed it and her sounds again were those of kissing and fast breath, and his hand was gentle on her breasts, under her loose white Mexican blouse. When he pushed it above her breasts she raised her shoulders and head and arms, and for an instant her face was inside its white, then it was gone and she was naked with him, save for her pants. When his hand went there she closed her legs and he kissed and softly sucked her breasts and she opened her legs to his hand, and lifted her hips; he pulled her pants away from her, then pushed them past her knees, and she drew one leg out of them and with that foot she pushed them down and over the other foot. He was on top of her, kissing, hard against her, and she drew back and twisted away.

"I can't."

"Please."

"I can't."

"Why?"

"I don't have anything."

"I do."

"No you don't."

She held him tightly and kissed him and it was touching her again; she moved with it, felt it slip between her lips, and she jerked back from it.

"In my room," he said. "I'll go get one."

"No. I can't. I won't."

"Please. I can't stop."

"Here. Move."

Holding his waist, she tenderly pushed him toward the back of the couch, and she shifted to its edge. When she held the cock, he lay on his back. She kissed him. She had never touched one, and its surface was smooth. She moved her hand up and down and he moaned. Now that she was not afraid, she wanted to give him his pleasure or his release from it; and warmly she kissed him, gently she moved her hand. Then he said: "Molly. Your mouth. Please."

She did not want to and she wanted to and this made her feel her drunkenness again, and the cocaine, and she moved with them, between his legs, and said What if I don't like it? then knew she had not said it aloud and she did not; she lowered her face, her hair falling down her cheeks and forehead, her jaws widening, and she saw a large bird, a swan, eating from the earth; then, as if she were beside the couch, she saw her mouth moving down and up. He squirmed and gasped and moaned, then it twitched: only a tiny spurt of salty liquid, it was nothing and it was over; but then she felt the rush beneath its skin and it convulsed and warm bitter liquid softly slapped the roof of her mouth, and then again, her mouth filled with it and the bitterness of lemon rind; she swallowed and oh shit oh God she had done it, it was in her, and her soul recoiled from her throat, from her heart, and lay soiled and sticky in her stomach while she swallowed again, then did not move. In her mouth it throbbed. She did not move; she kept her face hidden in her soft hair. Then his hands were on her cheeks, her shoulders, and he pulled her up to him, her face to his, and kissed her: her dirty mouth and fouled breath and her soul lying cold beneath her heart. She felt both abused and unworthy, so she gratefully received his kisses, and wept. He licked her tears. He was murmuring to her. She was beautiful, she was wonderful. His tongue went from her tears to her breasts, and he moved, and licked her belly and moved again and was licking her, she could hear him lapping juice, his tongue inside her, then on it, oh on it where at night in her bed and in the morning in her bed and afternoon in her bed her finger— She moved against and with his tongue and pressed his hair and head with her hands. Then she heard her voice, the girl's voice above her with its deep strange cry like a prayer as she became her climax and her voice grew louder with its chant: "Oh God —"

In the morning, heat woke her. She was naked and she got up and turned on the oscillating fan on her bureau at the foot of her bed, and knew from the angle of sunlight in her room that it was between eight and nine; as she went to the fan and back to bed she did not look at the clock. She opened her eyes only to the sunlight and the fan's switch, and closed them as she walked to the bed and lay on it and saw through her headache and nausea the cock in her mouth. His semen was in her blood. She was nearly asleep again; she had to piss and she tried to will her bladder to sleep too but it was insistent and now she was fully awake to the day she did not want to wake to. She got up and lit a cigarette and went to her bathroom and sat and sighed and shut her eyes and smoked. Then her bowels held her there, the Dos Equis leaving her with more solidity than they had in their bottles, all those bottles she had drunk, and with a stench that repulsed even her. Pain moved laterally through her stomach, and the next release weakened her, and her legs quivered. She sat and waited for her body to set her free so she could sleep, and regain that freedom too, from her knowledge that she deserved this punishment. Then she washed her hands and face, and studied its pallor and her dark eyes for a sign. There was none: only the fatigue in her eyes, and the drained skin and the expression of painless damage on her face. Only a hangover. *Gueule de bois*, the French called it. Mug of wood, Mrs. Conway said. Wooden face.

But she wanted a mark: deserved one, had earned one as Dorian Gray earned his. Late one night she had watched the old movie on television, in black and white until he pulled the cover from his portrait and it was in color; and sitting in the dark living room, she had exclaimed in horror; or her flesh had, her body tightening upright in the chair, and sending from her mouth an articulated gasp: *oh*. She rinsed her toothbrush glass and filled it with water and imagined her photograph on her mother's dresser: that eternal smile when she was fourteen changed by a downward turn of one corner of the mouth. She almost believed it, and felt the picture drawing her to her mother's bedroom, to gaze at the grim set of her lips. Then she saw her mother's mouth going down and up on a cock. From a bottle in the medicine cabinet she took three aspirins and swallowed them and gagged, on the tablets or the water, but she held her breath, then slowly released it, and leaning on the sink she told her body to relax, and she did not vomit.

In bed she smoked, to blend the flavor with the taste of toothpaste, to soothe her nerves and heart in their hung-over acceleration. Melted lemon rind in her mother's mouth, in her mother's breath and blood. *You feel like yourself alone among everyone else*, her mother had said. *With your body and your heart*. Then why did she feel like ashes? And not even five feet and four inches and a hundred and twelve pounds of contained ashes, but ashes scattered and blown among others, everywhere and so nowhere, and all that was left on her bed was her soul steeping in bitter semen. She slid her hand under the sheet she had pulled above her hips because even alone in her room she needed to cover her vagina. She closed her eyes to the sound of Bruce licking, to the image of them on the couch; she watched them from above and from the side and a close-up of his tongue on her like in the movie they had gathered the courage to rent, the four of them together in the store, and they watched it in Belinda's dark basement, Molly and Belinda and Dotty and Wanda: *They've got to be on drugs. That is sick!* and laughing and joking, then after the movie, in the first moments of dark, the four of them suddenly quiet on the couch, disgust and sorrow spreading like gas from their bodies pressed together, and all at once they each lit a cigarette and Belinda said *I guess nobody wants to suck a cock tonight* and the gas was compressed and released in jets of laughter. Now her finger was helpless against her mind, and she focused again on Bruce's tongue and inhaled from her cigarette as she came, the two pleasures drawing from her the moans she controlled from habit, muted to sighs of smoke.

Now she could sleep. But she took the ashtray to the wastebasket beside her dressing table and emptied it so she would not wake to its smell. She watched the ashes floating down to settle on wads of Kleenex and a crumpled shopping bag; yesterday she had bought music, cassettes in that bag. Yesterday: a Wednesday in summer. She looked at the mirror attached to the table. Not a mark. Even her hymen was in place. How could it be a Thursday you did not want to wake for, and how could you want it to be Wednesday again and buying Rickie Lee Jones, and nothing of those wishes showed, not even in your eyes? Her body was faithless. It only showed eating and colds and flu and the sun. *Yourself alone among everyone else. Your body and your heart.* Bullshit, she said to her eyes in the mirror, and turned from her reflected nakedness and went to bed, drew the sheet to her waist, and in the breeze of the fan, she slept.

Noon light was in her room when she woke. It was on the sheet and her breasts, her face in shadow still. She thought she was nauseated again, then knew it was hunger. She imagined the kitchen and her mother standing in it, and she wanted her mother there to smile at her, kiss her. Kiss her? She had given away her mouth. It would never be the same mouth for her mother; never, never. *If I don't get out of this bed I'm going to cry all afternoon.* Then she let it come, lying on her back, a forearm covering her eyes. When it stopped she was very hungry. She would eat on the sundeck and lie all afternoon in the sun. She would read. Choose a book that would make her forget, for those hours in the sun, last night and today and seeing Bruce tonight; would make her forget even her body, and her name. A book by a woman. She liked Edna O'Brien. She did not always understand the stories, but she loved their music. But she would not spend this afternoon with Edna O'Brien; she wanted the people in the book to have clothes on, and to be outdoors in sunlight.

Her stomach's demand was a childish distraction, and she denied it. She made the bed and gathered last night's clothes from the floor and stuffed them into the wicker basket in her bathroom. She would have to shower tonight to see Bruce, but she showered now for her soul, and when she stepped out of the tub her clean wet skin gave her a portion of hope, like a scent on the breeze. Showers were a delightful mystery: water, soap, water, and some transition occurred, something deeper than clean flesh. Her morning was in the past now. She could dress, move about the house, eat and drink; afternoon was here; night would come. Time had started its motion again, and she could enter it, with interest, with anticipation, and soon—she was sure of it now, as she dried before the steamed mirror and thought of what she would eat—she could enjoy again what time held for her: tonight with Bruce the ocean glittering and blue in the last of the sun, then darkening under the first stars in the fading color of the sky. She put on a maroon bikini bathing suit and went barefoot to her mother's room. The door was open. The bed was made, the windows behind it open to the smell of trees. She did not look at her photograph on the dressing table. She crouched at the bookcase and scanned the spines, then went downstairs. The living room was sunlit, warm; she moved slowly past the large bookcase, looking for a woman's name. But in the Hs she stopped at the five Hemingway books. Her mother had asked her to read *The Old Man and the Sea,* and she had liked it and had cried, last winter with snow. When she was a virgin. She was still a virgin. So last winter when she felt like one. Her mother's favorite was *For Whom the Bell Tolls*, but Molly had not wanted to read it because it was long. But this afternoon was long. She took it from the shelf and went to the kitchen.

Its emptiness felt larger than the room itself. She wanted her mother there. She had not realized how often she thought of her mother as the cheerful and pretty woman in the kitchen. Suddenly the emptiness within the walls shifted, spread out laterally, and extended itself beyond the house and lawn, out into the world, and it drew her with it as powerfully as an undertow. She dropped the book and her cigarettes and lighter on the table and gripped the edge of it. She could feel California beside her, and her father out there, living his morning. With her first tears the room became itself again, walls that contained her and sunlight, and air to breathe. When she stopped crying she said: "Fuck him."

But her words and her voice in the empty kitchen pierced her, and she sat at the table and her face dropped to her folded arms and she cried on her flesh: for having no memory of Norman, for Norman not loving her and not giving her even a memory, and never a visit or a phone call or even a letter; cried on her brown forearm for herself at three kissing her daddy goodbye. Her father. She had no memory of that, but her mother told her she had kissed him, he had held her in his arms and hugged her and she had hugged him around his neck with her little arms and kissed his mouth and said *Bye-bye, Daddy*, and her mother told her she had looked puzzled and frightened but not sad. *And how did he look? Very sad. Did he cry? No; but he never did.* But later she was sad, as days passed and each morning she asked *Where's Daddy?* and her mother told her again he was gone and her mother cried, not for herself, she said, but for Molly. Then it was weeks and she was not eating well and sometimes she was quiet for too long and other times she was ill-tempered and yelled at her mother and struck her. Her father. Norman. How could he leave that little girl and break her heart so soon? And not be here now. To see her. Not to know about last night, not even to know her as her mother did, but to be here with his man's voice and smells and touch, to look at her with love. She felt the loneliness of one who is not even hated, but worse: ignored; and she grieved too much for Molly at three to be angry, to hate him for giving her life, then only three years later turning away from her and leaving so he could be alone and, having that, still not giving her himself again, even for a Christmas or summer visit, not even a voice on the phone to love, an image of him to keep alive in school and with her friends and here in this house with her mother. No wonder her mother had never married again. He had done the same to her. The—. But she could not curse him again, could not bear the sorrow of it, the knowledge that he deserved her curse.

She rubbed her eyes on her forearm, then with her palms rubbed them again, and her cheeks, and left the table. In the refrigerator she found slices of ham and a small wheel of Vermont cheddar and made a sandwich. She took it to the sundeck with a Coke instead of the diet cola she had reached for, had even touched before re- alizing the comedy of drinking so many Dos Equis and then a Tab. She nearly smiled, even felt the beginning of laughter, the first breath of it in her breast. And it was not just the paradox of debauchery at night and vanity at noon. Something deeper that she could not define, could only know: after last night, in today's sun, the weight of her body, and whether her flesh was taut or flabby, had no importance at all. She read while she ate and she finished the sandwich and Coke and wanted a cigarette but they were in the kitchen and she did not move to get them. Not until she finished the first chapter, then she put her plate in the dishwasher and her bottle in the carton in the broomcloset and went out again, into the sun; but it was in Spain, and she was too, settled in the ham- mock, smoking, the sun glaring on the page that became in moments not white paper with black words but the smells of pine and garlic and tobacco smoke and wine, and cool dry air high in the hills, and a cave, and a magnificent ugly woman named Pilar, and a man with a strong and gentle heart, and a young woman only a few years older than Molly, a woman whose soul had been wounded too, and near mortally, through her body too; and the sun and the sky, and wood smoke from the fire in the cave where Molly lived too as her own sun moved in her sky; and between Maria and Robert the sudden and certain feeling that was falling in love. Pausing once, closing the book on her finger, she looked at the sky and saw their embrace in Spain, and death always so near that only the heft and length of the book assured her that it would not come; not yet. She closed her eyes and saw Maria and Robert making love, with death a very part of the air and trees around them, and not even birth control, as though indeed, for the first time in Molly's life, the old saying was true, was as solid and lasting as the large stone among the stand of poplars behind her house, was in fact the absolute and only truth: There's no tomorrow.

Then her own tomorrow, this day after last night's drugged and drunken filth on the couch, moved like this morning's nausea from her loins to her throat. She opened the book. At once, in the sag and scant sway of the hammock, she was in another country with people she loved. Her mother's car climbing the gravel driveway seemed not an intrusion but a sound from within the book, as though it came from a road beneath the hill and the cave. Then it was her mother's car, and the door of it opening and closing, and her mother's steps on the gravel, then silent on grass, and the screen door of the kitchen opening and closing, and steps again on the floor, then her name called into the rooms, the two floors of the house. She left the hammock, looked once more at the book as barefooted she crossed the warm floor of the sundeck, committed to memory the number of the page, and entered the kitchen: the cool of it, the diminished light. Her mother smiled and kissed her.

"*For Whom the Bell Tolls*? Well. Do you like it?"

"I love it."

"Sweetie? Are you all right?"

"No."

"What is it?"

"It's long. Maybe you'd better get your drink."

Her mother studied her face, then reached out, placed her palm on Molly's cheek.

"Okay. I'll get one."

She watched her mother make a gimlet, and she wanted one too, or wanted to want one. She did not want to drink. Leaving Maria and Robert and the hammock had aroused her hangover: the lethargy of her body and the anxiety of her mind, and her stomach's promise that if she swallowed alcohol it would spurt it back up her throat. But she liked the green-tinged color of the gimlet, and the cool and soothing look of the moist glass and ice and wedge of lime, and she wanted its effect: wanted the words for her mother to flow from her, without the fetters of shame. And she did not want to cry. She filled a tall glass with ice, took a Coke from the refrigerator, followed her mother to the couch, and as soon as she could free her hands of glass and bottle, lowering them to the coffee table, she lit a cigarette, and held the lighter for her mother, and felt that this small flame between them was a pact. She looked across the room, out the window at the crest of the wooded hill beyond the road. She heard her mother sip the drink; then her mother leaned forward and put the glass on the table and sat back again, and laid a hand on Molly's thigh.

"Tell me."

"I did coke last night. I've never done it before. I'll never do it again."

Her mother's hand gently patted. Molly saw the trees and hill through mist now; the afternoon was gone, Spain and Maria and Robert and danger were only a book she had been reading; the living room seemed to move in on her, a trick of distance and time, its walls and ceiling and floor shutting her in, severing her from the afternoon in the sun, distorting her memory so all she had felt for and with the people in the book was as distant as an aimless afternoon with friends a year ago. So were this morning's headache, and her humiliation on the toilet, her lust, and sleep again, and the shower. And Bruce was not a grateful boy murmuring *You're beautiful, you're wonderful,* and then in his gratitude and passion giving to her until she cried out in the dark that surrounded the couch. He was only it, in her mouth.

"I—"

Her mother's hand left her thigh, moved to her right shoulder, and the arm pressed her to her mother's body: the side of a breast, and soft flesh over ribs. She smiled against the mist that became droplets on the rims of her eyes.

"I turned into Ella Fitzgerald."

"You sang?"

"Your songs. A lot of them. I didn't even know I knew them." She sighed, and swallowed. The tears did not drip down her cheeks.

She blinked, flicked once at each eye with a finger, and there was only mist again. She breathed deeply once and knew that at least she would not cry. She looked into her mother's brown eyes, waiting like calm water for her to float on, or immerse herself in.

"I did fellatio."

The eyes received her; then her mother's flesh did, turning to her, holding her now with both arms, breasts pressing and yielding with hers; then gently the body drew back, the arms slid from her, and she was looking again into her mother's eyes.

"The first time?"

Molly nodded.

"Have you been with a boy before? Made love?"

"No. I would have told you."

"Do you love him?"

"It's Bruce."

Her mother nodded. They turned from each other, smoked, and together their hands descended to the ashtray, flicked ashes, and Molly watched their fingers, her mother's longer, more slender; then she looked at her mother's mouth, her eyes. Her mother's face was so near her own that Molly felt they shared the same air, their lungs synchronized so one exhaled as the other breathed in.

"Do you love him?"

"I don't know."

"It was just cocaine?"

"And beer."

"I mean why you did it."

"The cocaine. Yes. But maybe him too."

"What are you going to do? About him, I mean."

"We're going out tonight. To the beach. For the sunset."

"How is he? With you?"

"I don't know. I guess he's nice. There's just one thing I know. If doing that isn't wrong, then I don't know what is."

"It's my fault."

"Nothing's your fault."

"I'll tell you why it's my fault. If I'm wrong, stop me. Oral sex is—oh shit: I'm sorry I'm embarrassed. It's not you, do you understand? I don't feel *any* differently about you. You're my Molly. Just like yesterday. Always. I'm embarrassed because of what we're talking about, not what you did. You see the difference?"

"I think so."

"Because when I talk to you like this, I'm sharing with you. My own experiences with men. It's all I know. And it makes me blush, that's all. Am I blushing?"

"You were."

"Oral sex. Fellatio, cunnilingus—" Molly felt now the warmth rising to her own cheeks, and saw the recognition in her mother's eyes before they quickly lowered to her cigarette and she drew from it and looked again at Molly. "They're more advanced. God, what a word. They're for lovers. Who are in love with each other. Who need to explore each other. Each other's bodies. Give each other different pleasures. Receive them. There's nothing dirty about it. In the right context. And that's always the people. Just intercourse is dirty—I'm not talking about you, I've done it too, long ago, years ago—it can be dirty when you hardly know each other and you're drunk or—whatever: cocaine, other drugs—anything that makes you silent."

"Silent?"

"The deepest part of you. That wants to complete itself with another human being. When we silence that part we just become— we *can* just become—our sex organs. Not even our bodies. Just a meaningless desire between our legs. No heart; no brain."

"That's how it was. I think."

"No wonder you feel terrible. And it's my fault, because I should have known it would happen You *are* a woman, in a lot of ways. Certainly you look like one. So I should have faced it. Faced *you*. I should have gotten you a diaphragm. Because—stop me if I'm wrong—I think you got carried away, you weren't sober, and Bruce is a good-looking boy, and he seems nice—you said he was nice to you?"

"Yes. He was nice."

"Okay. And you went too far, and you couldn't stop, and you were afraid of getting pregnant. So instead of— Instead of *making* love, in the usual way, for a girl and boy, so young, you did the other. And—Molly, it's all good, when the two people are. But it takes a while, sometimes a very long while, for *that* to be good. Because it has to be your idea. Sometime when you know it's time, when you want to do it. Until then, it can be—I guess as awful as it was for you."

"He did it to me too."

"I thought so. And?"

She felt the blush again, and lowered her eyes.

"He was nice."

"Are you going to be his lover?"

"I don't know yet."

"Think about it. If it was just beer and cocaine, make yourself forget it. Like doing something silly you wouldn't do sober. I'm saying forgive yourself."

"I just don't know."

"Are you sure you should see him tonight?"

"I want to. I want to know things."

"What things?"

"About Bruce. Without beer or drugs."

"I think you should wait."

"For what?"

"I want to call Harry and get you fitted for a diaphragm."

"I'm not going to do anything tonight."

"That's easy to say in daylight. At night we change."

"I won't."

"I'll call Harry in the morning."

Molly looked out the window at the trees on the crest of the hill.

"He'll make time for you tomorrow."

"All right."

She was watching a crow perched on a branch near the top of a pine. Something in the book this afternoon: a bird flying.

"I wish you were happy," her mother said. "Not that you should be. Today."

"I will be."

"You're not just saying that?"

"No. I will be."

The crow was restless, watching for something.

"I wouldn't want you on the pill. Or an IUD. I've read too much about them; heard too much."

Molly nodded, and the crow spread its wings and climbed, large and glistening black against the blue sky.

"There used to be a rubber generation. I mean boys carried them. Before the pill. But a diaphragm's better. With the cream. It's—"

"Mom." The crow had risen out of her vision, above the window. "What?"

She watched the pine tree.

"What's going to happen?"

"I don't know."

"I mean what's going to happen to me?"

"It looks like—I guess you're going to have your first affair."

"My first affair."

"I guess, sweetie."

"Then what?"

"Maybe you'll learn something."

"And then I'll get married."

"Of course you will."

"So did you."

"It'll be different for you."

"Why?"

"You'll know more than I did."

"About sex?"

"About men. About yourself, most of all."

"I'm not off to a good start."

"You don't have to be. You're young. And Molly: this is a shitty time to say it, but I have to. I've let you drink at home. Wine at dinner. A beer sometimes. We even smoked a joint once."

"Twice."

"Twice. I wasn't very good at it."

"Neither am I. I don't smoke it anymore."

"Really? Not since then?"

"No."

"*That* makes me feel good. Since they were yours." Her mother's hand was on Molly's shoulder now, kneading it, and Molly knew from that touch that her mother's voice, when she spoke again, would be friendly, teasing, and it was: "Since you had these *joints* with you."

"That was last year. I smoked for a while. Then I thought it would be fun to turn you on." She looked at her mother, and blinked away the distant light and color of the pine against the sky. "To turn on with you."

"We got awfully hungry."

"It's dumb. A lot of stuff is dumb."

"I hope you mean that."

"Why else would I say it?"

"Sorry. I just want to ask you not to get drunk again. Or stoned, or whatever cocaine does."

"I told you I won't."

"I just have to say it. I know you and your friends drink a few beers."

"That's all. For me. From now on."

Her mother's arm was around her again, hugging, their temples and cheekbones touching, then pressing too.

"You'll be all right, Molly. You're strong. And you're wise. God, I was a silly, shallow little thing at fifteen."

Her mother's face moved back, then she stood and, holding Molly's hands, drew her up from the couch, and kissed her forehead, her eyes, her nose, and then her lips, and with that kiss Molly was inside her mother's mind—or was it only her own?—seeing her lips encircling Bruce's cock, and moving down and up, and sucking.

"And you'll be happy too."

"Yes," Molly said. "I will."

THREE

Molly sat at her dressing table, and when the polish on her fingernails had dried dark pink, she licked a finger and moistened an eyelid, chose the green eyeshadow, and colored her skin. When she finished her other eyelid, she lit a cigarette, then leaned forward and brushed mascara up onto her eyelashes. She squinted and with a finger pushed her lashes upward. She spread dark pink lipstick on her lips, then brushed the skin beneath her cheekbones with blush. She took the cigarette from the ashtray and drew on it, watching in the mirror, and as she returned the cigarette to its notch she looked at the lipstick on its filter. That stain of pink on the fawn tip, and the smoke rising between her face and the mirror that showed her brightened lashes and colored eyelids and, on her dark skin, the diagonal brushstrokes of pink rising to her cheekbones, and her lips like rose petals, made her sit erectly, and take a calm deep breath; and she felt that with the inhaled air, and its scents of cosmetics, and the aroma of cigarette smoke, she breathed an affirmation of her womanhood.

Her straightened back and shoulders pushed her breasts against her tight black shirt, so the button pulled against its hole at her cleavage. She did not wear a brassiere, and her nipples shaped the soft cotton of the shirt. They were small breasts, but certainly enough; certainly not flat; their proportion to her chest and shoulders and waist was good. *You're beautiful, you're wonderful.* She held the cigarette angling from her closed lips, and placed her hands on the table, tilted her head to the right, and lowered her face, so her black hair moved to her cheek and the corner of her left eye. Slightly she raised her eyes, watching Molly Cousteau in the glass. She withdrew the cigarette a moment before its lengthening ash changed her image from alluring to slovenly. She upturned a bottle of perfume onto her finger, and dabbed it behind her ears and on the arteries on either side of her neck and on the veins of her wrists. For a while longer she looked at herself, and turned her head from left to right to see fully the turquoise-on-silver earrings at her lobes. She was putting her make-up into her leather purse when she heard Bruce's car turning from the road and climbing the gravel driveway. She stood, in long soft leather boots under the tight legs of her jeans. The boots were dark brown, with high heels and toes that were sharply rounded, but not quite western. She went down the hall and stopped at her mother's door. Her mother sat at her dressing table, her back to Molly; she wore a beige dress and high heels and was applying lipstick. She stood and looked at Molly and said: "I'm glad I'm not one of those jealous mothers."

"Are there any?"

"So I've heard."

"Pretty shitty."

"I might not think so if you were a few years older."

"How many?"

The doorbell chimed.

"Ten?" her mother said. "Six? Face it: probably two. The way some of these men are. Is that Bruce?"

"In shining armor. If it's two, why not one?"

"What."

"Years."

"Oh."

"Or none."

"Because," her mother said, crossing the room now, pointing the tube of lipstick at Molly, a smile in her mother's eyes, and her lips mimicking scorn. "Because," she said, stopping, looking down, but with less angle of her neck now; soon, in a year, or two, they would look into each other's eyes. "You are an empty-headed girl. You could not talk to a grown man. You just want to eat junk, and listen to rock music—" But when she said eat junk the smile darted from her eyes, driven out by shame and guilt, and Molly felt them in her own eyes, and quickly said: "And get *stoned*, man; get wasted just all day long. And pop pimples."

Her mother's eyes, and her own, she knew, showed nothing now; but they would, in a second, and here it was and she felt it in her eyes too: the light of jest and merriment. Her mother said, "You're going to the beach? Don't you want to take a sweater? Or your shawl?"

"Maybe the shawl."

"Molly? Speaking of shining armor. Make him stop at a drug-store."

"He already has them."

"He has them." It was not a statement; it seemed to want to be a question, but her mother had controlled it, and was thinking now. Molly could see the images in her mind, hear the questions her mother would not allow to have sound: *If you know that, then he showed you or told you, so why fellatio? Or was it afterward? Did he say next time he would have rubbers? Because you— What did you do afterward? Spit it out? Cry? Get sick?*

"But he won't need them," Molly said.

"Molly."

"I'll be all right."

"I love you."

"I love you too."

"Should I go and tell Bruce hello?"

"No need."

"Give me a kiss, then."

Molly lifted her face and puckered her lips and they kissed, and Molly felt she was kissing from behind glass, not separating their lips but glass between her own heart and breasts.

"Bye-bye," she said.

"Twelve o'clock, sweetie."

As she went down the hall and stairs, she wondered how much she had lost or given away last night, or whether she had given or lost anything at all, and most of all she wondered how long she would feel like scattered pieces that were only contained in one body and soul when she was oblivious: asleep or lying in the sun on the hammock with Maria and Robert in Spain, among the smell of pines and the cool breath of dying in the sunlit air. It was her, not her mother; in her mother's eyes and mouth, in her voice and touch, there was nothing of accusation, or shame, or sorrow. Nothing but love, friendship—and yes: alliance, encouragement—in the face that had nearly wept two years ago when, after the birthday dinner, Molly had taken one of her mother's Winstons, and slowly, calmly, had tapped it and lit it: a performance that had concealed her fear of anger or, worse, ridicule, embarrassment; and Molly did not know that night when she gave in to her impulse, allowed it to become a choice that directed her fingers and lips, and still she did not know whether she was testing their friendship, or showing her trust in it.

Bruce stood looking out at the road, not at the screen, not into the kitchen, and tenderly she knew it was a pose, tenderly because at once she knew that he was not certain she would come to the door, and go with him. She stepped out and they stood on the concrete slab, close yet not touching, though her hands, her arms, started to rise and reach out to embrace him, but they stayed tensely at her sides. Then they spoke, the hello and how are you so tentative that quickly they laughed, with reddening cheeks, and they walked to the car, with between them a space, a foot or two of late-afternoon summer air and light that asserted itself, so Molly wanted to penetrate it, thrust her hand through it. But at the front of the blue Subaru they separated.

The interior of the car began to restore her, to draw back into her what had been dispersed. For here there was the ritual of pulling the seat belt over her shoulder and across her hips, watching their four juxtaposed hands pulling straps, pushing them into buckles; and lighting a cigarette and looking out her window and to the rear as he backed down the long driveway and paused, then backed into the road and shifted gears and drove away from the sun; past trees and the dairy farm, to the river, and east on the road where old trees grew on the bank, and across the road mowed hills rose to large houses. She had last seen him in this car, and sitting here in the passenger seat, with Dotty and Wanda in back, Wanda drinking a can of ginger ale and saying oh God it was good she puked, at least she wasn't sick anymore, and if she'd thrown up like that at home her mother might have heard her, and come to see if she had the flu or something, and one smell of her breath and it'd be all over, grounded, probably till she went to college. And she would never drink that much beer again. Never. It wasn't worth it. Bruce took her home first, then Dotty, quietly smoking a joint in the back seat, offering it again and again to Molly and Bruce, holding it between their shoulders, but they said no. At Dotty's house he waited at the curb, as he had at Wanda's, and watched Dotty standing under the lit porch light and unlocking the door and going inside. Then he drove to Molly's. But her house should have been first, it was between his and Dotty's and Wanda's. She was the one, though, who had taken the front seat. He had not arranged that, had only said he would drive the three of them home; he had brought them to the party, so there was nothing there either.

Nothing for any of her friends to see (yet she had chosen the front seat, and had not spoken when he drove toward Wanda's); and she thought and hoped there had been nothing they could see after she and Bruce dressed in the dark and, in a half-bathroom near the foot of the stairs leading to the bedrooms, she combed her hair and lipsticked her new mouth. Or perhaps old. For it felt older than she was, older than her time on earth, as if it had joined the mouths of women long dead, centuries dead, beyond electric lights and houses, all the way back to the dark of tents on deserts, beneath skies whose only light was the stars and moon. Bruce waited outside the bathroom door. When she came out, the light from above the mirror struck his face, and she saw her beauty in his humble eyes, his solemn lips. She switched off the light and moved a hand outward from her side in the dark and it met his moving toward her, and tightly their hands joined as they went through the dark and large dining room and through the kitchen, the bass of the music downstairs pulsing in the floor and the soles of her feet. At the door to the stairs they withdrew their hands, and he opened the door and went ahead of her down the stairs, into the light and music and smoke. As she descended, Molly looked over and beyond his shoulders scanning the people below, but she saw only dancers watching each other, and Belinda, with her back to Molly, standing at the couch across the room, talking to a seated girl, probably Wanda, though Molly could see only the girl's arms spread on top of the couch's back, one bare arm on either side of Belinda. She wondered how long she and Bruce had been upstairs. The first face to turn and look at her was a girl's, straightening up from the ice chest on the floor, twisting the cap from a Miller Lite. She was a senior, and Molly did not know her.

"I like your blouse," the girl said. "Your singing too."

"Thank you. I can't really sing. It was the coke."

"I don't do that anymore. It's dangerous shit. I've got a brother-in-law who's married to it. He's married to my sister too. But it's all shit now. You shouldn't do it anymore. You think these are addictive?" She held up her cigarette. "They're nothing. They'll maybe kill you. But my brother-in-law is soup. Babbling soup. My sister does everything: a job, the house, takes care of the kid. One day she'll walk out. When she sees it's all over. No hope. The asshole will be robbing banks soon, to pay for his shit. Maybe they'll shoot him and she can start living again. Jesus. I made a promise. I'd never *think* about them when I'm drinking. I can't take it, you know?"

"Yes."

"She's so *nice*. I'm fucked up. But not her. She's *get*ting fucked. You know? It's not *right*. Shit."

Molly bent over the chest and pulled a Dos Equis from the ice. She was in the world again: that was it: you did something, then it was over and you were back in the world. She looked at the girl's face, imagined her sorrow for her sister, imagined the sister coming home from work to a man she had loved, his body and mind and heart and tongue racing about, within the walls of their home with its littered floors. She wanted to embrace the girl. She said: "He'll either get himself cured, or your sister will leave him and marry somebody good."

"That's true. I believe it. It's just waiting for her to do it. That gets me. She doesn't even cry, my sister. When she talks to me. I'll tell you something about coke, though."

"What's that?"

"It doesn't give anybody a good voice. You can really sing. I'm going to the john. How does this stuff make you fat when it doesn't even stay in your body?"

Then she was gone, a pretty brown-haired girl walking with the concentrated steadiness of a drunk, around the corner to the room with the ping-pong table no one was using, and the bathroom where Molly knew there would be people waiting. She turned toward the room, the dancers; she had not felt Bruce close to her since she left the stairs. He was across the room, standing with Belinda at the couch, and yes it was Wanda sitting, smiling, holding a can of ginger ale. So Bruce had gone from the stairs to Belinda. Meaning what? That he was finished with her? Had been the first to hold her naked, and they had— No. He was being cool. She remembered his face in the light when she stepped out of the bathroom. She warily traversed the room to join him: angled from one person or group to another, stopped to talk, to smoke a cigarette, returned once to the chest for another beer, so that when finally she stood near him, with Belinda between them, she believed she had hidden any connections of time and space between her and Bruce, and their absence from the timeless swirl of the party. But Belinda said: "Where've you been?"

"Talking to a girl." She did not look past Belinda at Bruce. "A senior. About her brother-in-law. He's hooked on coke."

"That's Shelley," Bruce said.

Molly asked Wanda if she felt better; Wanda raised the ginger ale and nodded.

"Time for the Cinderellas to go home," Bruce said.

"Is it already?" Belinda said.

"Eleven-thirty. Where's Dotty?"

"I'll get her," Wanda said. "I want to see if I can walk. In case Dad's still watching a ballgame."

"This late?" Molly said.

Wanda pushed herself up from the couch.

"They're playing in California," she said. "I *always* check."

So as Wanda and Dotty and Molly approached the car, Molly quickened her last three strides and opened the front door, and Wanda followed Dotty into the back seat. Bruce drove out of the circular driveway and at the road turned right instead of left and Molly said nothing, waited in the sudden and brief quickening of her heart and breath, but Wanda and Dotty said nothing about the turn and the direction Bruce took, did not even give it an instant of divining silence: they kept talking and Dotty laughed at her fingers, said they were too drunk to roll a joint. Then Wanda and Dotty were gone and Bruce was driving to her house and Molly was trying to know what she ought to feel now, alone with him, or trying to feel what she ought to feel, or know what she did feel. She was not sober, and she was shy as with a stranger, and she tried to say something in the silence, and having to try tightened her stomach, and opened her to remorse and yearning. For they ought to be touching, and gentle, and they ought to fill the car with whatever sounds lovers made.

It was Bruce who finally spoke, when he stopped at the top of her driveway and turned off the engine and put his arms around her and kissed her, his lips open but his tongue withheld, a kiss so tender that it felt shy. Then he looked at her and asked if she would like to go to the beach tomorrow, in late evening, when the sun was setting and everyone had gone home and they could walk on it with the seagulls and sandpipers. She said yes and kissed him; a kiss she willed herself to give; yet when she felt and tasted his mouth her tension dissolved and she leaned into him, held him, and for those moments felt what she had wanted to, what she had believed during the quiet ride that she ought to: a yielding of herself to him, to his knowing her, and from his hard chest against her breasts she drew the comfort she was certain now that he gave. Then she went inside and heard his car start and back down over gravel as she climbed the stairs and quietly passed her mother's closed door, and went into her room. Almost at once she slept.

Now in the car with Bruce she sat again in tactile silence, and the car seemed strange too, smelling of an engine in the summer heat, and upholstery, and summer air coming through the windows, for until she actually entered it the car smelled forever in her mind of marijuana and cigarettes and the exhaled odor of beer; last night the windows had been closed; Bruce had said: *You can't open windows when girls are in the back seat.*

"I read all afternoon," she said.

"Really?"

"In the hammock."

"What did you read?"

"*For Whom the Bell Tolls*. Or a lot of it. By Hemingway."

"I know."

"Have you read it?"

"No. We read *A Farewell to Arms*. In English."

"Is it good?"

"It's sad. But it's good."

"I think this one will be sad too. It's so exciting, I can't stop reading it. But I don't understand what's going on."

"Why?"

"It's in Spain. In a civil war. I don't even know when."

"Neither do I."

"They're fighting the fascists."

"That's good."

He climbed up away from the river, through a neighborhood with old trees, toward the highway.

"And there are Communists. And Robert Jordan is an American fighting with them. He's a Spanish teacher. Can you believe it? From University of Montana. Can you see Howell going off to war?"

"I'm trying to."

He entered the three-lane highway and drove northeast; she had never ridden alone with him, on a drive in daylight, and she was relieved when he moved into the middle lane and stayed at fifty-five miles an hour while on both sides cars and trucks passed them.

"I don't know shit about history," she said. "I've never had a history course that got up to World War I."

"Neither have I. The school year ends."

"It's crazy. There was this important war going on, and everybody's ready to *die* for it. Even this American, Robert Jordan. And I don't know anything about it."

"Maybe it doesn't matter."

"Knowing about it? Or that it happened?"

"Knowing about it. It had to be important for the people in it."

She looked out her open window at the green hills and trees, then a dirt-streaked camper passed them, moving across her vision; the rear license plate was from North Carolina.

"Heading to Maine," she said. "Or Canada."

Bruce moved behind the camper, then left the highway and drove toward the sea, and quietly she watched the houses they passed: small yards, shaded by trees, most of them pines, and small houses: a juxtaposition of Americans she knew nothing about, people who were called working people because they did the real work, whatever that was, some fathers mowing lawns, others sitting with beer on their front steps, the wives probably inside cooking the dinners. Someone had told her that blue-collar people ate before six, then drank beer. Their children were on the lawns, with gloves and baseballs or toys, and she believed she could see in their faces some predetermined life, some boundary to their dreams, enclosed as tightly as their bodies were by their lawns and small houses. They were five minutes from the beach, these families, and Molly's notion was that they never went there. That they received the ocean's weather, and its smell too when the wind blew from the east, yet some routine of their lives—work, habit, or something of the spirit— held them at home as surely as it contained their hopes. She had never seen anyone like them at the beach. In the faces of a group of teenagers who stood under a tree and watched her and Bruce passing, she saw a dullness she thought was sculpted by years of television, of parents who at meals and in the evenings had nothing to say to them, nothing to teach them; and breathing now the first salt air coming through her window, she thanked her mother. Then the houses were behind her and on both sides of the car the tall grass of a salt marsh gently swayed, its green darkening in the setting sun, and she touched Bruce's shoulder, squeezed its hard width, and said: "Maybe I'll major in history."

He looked at her, and before he looked at the road again, the relieved expectancy in his eyes reminded her that this touch was their first since last night. She left her hand resting on his shoulder, moving with its motion as he steered.

"I don't know anything," she said. "It's like the whole world started fifteen years ago. My mother told me about Vietnam. And old movies."

"And old songs."

"Oh: those. They were before her time. She likes jazz."

"I've been wanting to tell you something for a long time. I'm sorry your father took off."

"I cursed him today."

"On the phone?"

"I've never talked to him on the phone. I cursed him at the kitchen table."

"What's it like? With just a mother?"

"I don't know. She's all I've ever had. Look, the tide's in."

They crossed a bridge over a tidal stream of rapid blue water moving at the tops of the banks. With her hand on his shoulder he turned north, then east, and parked facing a sand dune. In front of the car he took her hand and they climbed the dune. He was right: the beach was empty save for gulls standing in groups, their tails to the sea, and sandpipers darting across the sand. The surf was high and loud, and washed far up the slope of the beach. Beyond the white foam of the breakers and green of the shallow water the sea was deep blue to the horizon where it met the arcing cover of the sky, a clear and lighter blue. She wished she had remembered to bring her shawl, but her legs in denim and boots were warm; and her face, and her arms and body in the cotton shirt, still held that afternoon's slow burning in the sun, and the cool salt air soothed it. But soon she would be cold.

Holding hands, they descended the dune with short quick steps, then walked toward the surf. Sandpipers flew away from them, low over the beach; the seagulls in their path became restless, walked as a group farther up the beach; one flew ahead of the rest, then a second, and they both landed, but the others walked only far enough to allow Molly and Bruce to pass behind them. At the edge of the surf, where it hissed and spent itself at their feet, Molly shivered. Bruce put his arm around her and held her against his side.

"We should have brought sweatshirts," he said.

"Nobody knows what to wear to the beach."

"In New England, anyway. Let's keep moving."

She put her arm around his waist, and they walked south; his body shielded her from the breeze; in the distance she could see the ferris wheel at Salisbury, where the beach ended at the Merrimack River; in front of them the sandpipers flew and landed, and she said: "What are we doing?"

"Walking on the beach. Getting ready to freeze our asses off. Maybe we'll get hungry."

"I don't even know you."

"Only for eight years."

"Belinda's big brother. You don't know me."

"I know you're a fox."

"For eight years?"

"Three."

"So what are we doing?"

"I don't know."

"In the book. That I was reading this afternoon. They only have three days."

"Who?"

"The lovers."

"Why?"

"He has to blow up a bridge. Probably he'll get killed."

"How does he know that?"

"He doesn't. But he feels it. And a gypsy woman sees it in his hand. If we just had three days I'd know what we were doing. Did I tell you I'm a virgin? If you can call it that now."

"No. But I knew."

She stopped, releasing his waist, and faced him.

"*How?*" With a new shame now, seeing Shelley at the beer cooler—*I'm fucked up*—and probably she had made love for years, did it all the time with what's-his-name, and Bruce had been with girls like her—*I'm fucked up*—and then last night she had been on the couch, a naked clumsy frightened—

"Hey. Hey, Molly." He held her biceps. "I could just tell, that's all. I was surprised. I mean that you wanted to go upstairs. I thought that's why you wanted to go. And you took *me*. Out of all those guys."

"Was I that shitty?"

"Don't say that. It's—" He looked above her head at the sky, and squinted his eyes against the last of the sun. "Sweet," he said. "You're sweet."

"Really?"

"What do you think I'm here for? Not shitty, Molly. Sweet."

"Is that what you're here for?"

"Jesus. Let's walk back. When that sun goes, we'll freeze."

He turned her and held her on his lee side and they walked north.

She watched the rose and gold above the distant pine trees that hid the sun.

"I didn't come out here to make love," she said.

"Maybe I didn't either. Why did you?"

"To see if I wanted to. No. To understand last night. If it was just coke and beer. Can we just—"

Then she watched the sand ahead of their feet and listened to the roaring and smacking waves to her right and looked at the shadows cast now by the dunes. Far beyond them the pines in the sunset were darker; soon the red sky at their crowns would be twilight, the trees black.

"Just what?"

"I don't know. That's what's so bad. I don't know."

"Let's go to one of those beach stores. We'll get sweatshirts. With I Heart New Hampshire or something. Then let's go to Salisbury. Eat. Ride the roller coaster."

"No roller coaster."

"The ferris wheel."

"Okay."

Their sweatshirts were red with a white breaker on the chest and, beneath it, in white block letters: Seabrook Beach, N.H.; in the store, they pulled them over their heads, and when Bruce's hair and face pushed through the collar, he said: "Seabrook Beach, home of the nuclear power plant they can't get built; and if they do there are no—I repeat no—escape routes."

He paid for them, and as they walked to the car he said: "So maybe we just have three days anyway."

"It's not built yet," she said as he drove out of the parking lot: "And if we only had three days we wouldn't need that rubber."

"*What* rubber?"

"In your wallet."

"You didn't see that."

"I didn't have to."

"Holy shit. You know something?"

"What."

"This is the weirdest first date I've ever had in my fucking life."

"Me too," she said. "In my sucking life."

"*Molly.*"

She smiled and lit a cigarette, passed it to him, and lit one for herself. She did not know what it was: the darkness spreading in the sky, the headlights now of cars, her hunger for Italian sausage and egg rolls, but now they were all she knew and wanted, those and the ferris wheel circling above the lights and crowd and at its top showing you the white breakers and black sea and the paler dark sky at the horizon; and she felt too a control, a power, new and solid: she could tease him. She could do whatever she wished. When he stopped at a red light she leaned over and kissed him, mouths open, a brief kiss, and she felt she was his girl.

Felt it too with the taste of egg rolls and hot mustard and duck sauce in her mouth as the ferris wheel began its slow circle, and she was warm in her sweatshirt—was any material softer than a new sweatshirt?—and their seat went back and up, Bruce's arm around her shoulders, hers around his waist, tightly there between him and the wood of the seat as they rose above the people in the streets and the six policemen leaning against their motorcycles, and the buildings—bars and short-order restaurants and food and game stands—above the lights, but not beyond the voices of the crowd and the roller coaster's clacking roar and disco music from one of the hurtling rides, and the smells of hot grease and sausage; up to the top of the circle where for moments she saw the sea but not as she knew it and loved it. For the breakers were hidden by buildings and there were too many bright lights so all she saw was an expanse of black, too wide and its length forever, without horizon, for with so many lights there was only the low sky above the amusement park. It frightened her, that large black space that was not sea and sky at all, yet she stared at it, as though looking at the night of her death. Then the blackness was gone behind roofs and lighted walls and her legs hung over the street as backward she circled down past the man controlling the wheel, then up again, and as they rose she said to Bruce, loudly over the street voices and the roller coaster and screams from it and the cacophony of music from rides and booths and nightclubs: "Watch the ocean!"

Holding him tightly she watched it with him, her face beneath and parallel to his, and she glanced at his mouth and left eye to see if he saw it too, felt it, but she could not tell, and she looked again at that black space and tried to imagine fish in it, and ships on it, but all she saw was Molly Cousteau, not scattered ashes now, nor ashes drawn back and contained again by flesh and voice, and eyes with vision; but Molly as one tiny ash on the surface of the earth, looking into the depth of the universe, at the face of eternity.

So she told him. Not on the wheel, or when they left it and moved through the crowd on the streets to his car, and not while he slowly drove, changing gears, with the congestion of cars leaving Salisbury, then merging and increasing speed and the spaces between them, stopping once more at a traffic-lighted intersection, before dividing, taking separate roads to the north and south and west, and Bruce reached the highway and its middle lane, and she felt his body relax even as he lit a cigarette and settled in his seat. Felt like his girl again, as she told him of looking at death from the ferris wheel, felt like his girl when he listened, and said he had not felt it on the wheel, had felt only her against him, and her arm behind his waist, and her hand pressing his side, and himself holding her. But he had felt it before. Earlier in the summer, at night, in a strange mood, not sad or depressed or anything like that, but strange, and he wanted to be alone and drove without music to the sea and walked on the beach, at Seabrook, where they had walked at sunset, and he had stood looking at the ocean, at its huge deep blackness coming at him, coming straight to *him* till it stopped on the sand, and he was afraid. Really afraid. And he tried to talk himself out of it, because at first he thought what he feared was something stupid like a sudden tidal wave, the sea rising to take him and pull him away. Or that the sea could actually decide to drown him. That it was alive and could do it if it wanted to, just send in a big wave to knock him down and a current to take him under and out. Then he realized it wasn't drowning. It was that he felt so small. Tiny. And so empty. He tried to remember school, where he did well, and being class president, and having friends all around him. He did not have a girl then but he tried to remember old ones, their faces, the way they smiled at him. But he could not make the girls real so he could feel them, and he could not make school and his friends real, or even Belinda and his parents and his bedroom. So he could not feel himself. Except as that tiny empty breathing thing under stars in the biggest sky he had ever seen, frightened by the sound of the breaking waves and all that black out there. He turned his back on it and walked as quickly as he could over the sand. Only pride, as though he were being watched, kept him from running. On the ride home he played a cassette; the front windows were open, and his speakers were behind the back seat, and he turned the volume all the way up, so the music was louder than the rushing air.

She felt like his girl too when he parked on a country road not far from her house, and unbuckled his seat belt and she unbuckled hers. The car was on grass beside the road and under the branches of trees, and dark woods were on both sides of the road, a different darkness here, a quiet enclosing private dark that turned her to his lips and hands. His hands on her body were slow and as gentle as they could be, with the gearshift and hand brake between them. Then he stopped and pulled off his sweatshirt and she pulled off hers and they tossed them into the back seat. She received his tongue, and his hands unbuttoning her top button, then the next and the next until he reached her waist and she drew in her stomach muscles so he could unbutton the jeans, and with her legs she pushed herself upward so he could pull the zipper down. Then she pushed her jeans beneath her knees, until they stopped, and were crumpled at her feet, lower than the high leather calves of her boots, and she saw herself sitting on a toilet. But then he unbuttoned the lowest button of her shirt and helped her arms out of its sleeves and dropped it onto the back seat, and they embraced above the brake and gearshift, and she heard his side hitting the steering wheel. As they kissed she unbuttoned his shirt, unbuckled his belt, then he opened his door and took off his shirt and was gone, around the front of the car, his brown chest darker than the air above the road, lighter than the trees, as he moved to her door and opened it and with his toes pushed off his sneakers and stepped out of his jeans and scooped them and his shoes from the earth and shoved them behind her seat. Then he was holding the calves of her boots; and slowly still, gently, he turned her toward him, and pulled off one boot at a time and put it on the floor behind her, and lifted her jeans from her ankles and laid them in the back seat. The brake was against her back as he drew her pants down her legs and she watched them, pale in his hand above her, as he dropped them over the seat. He stepped out of his underpants and crouched to enter the car, then murmured something, not a word, only a sound like pain or anguish, a sound more intense than that of mere hurry in the quiet of the trees, and he reached into the back seat, and she listened to his wallet sliding out of denim, then the tearing of foil. Her back was still against the brake, and she said: "How do we —"

"Sit up." His voice was neither aloud nor a whisper: a moan, nearly plaintive, and her heart received it, felt the urgency that consumed him, as if the cock's tumescence drew all of him into it, diminishing his mind and soul to its length and circumference; but her body felt none of this, pinioned in static transition, seated naked, facing the windshield. She turned to watch him standing beside the car and unrolling the rubber, so white in the dark, onto his cock, and she remembered that she liked his waiting for Wanda and Dotty last night to get safely into their homes before he drove away, and she liked his walking between her and the breeze from the sea. Then he ducked and entered the car, bent over her, and he reached down between her legs and raised the lever under the seat and pushed it backward, and now he had space between her and the dashboard. She wanted to kiss him but his hand was between the door and her seat, his breath that of someone at work, and she heard plastic moving in a slot, and the back of the seat angled to the rear, but only a few degrees, and declined she sat and waited while he lifted her calves until her feet in socks pressed the dashboard.

Still he bent over her. Then he pulled her buttocks forward, and the cock touched her. He kissed her breasts. His hands pressed the back of the seat above her shoulders, and she held his swelling biceps, and wanted him now but in her bed, and was about to say: *Outside. On the ground.* So he would not be poised at the top of a push-up and they could lie together, slowly, and with grace; but then it was inside of her. Hard and pushing and she tried to jerk back from the pain but could not move; her hands left his biceps and loosely held his waist, and here it was again, the push against *her*, that small thin part that was her now; his pushes were rapid but still she had an instant to wait for each one's pain, and without seeing or even knowing numbers in her mind she counted, as if her hymen were counting and recording the assaults that would destroy it. The number was five and with that pain was a new one as the cock plunged and reamed, and she tried to move her hips and saw Belinda and Wanda and Dotty in their separate homes, or together in one, with music, and laughing—*No wonder they call it screwing.* Her jaws were tight against the pain, and the sound of it: *oh* and *oh* and *oh* held in her throat till it had the force of a scream. But she did not. Then he was saying it, his voice a boy's, high yet soft: Oh oh oh Molly oh Molly *oh*—

Then his right hand moved down, and he was out of her, holding his cock at its base, and she realized it was the rubber he held, the backflow of semen, and it just took one seed to work its way up and into her womb. Crouched above her, he stepped over her right leg, lost his balance leaving the car, but hopped and drew his other leg across her, then was standing on the grass, holding the rubber still, and in her pain she thought of blood on the seat and she swung her legs out of the car and stood facing him, standing in her socks, her feet pressing down the high and soft wild grass. Slowly he pulled off the rubber and dropped it and she looked at it lying on the grass. She wanted to step toward him and hold him, but her eyes, her face, would not move so she could not, and she looked down at that length of flat white draped over the dark blades. Then she turned to the car and leaned in to her purse on the floor in front of her seat, felt in it for Kleenex but everything she touched was hard or the leather of the purse. She looked over the seat, saw her pants lying on her clothes, and she reached around the seat and picked them up: soft cotton bikinis. They were pink. She stood and looked at Bruce's face: the same as last night when she stepped out of the bathroom and the light shone on him: not joyful or even happy, and not wicked, but humble and solemn. Then with her pants she touched the opening of her pain. Still she looked at his eyes. She dabbed the gentle warm flow; then wiped it, and her hair, and the tops of her inner thighs, but under the cotton they were dry. She looked down at the blood on her pants. Then she turned them and held Bruce's cock, hard still but angling downward, softening even as, with the clean side of her pants, she wiped it, then wiped her hand, and dropped the pants. She looked at them lying near the rubber.

When she looked up at Bruce his eyes and mouth had changed: a nuance of fear, of— Then she knew, or almost knew: something of awe, of responsibility; then she did know, felt it with a certainty as if he had spoken, had told her, or somehow his flesh naked under the dark of the trees had touched her own through the two feet of earth and air between them. He stood at the edge of remorse, and if she did not hold him, she would lightly push him over. He was all of Bruce again, his limp cock returning to him all those parts she had known for years, and perhaps now was loving as well. She stepped forward and tightly held him, her heart weeping but not with sorrow, her body quivering but without passion or fear. She kissed him, and closed her eyes, and breathed through her nose the smell of his face, and a sweetness of wild flowers, and the summer scents of grass and trees.

She would never forget holding him under those trees. The memory of the pain, renewed next morning by the doctor's cold probing and measuring while her mother sat in the waiting room, would fade until she no longer recalled it with the fear and helplessness she had felt that night. By the end of summer it seemed merely a brief and necessary suffering, and she could remember it as one remembers any rite of passage that is physically arduous and whose result is a change of the spirit, of the way one moves in the world. In fall she could laugh about it, talking with Belinda and Wanda and Dotty; mostly she talked to Belinda, though, for she was a virgin still, while Wanda and Dotty had been the first to lose their hymens and had long since lost the boys who broke them. So Molly felt closer to Belinda.

Even with Belinda she could not give words to what she had felt holding Bruce under the trees. She only knew she would never feel it again. Long after she had wept for Maria and Robert, reading in bed on a summer night, she could only think: *There is no Madrid*, but she could not say that to Belinda, or even to Bruce as they lay on her bed after school. His seed flowed from her as she sat on the toilet, and when her mother came home in the evenings Molly wondered if her own face bloomed as her mother's did the morning after a lover. But she never saw it in her face, and did not know whether this meant she was not in love, or whether her face did not change because she rarely came with Bruce, now that they made love; only when he licked her as he had on the couch last summer. But most of the time he did not pause for that, and after a while she pretended to come when he did, and though always she was impassioned on those afternoons and wanted to be naked with him and wanted him in her, she never again felt what she did that summer night when she looked up and saw in his face what he had done to her body forever, the first and last to do it, and then she held him and it was they who had done it, not just him.

On New Year's Eve her mother was at a party and Molly and Bruce were in Molly's bed and at midnight she kissed him and said Happy New Year. Then she knew. She rose from the bed and stood naked at the window and looked down at the snow on the earth, and the bare trees on the lawn. In the fall he would go to college and she would be a junior and she would lose him to a college girl. Then she knew she had always known it, and she closed her eyes and tried to see her and Bruce standing in the grass. From the bed he spoke her name. She still could not see them holding each other, with the rubber and her bloody pants near their feet, her body quivering with his. Bruce's voice gave her another image: a boy she did not even know; but faceless he waited for her, in the halls at school, and some afternoon or night he would lie on her bed and speak her name. Then she saw the others waiting, in high school and college and afterward, and she shivered and opened her eyes to the snow and the dark sky.

She tried to think of something new waiting for her, something that by her sixteenth year she had not done, but all she could imagine was pregnancy and childbirth and being a mother. She shivered again and he told her to get back under the covers. But now she was quietly crying. She would go to the bathroom and finish it there, because he was tender, he was always good to her, he would want to know why she wept, and he would kiss the tears on her cheeks, and kiss her eyes, as he did that night on Belinda's couch. And he would ask why she was sad, and as much as she wanted him to hold her, and to kiss her tears, she would hide them, because she would not be able to tell him. She wished she could. But blinking her eyes and looking once more at the snow, all she saw was her and Bruce in the car under the trees, on what she knew now was the last night of her girlhood, and she had no words to explain it to Bruce, or to herself, so she turned and hurried to the bathroom, switched on its lights, and shut the door and stood in the middle of the room and its brightness that dazzled her eyes, her heart.

Rose

In memory of Barbara Loden

SOMETIMES, WHEN I see people like Rose, I imagine them as babies, as young children. I suppose many of us do. We search the aging skin of the face, the unhappy eyes and mouth. Of course I can never imagine their fat little faces at the breast, or their cheeks flushed and eyes brightened from play. I do not think of them after the age of five or six, when they are sent to kindergartens, to school. There, beyond the shadows of their families and neighborhood friends, they enter the world a second time, their eyes blinking in the light of it. They will be loved or liked or disliked, even hated; some will be ignored, others singled out for daily abuse that, with a few adult exceptions, only children have the energy and heart to inflict. Some will be corrupted, many without knowing it, save for that cooling quiver of conscience when they cheat, when they lie to save themselves, when out of fear they side with bullies or teachers, and so forsake loyalty to a friend. Soon they are small men and women, with our sins and virtues, and by the age of thirteen some have our vices too.

There are also those unforgivable children who never suffer at all: from the first grade on, they are good at schoolwork, at play and sports, and always they are befriended, and are the leaders of the class. Their teachers love them, and because they are humble and warm, their classmates love them too, or at least respect them, and are not envious because they assume these children will excel at whatever they touch, and have long accepted this truth. They come from all manner of families, from poor and illiterate to wealthy and what passes for literate in America, and no one knows why they are not only athletic and attractive but intelligent too. This is an injustice, and some of us pause for a few moments in our middle-aged lives to remember the pain of childhood, and then we intensely dislike these people we applauded and courted, and we hope some crack of mediocrity we could not see with our young eyes has widened and split open their lives, the homecoming queen's radiance sallowed by tranquilized bitterness, the quarterback fat at forty wheezing up a flight of stairs, and all of them living in the same small town or city neighborhood, laboring at vacuous work that turns their memories to those halcyon days when the classrooms and halls, the playgrounds and gymnasiums and dance floors were theirs: the last places that so obediently, even lovingly, welcomed the weight of their flesh, and its displacement of air. Then, with a smile, we rid ourselves of that evil wish, let it pass from our bodies to dissipate like smoke in the air around us, and, freed from the distraction of blaming some classmate's excellence for our childhood pain, we focus on the boy or girl we were, the small body we occupied, watch it growing through the summers and school years, and we see that, save for some strengths gained here, some weaknesses there, we are the same people we first knew as ourselves; or the ones memory allows us to see, to think we know.

People like Rose make me imagine them in those few years their memories will never disclose, except through hearsay: *I was born in Austin. We lived in a garage apartment. When I was two we moved to Tuscaloosa. . . .* Sometimes, when she is drinking at the bar, and I am standing some distance from her and can watch without her noticing, I see her as a baby, on the second or third floor of a tenement, in one of the Massachusetts towns along the Merrimack River. She would not notice, even if she turned and looked at my face; she would know me, she would speak to me, but she would not know I had been watching. Her face, sober or drunk or on the way to it, looks constantly watched, even spoken to, by her own soul. Or by something it has spawned, something that lives always with her, hovering near her face. I see her in a tenement because I cannot imagine her coming from any but a poor family, though I sense this notion comes from my boyhood, from something I learned about America, and that belief has hardened inside me, a stone I cannot dissolve. Snobbishness is too simple a word for it. I have never had much money. Nor do I want it. No: it's an old belief, once a philosophy, which I've now outgrown: no one born to a white family with adequate money could end as Rose has.

I know it's not true. I am fifty-one years old, yet I cannot feel I am growing older because I keep repeating the awakening experiences of a child: I watch and I listen, I write in my journal, and each year I discover, with the awe of my boyhood, a part of the human spirit I had perhaps imagined, but had never seen or heard. When I was a boy, many of these discoveries thrilled me. Once in school the teacher told us of the men who volunteered to help find the cause of yellow fever. This was in the Panama Canal Zone. Some of these men lived in the room where victims of yellow fever had died; they lay on the beds, on sheets with dried black vomit, breathed and slept there. Others sat in a room with mosquitoes and gave their skin to those bites we simply curse and slap, and they waited through the itching and more bites, and then waited to die, in their agony leaving sheets like the ones that spared their comrades living in the room of the dead. This story, with its heroism, its infinite possibilities for human action, delighted me with the pure music of hope. I am afraid now to research it, for I may find that the men were convicts awaiting execution, or some other persons whose lives were so limited by stronger outside forces that the risk of death to save others could not have, for them, the clarity of a choice made with courage, and in sacrifice, but could be only a weary nod of assent to yet another fated occurrence in their lives. But their story cheered me then, and I shall cling to that. Don't you remember? When first you saw or heard or read about men and women who, in the face of some defiant circumstance, fought against themselves and won, and so achieved love, honor, courage?

I was in the Marine Corps for three years, a lieutenant during a time in our country when there was no war but all the healthy young men had to serve in the armed forces anyway. Many of us who went to college sought commissions so our service would be easier, we would have more money, and we could marry our girl-friends; in those days, a young man had to provide a roof and all that goes under it before he could make love with his girl. Of course there was lovemaking in cars, but the ring and the roof waited somewhere beyond the windshield.

Those of us who chose the Marines went to Quantico, Virginia, for two six-week training sessions in separate summers during col-lege; we were commissioned at graduation from college, and went back to Quantico for eight months of Officers' Basic School; only then would they set us free among the troops, and into the wise care of our platoon sergeants. During the summer training, which was called Platoon Leaders' Class, sergeants led us, harrassed us, and taught us. They also tried to make some of us quit. I'm certain that when they first lined us up and looked at us, their professional eyes saw the ones who would not complete the course: saw in a young boy's stiffened shoulders and staring and blinking eyes the flaw—too much fear, lack of confidence, who knows—that would, in a few weeks, possess him. Just as, on the first day of school, the bully sees his victim and eyes him like a cat whose prey has wan-dered too far from safety; it is not the boy's puny body that draws the bully, but the way the boy's spirit occupies his small chest, his thin arms.

Soon the sergeants left alone the stronger among us, and focused their energy on breaking the ones they believed would break, and ought to break now, rather than later, in that future war they probably did not want but never forgot. In another platoon, that first summer, a boy from Dartmouth completed the course, though in six weeks his crew-cut black hair turned gray. The boy in our platoon was from the University of Chicago, and he should not have come to Quantico. He was physically weak. The sergeants liked the smaller ones among us, those with short lean bodies. They called them feather merchants, told them You little guys are always tough, and issued them the Browning Automatic Rifle for marches and field exercises, because it weighed twenty pounds and had a

cumbersome bulk to it as well: there was no way you could comfortably carry it. But the boy from Chicago was short and thin and
weak, and they despised him.

Our platoon sergeant was a staff sergeant, his assistant a buck
sergeant, and from the first day they worked on making the boy
quit. We all knew he would fail the course; we waited only to see
whether he would quit and go home before they sent him. He did
not quit. He endured five weeks before the company commander
summoned him to his office. He was not there long; he came into
the squad bay where he lived and changed to civilian clothes, packed
the suitcase and seabag, and was gone. In those five weeks he had
dropped out of conditioning marches, forcing himself up hills in
the Virginia heat, carrying seventy pounds of gear—probably half
his weight—until he collapsed on the trail to the sound of shouted
derision from our sergeants, whom I doubt he heard.

When he came to Quantico he could not chin himself, nor do
ten push-ups. By the time he left he could chin himself five quivering times, his back and shoulders jerking, and he could do twenty
push-ups before his shoulders and chest rose while his small flat
belly stayed on the ground. I do not remember his name, but I
remember those numbers: five and twenty. The sergeants humil-
iated him daily, gave him long and colorful ass-chewings, but their
true weapon was his own body, and they put it to use. They ran
him till he fell, then ran him again, a sergeant running alongside
the boy, around and around the hot blacktop parade ground. They
sent him up and down the rope on the obstacle course. He never
climbed it, but they sent him as far up as he could go, perhaps
halfway, perhaps less, and when he froze, then worked his way
down, they sent him up again. That's the phrase: *as far up as he
could go*.

He should not have come to Virginia. What was he thinking?
Why didn't he get himself in shape during the school year, while
he waited in Chicago for what he must have known would be the
physical trial of his life? I understand now why the sergeants despised him, this weak college boy who wanted to be one of their
officers. Most nights they went out drinking, and once or twice a
week came into our squad bay, drunk at three in the morning, to
turn on the lights and shout us out of our bunks, and we stood at

attention and listened to their cheerful abuse. Three hours later, when we fell out for morning chow, they waited for us: lean and tanned and immaculate in their tailored and starched dungarees and spit-shined boots. And the boy could only go so far up the rope, up the series of hills we climbed, up toward the chinning bar, up the walls and angled poles of the obstacle course, up from the grass by the strength of his arms as the rest of us reached fifty, seventy, finally a hundred push-ups.

But in truth he could do all of it, and that is the reason for this anecdote while I contemplate Rose. One night in our fifth week the boy walked in his sleep. Every night we had fire watch: one of us walked for four hours through the barracks, the three squad bays that each housed a platoon, to alert the rest in case of fire. We heard the story next day, whispered, muttered, or spoken out of the boy's hearing, in the chow hall, during the ten-minute break on a march. The fire watch was a boy from the University of Alabama, a football player whose southern accent enriched his story, heightened his surprise, his awe. He came into our squad bay at three-thirty in the morning, looked up and down the rows of bunks, and was about to leave when he heard someone speak. The voice frightened him. He had never heard, except in movies, a voice so pitched by desperation, and so eerie in its insistence. He moved toward it. Behind our bunks, against both walls, were our wall lockers. The voice came from that space between the bunks and lockers, where there was room to stand and dress, and to prepare your locker for inspection. The Alabama boy stepped between the bunks and lockers and moved toward the figure he saw now: someone squatted before a locker, white shorts and white tee shirt in the darkness. Then he heard what the voice was saying. *I can't find it. I can't find it.* He closed the distance between them, squatted, touched the boy's shoulder, and whispered: *Hey, what you looking for?* Then he saw it was the boy from Chicago. He spoke his name, but the boy bent lower and looked under his wall locker. That was when the Alabama boy saw that he was not truly looking: his eyes were shut, the lids in the repose of sleep, while the boy's head shook from side to side, in a short slow arc of exasperation. *I can't find it*, he said. He was kneeling before the wall locker, bending forward to look under it for—what? any of the several small things the sergeant demanded we care for and have with our gear: extra shoelaces, a web strap from a haversack, a metal button for dungarees, any of these things that became for us as precious as talismans. Still on his knees, the boy straightened his back, gripped the bottom of the wall locker, and lifted it from the floor, six inches or more above it, and held it there as he tried to lower his head to look under it. The locker was steel, perhaps six feet tall, and filled with his clothes, boots, and shoes, and on its top rested his packed haversack and helmet. No one in the platoon could have lifted it while kneeling, using only his arms. Most of us could have bear-hugged it up from the floor, even held it there. *Gawd damn*, the fire watch said, rising from his squat; *Gawd damn, lemmee help you with it*, and he held its sides; it was tottering, but still raised. Gently he lowered it against the boy's resistance, then crouched again and, whispering to him, *like to a baby*, he told us, he said: *All rot, now. It'll be all rot now. We'll fin' that damn thing in the mawnin'*; as he tried to ease the boy's fingers from the bottom edge of the locker. Finally he pried them, one or two at a time. He pulled the boy to his feet, and with an arm around his waist, led him to his bunk. It was a lower bunk. He eased the boy downward to sit on it, then lifted his legs, covered him with the sheet, and sat down beside him. He rested a hand on the boy's chest, and spoke soothingly to him as he struggled, trying to rise. Finally the boy lay still, his hands holding the top of the sheet near his chest.

We never told him. He went home believing his body had failed; he was the only failure in our platoon, and the only one in the company who failed because he lacked physical strength and endurance. I've often wondered about him: did he ever learn what he could truly do? Has he ever absolved himself of his failure? His was another of the inspiring stories of my youth. Not *his* story so much as the story of his body. I had heard or read much about the human spirit, indomitable against suffering and death. But this was a story of a pair of thin arms, and narrow shoulders, and weak legs: freed from whatever consciousness did to them, they had lifted an unwieldy weight they could not have moved while the boy's mind was awake. It is a mystery I still do not understand.

Now, more often than not, my discoveries are bad ones, and if they inspire me at all, it is only to try to understand the unhappiness

186 · *The Last Worthless Evening*

and often evil in the way we live. A friend of mine, a doctor, told me never again to believe that only the poor and uneducated and usually drunk beat their children; or parents who are insane, who hear voices commanding them to their cruelty. He has seen children, sons and daughters of doctors, bruised, their small bones broken, and he knows that the children are repeating their parents' lies: they fell down the stairs, they slipped and struck a table. He can do nothing for them but heal their injuries. The poor are frightened by authority, he said, and they will open their doors to a social worker. A doctor will not. And I have heard stories from young people, college students who come to the bar during the school year. They are rich, or their parents are, and they have about them those characteristics I associate with the rich: they look healthy, as though the power of money had a genetic influence on their very flesh; beneath their laughter and constant talk there lies always a certain poise, not sophistication, but confidence in life and their places in it. Perhaps it comes from the knowledge that they will never be stranded in a bus station with two dollars. But probably its source is more intangible: the ambience they grew up in: that strange paradox of being from birth removed, insulated, from most of the world, and its agony of survival that is, for most of us, a day-to-day life; while, at the same time, these young rich children are exposed, through travel and—some of them—culture, to more of the world than most of us will ever see.

Years ago, when the students first found Timmy's and made it their regular drinking place, I did not like them, because their lives were so distant from those of the working men who patronize the bar. Then some of them started talking to me, in pairs, or a lone boy or girl, drinking near my spot at the bar's corner. I began enjoying their warmth, their general cheer, and often I bought them drinks, and always they bought mine in return. They called me by my first name, and each new class knows me, as they know Timmy's, before they see either of us. When they were alone, or with a close friend, they talked to me about themselves, revealed beneath that underlying poise deep confusion, and abiding pain their faces belied. So I learned of the cruelties of some of the rich: of children beaten, girls fondled by fathers who were never drunk and certainly did not smoke, healthy men who were either crazy or evil beneath their suits and briefcases, and their punctuality and calm confidence that crossed the line into arrogance. I learned of neglect: children reared by live-in nurses, by housekeepers who cooked; children in summer camps and boarding schools; and I saw the selfishness that wealth allows, a selfishness beyond greed, a desire to have children yet give them nothing, or very little, of oneself. I know one boy, an only child, whose mother left home when he was ten. She no longer wanted to be a mother; she entered the world of business in a city across the country from him, and he saw her for a weekend once a year. His father worked hard at making more money, and the boy left notes on the door of his father's den, asking for a time to see him. An appointment. The father answered with notes on the boy's door, and they met. Then the boy came to college here. He is very serious, very polite, and I have never seen him with a girl, or another boy, and I have never seen him smile.

So I have no reason to imagine Rose on that old stained carpet with places of it worn thin, nearly to the floor; Rose crawling among the legs of older sisters and brothers, looking up at the great and burdened height of her parents, their capacity, their will to love long beaten or drained from them by what they had to do to keep a dwelling with food in it, and heat in it, and warm and cool clothes for their children. I have only guessed at this part of her history. There is one reason, though: Rose's face is bereft of education, of thought. It is the face of a survivor walking away from a terrible car accident: without memory or conjecture, only shock, and the surprise of knowing that she is indeed alive. I think of her body as shapeless: beneath the large and sagging curve of her breasts, she has such sparse curvature of hips and waist that she appears to be an elongated lump beneath her loose dresses in summer, her old wool overcoat in winter. At the bar she does not remove her coat; but she unbuttons it and pushes it back from her breasts, and takes the blue scarf from her head, shakes her graying brown hair, and lets the scarf hang from her neck.

She appeared in our town last summer. We saw her on the streets, or slowly walking across the bridge over the Merrimack River. Then she found Timmy's and, with money from whatever source, became a regular, along with the rest of us. Sometimes, if someone drank beside her, she spoke. If no one drank next to her, she drank alone. Always screwdrivers. Then we started talking about her and, with that ear for news that impresses me still about small communities, either towns or city neighborhoods, some of us told stories about her. Rumors: she had been in prison, or her husband, or someone else in the family had. She had children but lost them. Someone had heard of a murder: perhaps she killed her husband, or one of the children did, or he or Rose or both killed a child. There was talk of a fire. And so we talked for months, into the fall, then early winter, when our leaves are gone, the reds and golds and yellows, and the trees are bare and gray, the evergreens dark green, and beyond their conical green we have lovely early sunsets. When the sky is gray, the earth is washed with it, and the evergreens look black. Then the ponds freeze and snow comes silently one night, and we wake to a white earth. It was during an early snowstorm when one of us said that Rose worked in a leather factory in town, had been there since she had appeared last summer. He knew someone who worked there and saw her. He knew nothing else.

On a night in January, while a light and pleasant snow dusted the tops of cars, and the shoulders and hats and scarves of people coming into Timmy's, Rose told me her story. I do not know whether, afterward, she was glad or relieved; neither of us has mentioned it since. Nor have our eyes, as we greet each other, sometimes chat. And one night I was without money, or enough of it, and she said *I owe you*, and bought the drinks. But that night in January she was in the state when people finally must talk. She was drunk too, or close enough to it, but I know her need to talk was there before vodka released her. I won't try to record our conversation. It was interrupted by one or both of us going to the bathroom, or ordering drinks (I insisted on paying for them all, and after the third round she simply thanked me, and patted my hand); interrupted by people leaning between us for drinks to bring back to booths, by people who came to speak to me, happy people oblivious of Rose, men or women or students who stepped to my side and began talking with that alcoholic lack of manners or awareness of intruding that, in a neighborhood bar, is not impolite but a part of the fabric of conversation. Interrupted too by the radio behind the bar, the speakers at both ends of the room, the loud rock music from an FM station in Boston.

It was a Friday, so the bar closed at two instead of one; we started talking at eleven. Gradually, before that, Rose had pushed her way down the bar toward my corner. I had watched her move to the right to make room for a couple, again to allow a man to squeeze in beside her, and again for some college girls; then the two men to my left went home, and when someone else wedged his arms and shoulders between the standing drinkers at the bar, she stepped to her right again and we faced each other across the corner. We talked about the bartender (we liked him), the crowd (we liked them: loud, but generally peaceful) and she said she always felt safe at Timmy's because everybody knew everybody else, and they didn't allow trouble in here.

"I can't stand fighting bars," she said. "Those young punks that have to hit somebody."

We talked about the weather, the seasons. She liked fall. The factory was too hot in summer. So was her apartment. She had bought a large fan, and it was so loud you could hear it from outside, and it blew dust from the floor, ashes from ashtrays. She liked winter, the snow, and the way the cold made her feel more alive; but she was afraid of it too: she was getting old, and did not want to be one of those people who slipped on ice and broke a hip.

"The old bones," she said. "They don't mend like young ones."

"You're no older than I am."

"Oh yes I am. And you'd better watch your step too. On that ice," and she nodded at the large front window behind me.

"That's snow," I said. "A light, dry snow."

She smiled at me, her face affectionate, and coquettish with some shared secret, as though we were talking in symbols. Then she finished her drink and I tried to get Steve's attention. He is a large man, and was mixing drinks at the other end of the bar. He did not look our way, so finally I called his name, my voice loud enough to be heard, but softened with courtesy to a tenor. Off and on, through the years, I have tended bar, and I am sensitive about the matter of ordering from a bartender who is making several drinks and, from the people directly in front of him, hearing requests for more. He heard me and glanced at us and I raised two fingers; he nodded. When I looked at Rose again she was gazing down into her glass, as though studying the yellow-filmed ice.

"I worry about fires in winter," she said, still looking down. "Sometimes every night."

"When you're going to sleep? You worry about a fire?"

She looked at me.

"Nearly every night."

"What kind of heat does your building have?"

"Oil furnace."

"Is something wrong with it?"

"No."

"Then—" Steve is very fast; he put my beer and her screwdriver before us, and I paid him; he spun, strode to the cash register, jabbed it, slapped in my ten, and was back with the change. I pushed a dollar toward him, and he thanked me and was gone, repeating an order from the other end of the bar, and a rock group sang above the crowd, a ceiling of sound over the shouts, the laughter, and the crescendo of juxtaposed conversations.

"Then why are you worried?" I said. "Were you in a fire? As a child?"

"I was. Not in winter. And I sure wasn't no child. But you hear them. The sirens. All the time in winter."

"Wood stoves," I said. "Faulty chimneys."

"They remind me. The sirens. Sometimes it isn't even the sirens. I try not to think about them. But sometimes it's like they think about me. They do. You know what I mean?"

"The sirens?"

"*No.*" She grabbed my wrist and squeezed it, hard as a man might; I had not known the strength of her hands. "The flames," she said.

"The flames?"

"I'm not doing anything. Or I'm at work, packing boxes. With leather. Or I'm going to sleep. Or right now, just then, we were talking about winter. I try not to think about them. But here they come, and I can see them. I feel them. Little flames. Big ones. Then—"

She released my wrist, swallowed from her glass, and her face changed: a quick recognition of something forgotten. She patted my hand.

"Thanks for the drink."

"I have money tonight."

"Good. Some night you won't, and I will. You'll drink on me."

"Fine."

"Unless you slip on that ice," nodding her head toward the window, the gentle snow, her eyes brightening again with that shared mystery, their luster near anger, not at me but at what we shared.

"Then what?" I said.

"What?"

"When you see them. When you feel the fire."

"My kids."

"No."

"Three kids."

"No, Rose."

"Two were upstairs. We lived on the third floor."

"Please: no stories like that tonight."

She patted my hand, as though in thanks for a drink, and said: "Did you lose a child?"

"Yes."

"In a fire?"

"A car."

"You poor man. Don't cry."

And with her tough thumbs she wiped the beginning of my tears from beneath my eyes, then standing on tiptoe she kissed my cheek, her lips dry, her cheek as it brushed mine feeling no softer than my own, save for her absence of whiskers.

"Mine got out," she said. "I got them out."

I breathed deeply and swallowed beer and wiped my eyes, but she had dried them.

"And it's the only thing I ever did. In my whole fucking life. The only thing I ever did that was worth a shit."

"Come on. Nobody's like that."

"No?"

"I hope nobody is."

I looked at the clock on the opposite wall; it was near the speaker that tilted downward, like those mirrors in stores, so cashiers can watch people between shelves. From the speaker came a loud electric guitar, repeating a series of chords, then two or more frenetic saxophones blowing their hoarse tones at the heads of the drinkers, like an indoor storm without rain. On that clock the time was two minutes till midnight, so I knew it was eleven thirty-eight; at Timmy's they keep the clock twenty minutes fast. This allows them time to give last call and still get the patrons out by closing. Rose was talking. Sometimes I watched her; sometimes I looked away, when I could do that and still hear. For when I listened while watching faces I knew, hearing some of their voices, I did not see everything she told me: I saw, but my vision was dulled, given distance, by watching bearded Steve work, or the blond student Ande laughing over the mouth of her beer bottle, or old gray-haired Lou, retired from his job as a factory foreman, drinking his shots and drafts, and smoking Camels; or the young owner Timmy, in his mid-thirties, wearing a leather jacket and leaning on the far corner of the bar, drinking club soda and watching the hockey game that was silent under the sounds of rock.

But most of the time, because of the noise, I had to look at her eyes or mouth to hear; and when I did that, I saw everything, without the distractions of sounds and faces and bodies, nor even the softening of distance, of time: I saw the two little girls, and the little boy, their pallid terrified faces; I saw their father's big arm and hand arcing down in a slap; in a blow with his fist closed; I saw the five-year-old boy, the oldest, flung through the air, across the room, to strike the wall and drop screaming to the couch against it. Toward the end, nearly his only sounds were screams; he virtually stopped talking, and lived as a frightened yet recalcitrant prisoner. And in Rose's eyes I saw the embers of death, as if the dying of her spirit had come not with a final yielding sigh, but in a blaze of recognition.

It was long ago, in a Massachusetts town on the Merrimack River. Her husband was a big man, with strongly muscled arms, and the solid rounded belly of a man who drinks much beer at night and works hard, with his body, five days a week. He was handsome, too. His face was always reddish-brown from his outdoor work, his hair was thick and black, and curls of it topped his forehead, and when he wore his cap on the back of his head, the visor rested on his curls. He had a thick but narrow mustache, and on Friday and Saturday nights, when they went out to drink and dance, he dressed in brightly colored pants and shirts that his legs and torso and arms filled. His name was Jim Cormier, his grandfather Jacques had come from Quebec as a young man, and his father was Jacques Cormier too, and by Jim's generation the last name was pronounced *Cormeer*, and he was James. Jim was a construction worker, but his physical strength and endurance were unequally complemented by his mind, his spirit, whatever that element is that draws the attention of other men. He was best at the simplest work, and would never be a foreman, or tradesman. Other men, when he worked with them, baffled him. He did not have the touch: could not be entrusted to delegate work, to plan, to oversee, and to handle men. Bricks and mortar and trowels and chalk lines baffled him too, as did planes and levels; yet, when he drank at home every night— they seldom went out after the children were born—he talked about learning to operate heavy equipment.

Rose did not tell me all this at first. She told me the end, the final night, and only in the last forty minutes or so, when I questioned her, did she go further back, to the beginning. Where I start her story, so I can try to understand how two young people married, with the hope of love—even, in those days before pandemic divorce, the certainty of love—and within six years, when they were still young, still in their twenties, their home had become a horror for their children, for Rose, and yes: for Jim. A place where a boy of five, and girls of four and three, woke, lived, and slept in isolation from the light of a child's life: the curiosity, the questions about birds, appliances, squirrels and trees and snow and rain, and the first heart-quickening of love for another child, not a sister or brother, but the boy or girl in a sandbox or on a tricycle at the house down the street. They lived always in darkness, deprived even of childhood fears of ghosts in the shadowed corners of the rooms where they slept, deprived of dreams of vicious and carnivorous monsters. Their young memories and their present consciousness were the tall broad man and his reddening face that shouted and hissed, and his large hands. Rose must have had no place at all, or very little, in their dreams and in their wary and apprehensive minds when they were awake. Unless as a wish: I imagine them in their beds, in the moments before sleep, hoping for Rose to take them in her arms, carry them one by one to the car while the giant slept drunkenly in the bed she shared with him, Rose putting their toys and clothes in the car's trunk, and driving with them far away to a place—what place could they imagine? What place not circumscribed by their apartment's walls, whose very colors and hanging pictures and calendar were for them the dark gray of fear and pain? Certainly, too, in those moments before sleep, they must have wished their father gone. Simply gone. The boy may have thought of, wished for, Jim's death. The younger girls, four and three, only that he vanish, leaving no trace of himself in their home, in their hearts, not even guilt. Simply vanish.

Rose was a silent partner. If there is damnation, and a place for the damned, it must be a quiet place, where spirits turn away from each other and stand in solitude and gaze haplessly at eternity. For it must be crowded with the passive: those people whose presence in life was a paradox; for, while occupying space and moving through it and making sounds in it they were obviously present, while in truth they were not: they witnessed evil and lifted neither an arm nor a voice to stop it, as they witnessed joy and neither sang nor clapped their hands. But so often we understand them too easily, tolerate them too much: they have universality, so we forgive the man who watches injustice, a drowning, a murder, because he reminds us of ourselves, and we share with him the loyal bond of cowardice, whether once or a hundred times we have turned away from another's suffering to save ourselves: our jobs, our public selves, our bones and flesh. And these people are so easy to pity. We know fear as early as we know love, and fear is always with us. I have friends my own age who still cannot say what they believe, except in the most intimate company. Condemning the actively evil man is a simple matter, though we tend not only to forgive but cheer him if he robs banks or Brink's, and outwits authority: those unfortunate policemen, minions whose uniforms and badges and revolvers are, for many of us, a distorted symbol of what we fear: not a fascist state but a Power, a God, who knows all our truths, believes none of our lies, and with that absolute knowledge will both judge and exact punishment. For we see to it that no one absolutely knows us, so at times the passing blue figure of a policeman walking his beat can stir in us our fear of discovery. We like to see them made into dupes by the outlaw.

But if the outlaw rapes, tortures, gratuitously kills, or if he makes children suffer, we hate him with a purity we seldom feel: our hatred has no roots in prejudice, or self-righteousness, but in horror. He has done something we would never do, something we could not do even if we wished it; our bodies would not obey, would not tear the dress, or lift and swing the axe, pull the trigger, throw the screaming child across the room. So I hate Jim Cormier, and cannot understand him; cannot with my imagination cross the distance between myself and him, enter his soul and know how it felt to live even five minutes of his life. And I forgive Rose, but as I write I resist that compassion, or perhaps merely empathy, and force myself to think instead of the three children, and Rose living there, knowing what she knew. She was young.

She is Irish: a Callahan till marriage, and she and Jim were Catholic. Devout Catholics, she told me. By that, she did not mean they strived to live in imitation of Christ. She meant they did not practice artificial birth control, but rhythm, and after their third year of marriage they had three children. They left the Church then. That is, they stopped attending Sunday Mass and receiving Communion. Do you see? I am not a Catholic, but even I know that they were never truly members of that faith, and so could not have left it. There is too much history, too much philosophy involved, for the matter of faith to rest finally and solely on the use of contraceptives. That was long ago, and now my Catholic friends tell me the priests no longer concern themselves with birth control. But we must live in our own time; Thomas More died for an issue that would have no meaning today. Rose and Jim, though, were not Thomas Mores. They could not see a single act as a renunciation or affirmation of a belief, a way of life. No. They had neither a religion nor a philosophy; like most people I know, their philosophies were simply their accumulated reactions to their daily circumstance, their lives as they lived them from one hour to the next. They were not driven, guided, by either passionate belief or strong resolve. And for that I pity them both, as I pity the others who move through life like scraps of paper in the wind.

With contraception they had what they believed were two years of freedom. There had been a time when all three of their children wore diapers, and only the boy could walk, and with him holding her coat or pants, moving so slowly beside her, Rose went daily to the laundromat, pushing two strollers, gripping a paper grocery bag of soiled diapers, with a clean bag folded in her purse. Clorox rested underneath one stroller, a box of soap underneath the other. While she waited for the diapers to wash, the boy walked among the machines, touched them, watched them, and watched the other women who waited. The oldest girl crawled about on the floor. The baby slept in Rose's lap, or nursed in those days when mothers did not expose their breasts, and Rose covered the infant's head, and her breast, with her unbuttoned shirt. The children became hungry, or tired, or restless, and they fussed, and cried, as Rose called to the boy to leave the woman alone, to stop playing with the ashtray, the soap, and she put the diapers in the dryer. And each day she felt that the other women, even those with babies, with crawling and barely walking children, with two or three children, and one pregnant with a third, had about them some grace, some calm, that kept their voices soft, their gestures tender; she watched them with shame, and a deep dislike of herself, but no envy, as if she had tried out for a dance company and on the first day had entered a room of slender professionals in leotards, dancing like cats, while she clumsily moved her heavy body clad in gray sweatclothes. Most of the time she changed the diaper of at least one of the children, and dropped it in the bag, the beginning of tomorrow's load. If the baby slept in her stroller, and the older girl and the boy played on the floor, Rose folded the diapers on the table in the laundromat, talking and smoking with the other women. But that was rare: the chance that all three small children could at the same time be peaceful and without need, and so give her peace. Imagine: three of them with bladders and bowels, thirst, hunger, fatigue, and none of them synchronized. Most days she put the hot unfolded diapers in the clean bag and hurried home.

Finally she cried at dinner one night for a washing machine and a dryer, and Jim stared at her, not with anger, or impatience, and not refusal either: but with the resigned look of a man who knew he could neither refuse it nor pay for it. It was the washing machine; he would buy it with monthly payments, and when he had done that, he would get the dryer. He sank posts in the earth and nailed boards across their tops and stretched clotheslines between them. He said in rain or freezing cold she would have to hang the wet diapers over the backs of chairs. It was all he could do. Until he could get her a dryer. And when he came home on those days of rain or cold, he looked surprised, as if rain and cold in New England were as foreign to him as the diapers that seemed to occupy the house. He removed them from the rod for the shower curtain, and when he had cleaned his work from his body, he hung them again. He took them from the arms and back of his chair and laid them on top of others, on a chair, or the edges of the kitchen table. Then he sat in the chair whose purpose he had restored; he drank beer and gazed at the drying diapers, as if they were not cotton at all, but the whitest of white shades of the dead, come to haunt him, to assault him, an inch at a time, a foot, until they won, surrounded him where he stood in some corner of the bedroom, the bathroom, in the last place in his home that was his. His *querençia:* his cool or blood-smelling sand, the only spot in the bull-ring where he wanted to stand and defend, to lower his head and wait.

He struck the boy first, before contraception and the freedom and new life it promised, as money does. Rose was in the kitchen, chopping onions, now and then turning her face to wipe, with the back of her wrist, the tears from her eyes. The younger girl was asleep; the older one crawled between and around Rose's legs. The boy was three. She had nearly finished the onions and could put them in the skillet and stop crying, when she heard the slap, and knew what it was in that instant before the boy cried: a different cry: in it she heard not only startled fear, but a new sound: a wail of betrayal, of pain from the heart. Wiping her hands on her apron, she went quickly to the living room, into that long and loudening cry, as if the boy, with each moment of deeper recognition, raised his voice until it howled. He stood in front of his seated father. Before she reached him, he looked at her, as though without hearing footsteps or seeing her from the corner of his blurred wet vision, he knew she was there. She was his mother. Yet when he turned his face to her, it was not with appeal: above his small reddened cheeks he looked into her eyes; and in his, as tears ran from them, was that look whose sound she had heard in the kitchen. Betrayal.

Accusing her of it, and without anger, only with dismay. In her heart she felt something fall between herself and her son, like a glass wall, or a space that spanned only a few paces, yet was infinite, and she could never cross it again. Now his voice had attained the howl, and though his cheeks were wet, his eyes were dry now; or anyway tearless, for they looked wet and bright as pools that could reflect her face. The baby was awake, crying in her crib. Rose looked from her son's eyes to her husband's. They were dark, and simpler than the boy's: in them she saw only the ebb of his fury: anger, and a resolve to preserve and defend it.

"I told him not to," he said.

"Not to what?"

"Climbing on my legs. Look." He pointed to a dark wet spot on the carpet. "He spilled the beer."

She stared at the spot. She could not take her eyes from it. The baby was crying, and the muscles of her legs tried to move toward that sound. Then she realized her son was silent. She felt him watching her, and she would not look at him.

"It's nothing to cry about," Jim said.

"You *slapped* him."

"Not *him*. You."

"Me? That's onions."

She wiped her hands on her apron, brushed her eyes with the back of her wrist.

"Jesus," she said. She looked at her son. She had to look away from those eyes. Then she saw the older girl: she had come to the doorway, and was standing on the threshold, her thumb in her mouth; above her small closed fist and nose, her frightened eyes stared, and she looked as though she were trying not to cry. But, if she was, there could be only one reason for a child so young: she was afraid for her voice to leave her, to enter the room, where now Rose could feel her children's fear as tangibly as a cold draft blown through a cracked windowpane. Her legs, her hips, strained toward the baby's cry for food, a dry diaper, for whatever acts of love they need when they wake, and even more when they wake before they are ready, when screams smash the shell of their sleep. "Jesus," she said, and hurried out of the room where the pain in her son's heart had pierced her own, and her little girl's fearful silence pierced it again; or slashed it, for she felt as she bent over the crib that she was no longer whole, that her height and breadth and depth were in pieces that somehow held together, did not separate and drop to the floor, through it, into the earth itself.

"I should have hit him with the skillet," she said to me, so many years later, after she had told me the end and I had drawn from her the beginning, in the last half-hour of talk.

She could not hit him that night. With the heavy iron skillet, with its hot oil waiting for the onions. For by then something had flowed away from Rose, something of her spirit simply wafting willy-nilly out of her body, out of the apartment, and it never came back, not even with the diaphragm. Perhaps it began to leave her at the laundromat, or in bed at night, at the long day's end not too tired for lust, for rutting, but too tired for an evening of desire that began with dinner and crested and fell and crested again through the hours as they lay close and naked in bed, from early in the night until finally they slept. On the car seat of courtship she had dreamed of this, and in the first year of marriage she lived the dream: joined him in the shower and made love with him, still damp, before they went to the dinner kept warm on the stove, then back to the bed's tossed sheets to lie in the dark, smoking, talking, touching, and they made love again; and, later, again, until they could only lie side by side waiting for their breathing to slow, before they slept. Now at the tired ends of days they took release from each other, and she anxiously slept, waiting for a baby to cry.

Or perhaps it left her between the shelves of a supermarket. His payday was Thursday, and by then the refrigerator and cupboard were nearly empty. She shopped on Friday. Unless a neighbor could watch the children, Rose shopped at night, when Jim was home; they ate early and she hurried to the store to shop before it closed. Later, months after he slapped the boy, she believed his rage had started then, alone in the house with them, changing the baby and putting her in the crib while the other girl and the boy spat and flung food from their highchairs where she had left them, in her race with time to fill a cart with food Jim could afford: she looked at the price of everything she took from a shelf. She did not believe, later, that he struck them on those nights. But there must have been rage, the frightening voice of it; for he was tired, and confused, and overwhelmed by three small people with wills of their own, and no control over the needs of their bodies and their spirits. Certainly he must have yelled; maybe he squeezed an arm, or slapped a rump. When she returned with the groceries, the apartment was quiet: the children slept, and he sat in the kitchen, with the light out, drinking beer. A light from the living room behind him and around a corner showed her his silhouette: large and silent, a cigarette glowing at his mouth, a beer bottle rising to it. Then he would turn on the light and put down his beer and walk past her, to the old car, to carry in the rest of the groceries.

When finally two of the children could walk, Rose went to the supermarket during the day, the boy and girl walking beside her, behind her, away from her voice whose desperate pitch embarrassed her, as though its sound were a sign to the other women with children that she was incompetent, unworthy to be numbered among them. The boy and girl took from shelves cookies, crackers, cereal boxes, cans of vegetables and fruit, sometimes to play with them, but at other times to bring to her, where holding the cart they pulled themselves up on the balls of their feet and dropped in the box, or the can. Still she scolded them, jerked the can or box from the cart, brought it back to its proper place; and when she did this, her heart sank as though pulled by a sigh deeper into her body. For she saw. She saw that when the children played with these things whose colors or shapes drew them so they wanted to sit on the floor and hold or turn in their hands the box or can, they were simply being children whom she could patiently teach, if patience were still an element in her spirit. And that when they brought things to her, to put into the cart, repeating the motions of their mother, they were joining, without fully knowing it, the struggle of the family, and without knowing the struggle that was their parents' lives. Their hearts, though, must have expected praise; or at least an affectionate voice, a gentle hand, to show that their mother did not need what they had brought her. If only there were time: one extra hour of grocery shopping to spend in this gentle instruction. Or if she had strength to steal the hour anyway, despite the wet and tired and staring baby in the cart. But she could not: she scolded, she jerked from the cart or their hands the things they had brought, and the boy became quiet, the girl sucked her thumb and held Rose's pants as the four of them moved with the cart between the long shelves. The baby fussed, with that unceasing low cry that was not truly crying, only wordless sounds of fatigue. Rose recognized it, understood it, for by now she had learned the awful lesson of fatigue, which as a young girl she had never felt. She knew that it was worse than the flu, whose enforced rest at least left you the capacity to care for someone else, to mutter words of love; but that, healthy, you could be so tired that all you wanted was to lie down, alone, shut off from everyone. And you would snap at your husband, or your children, if they entered the room, probed the solace of your complete surrender to silence and the mattress that seductively held your body. So she understood the baby's helpless sounds for *I want to lie in my crib and put my thumb in my mouth and hold Raggedy Ann's dirty old apron and sleep.* The apron was long removed from the doll, and the baby would not sleep without its presence in her hand. Rose understood this, but could not soothe the baby. She could not have soothed her anyway; only sleep could. But Rose could not try, with hugs, with petting, with her softened voice. She was young.

Perhaps her knowledge of her own failures dulled her ears and eyes to Jim after he first struck the boy, and on that night lost for the rest of his life any paternal control he might have exerted in the past over his hands, finally his fists. Because more and more now he spanked them; with a chill Rose tried to deny, a resonant quiver up through her body, she remembered that her parents had spanked her too. That all, or probably all, parents spanked their children. And usually it was the father, the man of the house, the authority and judge, and enforcer of rules and discipline the children would need when they reached their teens. But now, too, he held them by the shoulders, and shook their small bodies, the children sometimes wailing, sometimes frighteningly silent, until it seemed their heads would fly across the room then roll to rest on the floor, while he shook a body whose neck had snapped in two like a dried branch. He slapped their faces, and sometimes he punched the boy, who was four, then five, with his fist. They were not bad children; not disobedient; certainly they were not loud. When Jim yelled and shook them, or slapped or punched, they had done no more than they had in the supermarket, where her voice, her snatching from their hands, betrayed her to the other women. So maybe that kept her silent.

But there was more: she could no longer feel love, or what she had believed love to be. On the few nights when she and Jim could afford both a sitter and a nightclub, they did not dance. They sat drinking, their talk desultory: about household chores, about Jim's work, pushing wheelbarrows, swinging a sledgehammer, thrusting a spade into the earth or a pile of gravel or sand. They listened to the music, watched the band, even drummed their fingers on the table dampened by the bottoms of the glasses they emptied like thirsty people drinking water; but they thirsted for a time they had lost. Or not even that: for respite from their time now, and their knowledge that, from one day to the next, year after year, their lives would not change. Each day would be like the one they had lived before last night's sleep; and tomorrow was a certain and already draining repetition of today. They did not decide to sit rather than dance. They simply did not dance. They sat and drank and watched the band and the dancing couples, as if their reason for dancing had been stolen from them while their eyes had been jointly focused on something else.

She could no longer feel love. She ate too much and smoked too much and drank too much coffee, so all day she felt either lethargic from eating or stimulated by coffee and cigarettes, and she could not recall her body as it had once been, only a few years ago, when she was dating Jim, and had played softball and volleyball, had danced, and had run into the ocean to swim beyond the breakers. The ocean was a half-hour away from her home, yet she had not seen it in six years. Rather than love, she felt that she and Jim only worked together, exhausted, toward a nebulous end, as if they were digging a large hole, wide as a house, deeper than a well. Side by side they dug, and threw the dirt up and out of the hole, pausing now and then to look at each other, to wait while their breathing slowed, and to feel in those kindred moments something of why they labored, of why they had begun it so long ago—not in years, not long at all—with their dancing and lovemaking and finally marriage: to pause and look at each other's flushed and sweating faces with as much love as they could feel before they commenced again to dig deeper, away from the light above them.

On a summer night in that last year, Jim threw the boy across the living room. Rose was washing the dishes after dinner. Jim was watching television, and the boy, five now, was playing on the floor between Jim and the set. He was on the floor with his sisters and wooden blocks and toy cars and trucks. He seldom spoke directly to his father anymore; seldom spoke at all to anyone but his sisters. The girls were too young, or hopeful, or were still in love. They spoke to Jim, sat on his lap, hugged his legs, and when he hugged them, lifted them in the air, talked with affection and laughter, their faces showed a happiness without memory. And when he yelled at them, or shook or spanked them, or slapped their faces, their memory failed them again, and they were startled, frightened, and Rose could sense their spirits weeping beneath the sounds of their crying. But they kept turning to him, with open arms, and believing faces.

"Little flowers," she said to me. "They were like little flowers in the sun. They never could remember the frost."

Not the boy, though. But that night his game with his sisters absorbed him, and for a short while—nearly an hour—he was a child in a home. He forgot. Several times his father told him and the girls to be quiet or play in another room. Then for a while, a long while for playing children, they were quiet: perhaps five minutes, perhaps ten. Each time their voices rose, Jim's command for quiet was abrupt, and each time it was louder. At the kitchen sink Rose's muscles tensed, told her it was coming, and she must go to the living room now, take the children and their blocks and cars and trucks to the boy's bedroom. But she breathed deeply and rubbed a dish with a sponge. When she finished, she would go down to the basement of the apartment building, descend past the two floors of families and single people whose only sounds were music from radios, voices from television, and sometimes children loudly playing and once in a while a quarrel between a husband and wife. She would go into the damp basement and take the clothes from the washing machine, put them in the dryer that Jim was now paying for with monthly installments. Then she heard his voice again, and was certain it was coming, but could not follow the urging of her muscles. She sponged another dish. Then her hands came out of the dishwater with a glass: it had been a jelly jar, and humanly smiling animals were on it, and flowers, and her children liked to drink from it, looked for it first when they were thirsty, and only if it was dirty in the sink would they settle for an ordinary glass for their water, their juice, or Kool-Aid or milk. She washed it slowly, and was for those moments removed; she was oblivious of the living room, the children's voices rising again to the peak that would bring either Jim's voice or his body from his chair. Her hands moved gently on the glass. She could have been washing one of her babies. Her heart had long ago ceased its signals to her; it lay dormant in despair beyond sorrow; standing at the sink, in a silence of her own making, lightly rubbing the glass with the sponge, and her fingers and palms, she did not know she was crying until the tears reached her lips, salted her tongue.

With their wooden blocks, the children were building a village, and a bridge leading out of it to the country: the open spaces of the living-room carpet, and the chairs and couch that were distant mountains. More adept with his hands, and more absorbed too in the work, the boy often stood to adjust a block on a roof, or the bridge. Each time he stood between his father and the television screen, he heard the quick command, and moved out of the way. They had no slanted blocks, so the bridge had to end with two sheer walls; the boy wanted to build ramps at either end, for the cars and trucks to use, and he had only rectangles and squares to work with. He stood to look down at the bridge. His father spoke. He heard the voice, but a few seconds passed before it penetrated his concentration and spread through him. It was too late. What he heard next was not words, or a roar, but a sustained guttural cry, a sound that could be either anguish or rage. Then his father's hands were on him: on him and squeezing his left thigh and left bicep so tightly that he opened his mouth to cry out in pain. But he did not. For then he was above his father's head, above the floor and his sisters, high above the room itself and near the ceiling he glimpsed; and he felt his father's grip and weight shifting and saw the wall across the room, the wall above the couch, so that when finally he made a sound it was of terror, and it came from him in a high scream he heard as he hurtled across the room, seeing always the wall, and hearing his own scream, as though his flight were prolonged by the horror of what he saw and heard. Then he struck it. He heard that, and the bone in his right forearm snap, and he fell to the couch. Now he cried with pain, staring at the swollen flesh where the bone tried to protrude, staring with astonishment and grief at this part of his body. Nothing in his body had ever broken before. He touched the flesh, the bone beneath it. He was crying as, in his memory, he had never cried before, and he not only did not try to stop, as he always had, with pride, with anger; but he wanted to cry this deeply, his body shuddering with it, doubling at his waist with it, until he attained oblivion, invisibility, death. Somehow he knew his childhood had ended. In his pain, he felt relief too: now on this couch his life would end.

He saw through tears but more strongly felt his sisters standing before him, touching him, crying. Then he heard his mother. She was screaming. And in rage. At his father. He had never heard her do that, but still her scream did not come to him as a saving trumpet. He did not want to live to see revenge. Not even victory. Then he heard his father slap her. Through his crying he listened then for her silence. But her voice grew, its volume filled the world. Still he felt nothing of hope, of vengeance; he had left that world, and lived now for what he hoped and believed would be only a very short time. He was beginning to feel the pain in his head and back and shoulders, his elbows and neck. He knew he would only have to linger a while in this pain, until his heart left him, as though disgorged by tears, and went wherever hearts went. A sister's hand held his, and he squeezed it.

When he was above his father's head, the boy had not seen Rose. But she was there, behind Jim, behind the lifted boy, and she had cried out too, and moved: as Jim regained his balance from throwing the boy, she turned him, her hand jerking his shoulder, and when she could see his face she pounded it with her fists. She was yelling, and the yell was words, but she did not know what they were. She hit him until he pushed her back, hard, so she nearly fell. She looked at his face, the cheeks reddened by her blows, saw a trickle of blood from his lower lip, and charged it: swinging at the blood, the lip. He slapped her so hard that she was sitting on the floor, with no memory of falling, and holding and shaking her stunned and buzzing head. She stood, yelling words again that she could not hear, as if their utterance had been so long coming, from whatever depth in her, that her mind could not even record them as they rushed through her lips. She went past Jim, pushing his belly, and he fell backward into his chair. She paused to look at that. Her breath was deep and fast, and he sat glaring, his breathing hard too, and she neither knew nor cared whether he had desisted or was preparing himself for more. At the bottom of her vision, she saw his beer bottle on the floor beside the chair. She snatched it up, by its neck, beer hissing onto her arm and breast, and in one motion she turned away from Jim and flung the bottle smashing through the television screen. He was up and yelling behind her, but she was crouched over the boy.

She felt again what she had felt in the kitchen, in the silence she had made for herself while she bathed the glass. Behind and above her was the sound of Jim's fury; yet she stroked the boy's face: his forehead, the tears beneath his eyes; she touched the girls too, their hair, their wet faces; and she heard her own voice: soft and soothing, so soft and soothing that she even believed the peace it promised. Then she saw, beneath the boy's hand, the swollen flesh; gently she lifted his hand, then was on her feet. She stood into Jim's presence again: his voice behind her, the feel of his large body inches from her back. Then he gripped her hair, at the back of her head, and she shook her head but still he held on.

"His *arm's* broken."

She ran from him, felt hair pulling from her scalp, heard it, and ran to her bedroom for her purse but not a blanket, not from the bed where she slept with Jim; for that she went to the boy's, and pulled his thin summer blanket from his bed, and ran back to the living room. Where she stopped. Jim stood at the couch, not looking at the boy, or the girls, but at the doorway where now she stood holding the blanket. He was waiting for her.

"You crazy fucking bitch."

"*What?*"

"The fucking TV. Who's going to buy one? You? You fucking cunt. You've never had a fucking job in your life."

It was madness. She was looking at madness, and it calmed her. She had nothing to say to it. She went to the couch, opening the blanket to wrap around the boy.

"It's the only fucking peace I've *got*."

She heard him, but it was like overhearing someone else, in another apartment, another life. She crouched and was working the blanket under the boy's body when a fist knocked loudly on the door. She did not pause, or look up. More knocking, then a voice in the hall: "Hey! Everybody all right in there?"

"Get the fuck away from my door."

"You tell me everybody's all right."

"Get the fuck *away*."

"I want to hear the woman. And the kid."

"You want me to throw you down the fucking stairs?"

"I'm calling the cops."

"Fuck you."

She had the boy in her arms now. He was crying still, and as she carried him past Jim, she kissed his cheeks, his eyes. Then Jim was beside her. He opened the door, swung it back for them. She did not realize until weeks later that he was frightened. His voice was low: "Tell them he fell."

She did not answer. She went out and down the stairs, past apartments; in one of them someone was phoning the police. At the bottom of the stairs she stopped short of the door, to shift the boy's weight in her arms, to free a hand for the knob. Then an old woman stepped out of her apartment, into the hall, and said: "I'll get it."

An old woman with white hair and a face that knew everything, not only tonight, but the years before this too, yet the face was neither stern nor kind; it looked at Rose with some tolerant recognition of evil, of madness, of despair, like a warrior who has seen and done too much to condemn, or even try to judge; can only nod in assent at what he sees. The woman opened the door and held it, and Rose went out, across the small lawn to the car parked on the road. There were only two other cars at the curb; then she remembered that it was Saturday, and had been hot, and before noon she had heard most of the tenants separately leaving for beaches or picnic grounds. They would be driving home now, or stopping to eat. The sun had just set, but most windows of the tenements on the street were dark. She stopped at the passenger door, started to shift the weeping boy's weight, then the old woman was beside her, trying the door, asking for the key. Rose's purse hung from her wrist. The woman's hands went into it, moved in there, came out with the ring of keys, held them up toward the streetlight, and found the one for the car. She opened the door, and Rose leaned in and laid the boy on the front seat. She turned to thank the woman but she was already at the front door of the building, a square back and short body topped by hair like cotton.

Rose gently closed the car door, holding it, making certain it was not touching the boy before she pushed it into place. She ran to the driver's side, and got in, and put the key in the ignition slot. But she could not turn it. She sat in the boy's crying, poised in the moment of action the car had become. But she could not start it.

"Jimmy," she said. "Jimmy, listen. Just hang on. I'll be right back. I can't leave the girls. Do you hear me?"

His face, profiled on the seat, nodded.

"I've got to get them."

She pushed open the door, left the car, closed the door, the keys in her hands, not out of habit this time; no, she clung to them as she might to a tiny weapon, her last chance to be saved. She was running to the building when she saw the flames at her windows, a flare of them where an instant before there had been only lamplight. Her legs now, her body, were weightless as the wind. She heard the girls screaming. Then the front door opened and Jim ran out of it, collided with her, and she fell on her back as he stumbled and sidestepped and tried to regain balance and speed and go around her. Her left hand grabbed his left ankle. Then she turned with his pulling, his weight, and, on her stomach now, she held his ankle with her right hand too, and pulled it back and up. He fell. She dived onto his back, saw and smelled the gasoline can in his hand, and in her mind she saw him going down to the basement for it, and back up the stairs. She twisted it away from his fingers on the handle, and kneeled with his back between her legs, and as he lifted his head and shoulders and tried to stand, she raised the can high with both hands and brought it down, leaning with it, into it, as it struck his skull. For a moment he was still, his face in the grass. Then he began to struggle again, and said into the earth: "Over now. All over."

She hit him three more times, the sounds hollow, metallic. Then he was still, save for the rise and fall of his back. Beneath his other hand she saw his set of car keys. She scooped them from the grass and stood and threw them across the lawn, whirling now into the screams of the girls, and windows of fire. She ran up the stairs. The white-haired woman was on the second-floor landing. Rose passed her, felt her following, and the others: she did not know how many, nor who they were. She only heard them behind her. No one passed her. She was at the door, trying to turn the knob, while her left arm and hand pressed hot wood.

"I called the fire department," a man said, behind her in the hall.

"So did we," a woman said.

Rose was calling to the girls to open the door.

"They can't," another man said. "That's where the fire is." Then he said: "Fuck this," and pulled her away from the door where she was turning the knob back and forth and calling through the wood to the screams from the rear of the apartment, their bedroom. She was about to spring back to the door, but stopped: the man faced it, then stepped away. She knew his name, or had known it; she could not say it. He lived on the second floor; it was his wife who had said *So did we*. He stepped twice toward the door, then kicked, his leg horizontal, the bottom of his shoe striking the door, and it swung open, through the flames that filled the threshold and climbed the doorjambs. The man leaped backward, his forearms covering his face, while Rose yelled to the girls: *We're coming, we're coming*. The man lowered his head and sprinted forward. Or it would have been a sprint. Certainly he believed that, believed he would run through fire to the girls and get them out. But in his third stride his legs stopped, so suddenly and autonomously that he nearly fell forward into the fire. Then he backed up.

"They'll have a net," he said. He was panting. "We'll get them to jump. We'll get them to a window, and get them to jump."

A man behind Rose was holding her. She had not known it till now. Nor had she known she was straining forward. The man tightly held her biceps. He was talking to her and now she heard that too, and was also aware that people were moving away, slowly but away, down the hall toward the stairs. He was saying, "You can't. All you'll do is get yourself killed."

Then she was out of his hands, as though his fingers were those of a child, and, with her breath held and her arms shielding her face, and her head down, she was in motion, through the flames and into the burning living room. She did not feel the fire, but even as she ran through the living room, dodging flames, running through them, she knew that very soon she would. It meant no more to her than knowing that she was getting wet in a sudden rain. The girls were standing on the older one's bed, at the far side of the room, holding each other, screaming, and watching their door and the hall beyond it where the fire would come. She filled the door, their vision, then was at the bed and they were crying: *Mommy! Mommy!* She did not speak. She did not touch them either. She pulled the blanket from under them, and they fell onto the bed. Running again, she grabbed the blanket from the younger girl's bed, and went into the hall where there was smoke but not fire yet, and across it to the bathroom where she turned on the shower and held the blankets under the spray. They soaked heavily in her hands. She held her breath leaving the bathroom and exhaled in the girls' room. They were standing again, holding each other. Now she spoke to them. Again, as when she had crouched with them in front of Jimmy, her voice somehow came softly from her. It was unhurried, calm, soothing: she could have been helping them put on snowsuits. They stopped screaming, even crying; they only sniffled and gasped as she wound a blanket around each of them, covering their feet and heads too, then lifted them, pressing one to each breast. Then she stopped talking, stopped telling them that very soon, before they even knew it, they would be safe outside. She turned and ran through smoke in the hall, and into the living room. She did not try to dodge flames: if they were in front of her, she spun and ran backward through them, hugging the girls against each other, so nothing of their bodies would protrude past her back, her sides; then spun and ran forward again, fearful of an image that entered her mind, though in an instant she expelled it: that she would fall with them, into fire. She ran backward through the door, and her back hit the wall. She bounced off it; there was fire in the hall now, moving at her ankles, and she ran, leaping, and when she reached the stairs she smelled the scorched blankets that steamed around the girls in her arms. She smelled her burned hair, sensed that it was burning still, crackling flames on her head. It could wait. She could wait. She was running down the stairs, and the fire was behind her, above her, and she felt she could run with her girls all night. Then she was on the lawn, and her arms took the girls, and a man wrestled her to the ground and rolled with her, rolled over and over on the grass. When she stood, someone was telling her an ambulance would— But she picked up her girls, unwrapped now, and looked at their faces: pale with terror, with shock, yes; but no burns. She carried them to the car.

"*No*," she heard. It was a man's voice, but one she did not know. Not for a few moments, as she laid the girls side by side on the back seat. Then she knew it was Jim. She was startled, as though she had not seen him for ten years. She ran around the car, got behind the wheel, reached over Jimmy, who was silent now and she thought unconscious until she saw his eyes staring at the dashboard, his teeth gritting against his pain. Leaning over his face, she pushed down the latch on his side. Then she locked her door. It was a two-door car, and they were safe now and they were going to the hospital. She started the engine.

Jim was at her window, a raging face, but a desperate one too, as though standing outside he was locked in a room without air. Then he was motion, on her left, to her front, and he stood at the middle of the car, slapped his hands onto the hood, and pushed. He bulged: his arms and chest and reddened face. With all his strength he pushed, and she felt the car rock backward. She turned on the headlights. The car rocked forward as he eased his pushing and drew breath. Then he pushed again, leaning, so all she could see of him was his face, his shoulders, his arms. The car rocked back and stopped. She pushed the accelerator pedal to the floor, waited two or three seconds in which she either did not breathe or held what breath she had, and watched his face above the sound of the racing engine. Then, in one quick motion, she lifted her foot from the clutch pedal. He was gone as she felt the bumper and grille leap through his resistance. She stopped and looked in the rear-view mirror; she saw the backs of the girls' heads, their long hair; they were kneeling on the seat, looking quietly out the back window. He lay on his back. Rose turned her wheels to the right, as though to back into a parking space, shifted to reverse, and this time without racing the engine, she slowly drove. She did not look through the rear window; she looked straight ahead, at the street, the tenements, the darkening sky. Only the rear tires rolled over him, then struck the curb. She straightened the front wheels and drove forward again. The car bumped over him. She stopped, shifted gears, and backed up: the bump, then the tires hitting the curb. She was still driving back and forth over his body, while beyond her closed windows people shouted or stared, when the sirens broke the summer sky: the higher wail of the police called by the neighbor, and the lower and louder one of the fire engine.

She was in the hospital, and by the time she got out, her three brothers and two sisters had found money for bail. Her parents were dead. Waiting for the trial, she lived with a married sister; there were children in the house, and Rose shied away from them. Her court-appointed lawyer called it justifiable homicide, and the jury agreed. Long before the trial, before she even left the hospital, she had lost the children. The last time she saw them was that night in the car, when finally she took them away: the boy lying on the front seat, his left cheek resting on it as he stared. He did not move while she drove back and forth over his father. She still does not know whether he knew then, or learned it from his sisters. And the two girls kneeling, their chests leaning on the back of the seat, watching their father appear, then vanish as a bump beneath them. They all went to the same foster home. She did not know where it was.

"Thanks for the drinks," she said, and patted my hand. "Next time you're broke, let me know."

"I will."

She adjusted the blue scarf over her hair, knotted it under her face, buttoned her coat, and put on her gloves. She stepped away from the bar, and walked around and between people. I ordered a beer, and watched her go out the door. I paid and tipped Steve, then left the bottle and glass with my coat and hat on the bar, and moved through the crowd. I stepped outside and watched her, a half-block away now. She was walking carefully in the lightly falling snow, her head down, watching the sidewalk, and I remembered her eyes when she talked about slipping on ice. But what had she been sharing with me? Age? Death? I don't think so. I believe it was the unexpected: chance, and its indiscriminate testing of our bodies, our wills, our spirits. She was walking toward the bridge over the Merrimack. It is a long bridge, and crossing it in that open air she would be cold. I was shivering. She was at the bridge now, her silhouette diminishing as she walked on it. I watched until she disappeared.

I had asked her if she had tried to find her children, had tried an appeal to get them back. She did not deserve them, she said. And after the testimony of her neighbors, she knew she had little hope anyway. She should have hit him with the skillet, she said; the first time he slapped the boy. I said nothing. As I have written, we have talked often since then, but we do not mention her history, and she does not ask for mine, though I know she guesses some of it. All of this is blurred; nothing stands out with purity. By talking to social workers, her neighbors condemned her to lose her children; talking in the courtroom, they helped save her from conviction.

I imagine again those men long ago, sitting among mosquitoes in a room, or sleeping on the fouled sheets. Certainly each of them hoped that it was not the mosquito biting his arm, or the bed he slept on, that would end his life. So he hoped for the men in the other room to die. Unless he hoped that it was neither sheets nor mosquitoes, but then he would be hoping for the experiment to fail, for yellow fever to flourish. And he had volunteered to stop it. Perhaps though, among those men, there was one, or even more, who hoped that he alone would die, and his death would be a discovery for all.

The boy from Chicago and Rose were volunteers too. I hope that by now the man from Chicago has succeeded at something—love, work—that has allowed him to outgrow the shame of failure. I have often imagined him returning home a week early that summer, to a mother, to a father; and having to watch his father's face as the boy told him he had failed because he was weak. A trifling incident in a whole lifetime, you may say. Not true. It could have changed him forever, his life with other men, with women, with daughters, and especially sons. We like to believe that in this last quarter of the century, we know and are untouched by everything; yet it takes only a very small jolt, at the right time, to knock us off balance for the rest of our lives. Maybe—and I hope so—the boy learned what his body and will could do: some occurrence he did not have time to consider, something that made him act before he knew he was in action.

Like Rose. Who volunteered to marry; even, to a degree, to practice rhythm, for her Catholic beliefs were not strong and deep, else she could not have so easily turned away from them after the third child, or even early in that pregnancy. So the life she chose slowly turned on her, pressed against her from all sides, invisible, motionless, but with the force of wind she could not breast. She stood at the sink, holding the children's glass. But *then*—and now finally I know why I write this, and what does stand out with purity—she reentered motherhood, and the unity we all must gain against human suffering. This is why I did not answer, at the bar, when she told me she did not deserve the children. For I believe she did, and does. She redeemed herself, with action, and with less than thirty minutes of it. But she could not see that, and still cannot. She sees herself in the laundromat, the supermarket, listlessly drunk in a nightclub where only her fingers on the table moved to the music. I see her young and strong and swift, wrapping the soaked blankets around her little girls, and hugging them to her, and running and spinning and running through the living room, on that summer night when she was touched and blessed by flames.